EVS

FICA-

LEFI,

æresim, vt *S. Mag*

entissima

ns,

THE
WITCH'S TRINITY

THE
WITCH'S
TRINITY

a novel

ERIKA
MAILMAN

CROWN PUBLISHERS
NEW YORK

This is a work of fiction. Names, characters, places, and incidents either are the product of the author's imagination or are used fictitiously. Any resemblance to actual persons, living or dead, events, or locales is entirely coincidental.

Copyright © 2007 by Erika Mailman

Published in the United States by Crown Publishers,
an imprint of the Crown Publishing Group,
a division of Random House, Inc., New York.
www.crownpublishing.com

CROWN is a trademark and the Crown colophon is a registered trademark of Random House, Inc.

Library of Congress Cataloging-in-Publication Data
Mailman, Erika.
The witch's trinity : a novel / Erika Mailman. — 1st ed.
1. Famines—Fiction.   2. Germany—History — 1273–1517 — Fiction.
3. Witches—Fiction.   I. Title.
PS3613.A349345W58 2007
813'.6—dc22   2006103292

ISBN 978-0-307-35152-4

Printed in the United States of America

Design by Jo Anne Metsch

10 9 8 7 6 5 4 3 2 1

First Edition

To Mary Bliss Parsons

After she has been consigned to prison in this way,

the promise to spare her life should be kept for a time,

but after a certain period she should be burned.

— MALLEUS MALEFICARUM

*I*t has indeed lately come to Our ears, not without afflicting Us
with bitter sorrow, that in some parts of Northern Germany, as well
as in the provinces, townships, territories, districts, and dioceses of
Mainz, Cologne, Trèves, Salzburg, and Bremen, many persons of both
sexes, unmindful of their own salvation and straying from the
Catholic Faith, have abandoned themselves to devils, incubi and
succubi, and by their incantations, spells, conjurations, and other
accursed charms and crafts, enormities and horrid offences, have slain
infants yet in the mother's womb, as also the offspring of cattle, have
blasted the produce of the earth, the grapes of the vine, the fruits of the
trees, nein, men and women, beasts of burthen, herd-beasts, as well as
animals of other kinds, vineyards, orchards, meadows, pasture-land,
corn, wheat, and all other cereals; these wretches furthermore afflict
and torment men and women, beasts of burthen, herd-beasts, as well as
animals of other kinds, with terrible and piteous pains and sore
diseases, both internal and external; they hinder men from performing
the sexual act and women from conceiving, whence husbands cannot
know their wives nor wives receive their husbands; over and above this,
they blasphemously renounce that Faith which is theirs by the Sacrament of Baptism, and at the instigation of the Enemy of Mankind
they do not shrink from committing and perpetrating the foulest
abominations and filthiest excesses to the deadly peril of their own
souls, whereby they outrage the Divine Majesty and are a cause of
scandal and danger to very many.

—From the papal bull of Innocent VIII, 1484

THE
WITCH'S TRINITY

1

It was a winter to make bitter all souls. So cold the birds froze midcall and our little fire couldn't keep ice from burrowing into bed with us. The fleas froze in the straw beds, bodies swollen with chilled blood.

We were hungry.

It had been a poor year for grain, like the year before, and the blasted field was now covered with snow. What game there was starved too, their ribs plain as kindling. But soon enough we ate all of those and there were no longer claw marks leading us along their little paths.

The lord's mill, which Jost ran, hadn't been in use for years. When I looked upon the mill wheel a fortnight ago, a cobweb stretched from the hub to the teeth. No one had any grain to grind and so our barter was based on "next harvest." Last year, the lord had released the vassals from obligation and we had all walked the furrows of the tilled earth many times, seeking a scrap thought useless before, even chaff, something to put into our mouths. The soil was as if salted. Seeds went into it only to fester and wither. We did all manner of things to change our fortune. We prayed in the way that the priest asked us to, with the Lord's Prayer, raising our eyes to heaven as we spake of the daily loaf God might grant us. Incense cloyed our throats as we prayed again and again, asking Mary's help as well. We became as gaunt as the saints carved onto the boards of the altar.

And we also did what the priest asked us not to do. Facing to the west, where the sun sets, we slaughtered beasts and poured the blood onto the soil. We dabbed blood into the middle of our palms to represent the harvest we wished to hold. We sang the old songs, our voices hushed so that the ancient music would not drift back to the church. We could not eat the meat of the ritual beasts, and so with tears in our eyes we burned the goats we might have eaten. We watched the smoke drift with the cold wind, incense the earth might prefer to the sweetish cloud from the censer.

We scolded the fields as if they were children; we threw the silt at the sky in a dusty haze and screamed. Künne Himmelmann slept with a clod beneath her pillow.

And nothing changed.

Nothing changed except that snow fell.

My son, Jost, and his wife, Irmeltrud, never spake in jest anymore; never did they laugh. No one did. I felt worst for the young ones. I had already had a lifetime when food was plentiful and neighbors bantered with each other, but they had not known lightness, only heavy, stolid days. I tried now and then to tell funny stories to Alke and Matern, my grandchildren, stories my parents had once told me, of old Lenne kissing her brother by mistake, deep in her cups, or the year the maypole came crashing down and all the girls were cross for thought of the bad luck it brought. But I was the only one who made such effort, and after a time of watching the move-less faces of my family, I ceased myself. Alke and Matern were always solemn. Because they were so thin, they didn't have the strength to race each other into the woods as children should. They played their games close to the fire, and often-times their shoulders were joined. I knew they sat that way to keep each other warm.

Alke, the elder, would have no doubt been the prettiest one in the village if only there were color and plumpness to her cheeks. But her blond hair, which should have shone like poppy oil, was lusterless. She had not much spirit to her. In several seasons, she would be marriageable, but would she be able to flirt at Mayfest to gain a lover, as Künne and I had done so shamelessly when we were her age?

And Matern, the boy, was made like a girl by these cir-cumstances. Tears came to his eyes easily and he was hurt by the smallest slight. The idea of him cleaving to a woman and taking care of all the household's needs—hunting and wood getting—seemed an impossibility. Matern would always be helpless, an eternal child created by the absence on the table. And so we all did our best to exist in the same cottage with-out food, letting the silence fall upon all of us. If my Hensel had been yet here, he'd have made them merry, but he died when Jost was yet a child, turning the world upside down like a plate.

———

"Mutter, Großmutter has hardly any soup," said Matern, eye-ing my bowl.

"Soup's for those who work," said Irmeltrud. "Those who barely move all the day long need little to sustain them." Jost tried to catch her eye, but she wouldn't let him. Such a thing was true, but she was ashamed to have spoken it.

We all sat at the table, backs straight in the formal wish that there might be real food served upon it. Members of my family had sat upon these benches for so many generations, I felt the grooves placed by their more ample bodies. Of course, they had assembled for several meals each day, while we now gathered in the late afternoon for our sole serving.

The soup looked hardly worth the having, coins of carrot floating in water barely flavored with rosemary. The sojourn in the soup pot had likely not softened these rough roots. We had not had meat since Michaelmas. When Irmeltrud turned her back to fill Matern's bowl, Jost poured some of his soup into mine. "No, son," I said in a low voice. He set his jaw. When Irmeltrud sat down, I saw her notice the sudden difference in my bowl. Her eyes narrowed and I thought, as I often had, how her face expressed the very fume of Eve when she realized the apple had undone all the good. Years ago, Irmeltrud used to smile at me, thinking that earning Jost's favor required mine. She asked my advice in all things and was hesitant as a midafternoon spider. As soon as the marriage banns were read, however, a sourness crept into her face and she has been so with me ever since.

We all held hands while Jost said the prayer of thanks. Alke's fingers were impatient in my right hand, while my left stretched across the table to capture Matern's. And then we all picked up our spoons and wetted our tongues.

At least it was hot.

Heat added flavor to things that had none, we had learned.

I took a spoonful into my mouth and simply sat with it, one carrot coin sitting on my tongue like a communion crumb. I closed my eyes to fully sense it, the meager gift of water with a ghost of taste. Everyone else plunged in with quick spoons, as if it would wink at them and run out the door if they did not hurry.

"What has Ramwold said this day?" asked Irmeltrud, in between gulps. Jost and the other village men had gone to hear him read the runes.

"He said the winter is yet to stretch more grievous," said Jost. Some *Suppe* dribbled from his mouth from the haste. He used no cloth to wipe his face, only his own tongue, to not waste even a drop.

"Can it be so?" asked Irmeltrud in a horrified tone. "What have we done to bring this?"

"I know not, but there is talk of a hunting party to gather together. The woods here are emptied."

"Better to solve the reason for our hunger than to lose yourselves to a boar's tusks or worse betides. The woods are full of the devil's minions."

"Solve it, Mutter? How?" asked Matern with wide eyes.

"By seeking the source of the evil and suppressing it," said Irmeltrud. She had already reached the bottom of her bowl, despite her talking, and clapped it down on the board. Her eyes snaked over to mine. "Someone is making mischief and bringing misery to this village," she said. "One who has made a bargain with the devil and benefits from our distress."

"We all toil in sin," said Jost. "Yet I know of no one who would have struck such a bargain."

"Not all toil," she said, and looked into my eyes. I saw no warmth there. "There's talk of old Künne Himmelmann."

"What manner of talk?" Jost's voice took on an edge of anger.

"The Töpfers say their hen has stopped laying. She is simply dried of eggs. And this happened after Künne sat down on a rock by their door."

"Everyone sits at that rock," said Jost. "The children sit there to play, the women sit on that rock to card their wool. And an old one such as Künne, to be walking the road, she'd have to tarry a bit to rest her feet."

"But the hen?"

"The hen is as hungry as the rest of us and hasn't the will to push out eggs," said Jost.

I stared down at the rind of carrot spinning slowly in my bowl. Künne was my friend. I remembered when her hair had been flaxen, her braids thick as a goose neck. Now they were thin and gray, straggled like mine. I had taken only one sip from the bowl but could eat no more. If Künne was being talked of in this way, she was in danger. A Dominican friar had come to our village a week ago—he had been the one to speak of God punishing one of our villagers by withholding the harvest from everyone. I nodded to Jost and began to push my bowl across the board to him. He smiled weakly, knowing what Künne was to me. My shaky fingers, barely recognizable to me now as those that once easily did my bidding, pushed too hard and the bowl spilled.

"Fool!" said Irmeltrud as she stood and tried to scoop the liquid back into the bowl. "You've wasted an entire bowl.

Would that you worked for it yourself, you'd treat it a little more carefully!"

It was true. I'd done naught to prepare for this repast. My fingers were too shaky for the knife to cut the carrots and my frame too frail to carry water to the cauldron.

The soup dripped down onto the dirt below. Jost's face registered the regret that he had given me of his, and now it was lost to both.

"I don't know how we're to keep all these mouths full, Jost," said Irmeltrud, turning her ire to him. "It's barely enough to even wet the teeth. There's too many in this house."

"Calm yourself. All's here that needs to be, and we will fill our stomachs when winter passes, God willing," he said.

"I can barely think, I'm so hungry!" she yelled, and both children jumped at the loud bark of her tone. "And here she sits all the day, doing nothing but dreaming! All her age have already gone! *My* parents died many years ago! Yet *she* keeps sitting at our table, opening her mouth for whatever food we have!"

Jost got up from the table. "She is my mother, wife. Pray that Matern treats you kindly when you are gray. Have pity; she's worked her entire life and now she deserves her rest." He put on his cloak and hat and brushed past her to go out the door. A shattering wind came in and swirled around us before the door shut.

For a moment I thought Jost's words had shamed her. She stared down at the table. Then she got up to get a kitchen cloth, which she pressed to the wet board to soak up the soup, then put in Matern's mouth to suck. "You need to earn your keep, old woman," she said in a tired voice. She reached across and cradled Alke's cheek in her hand. Alke concentrated only on the thin sheen of soup on her spoon.

"Look at my hands," I whispered. "Scarcely more useful than those buried in the graveyard, and with little more flesh on them. How can I put them to use?"

"By holding them out flat for alms. Beg for your meal, old woman. I'm through with feeding you."

I stared.

"That's right, Güde. Get your garments on and beg from the village. Get these children some food!"

Alke now licked the bowl that had been spilled, her pink tongue darting down to the bottom to catch the halfway salty flavor. Matern stared at his mother solemnly, still suckling the cloth she had placed in his mouth.

I stood to go to my straw mattress in the corner and shun her wrath, but she put her hands on my shoulders and funneled me to the door. "Here then! Here's your scarf, there, and there," she said as she wrapped it around my head and neck. She thrust my cloak at me.

"You're sending me out to beg?" I asked. Even though my voice had gotten reedy as I aged, I was surprised at the frail sound coming from me.

"Your mind is going along with your body," said she. "Haven't I said it clearly?"

She pushed me outside and I shivered instantly in the shock of cold. The sky was a large gray stone pressing down upon the treetops. I turned to press my hand to the door to stop her, but she was stronger and it closed.

I stared at the wood in disbelief.

I banged my palm against the door. "Irmeltrud," I called. "Please let me in. It is freezing as night out here. It's snowing."

She made no reply.

"Please," I cried. I curled both hands into fists and battered them against the door.

My fists stilled and I listened to the wind. Inside I heard Matern begin to wail. I hammered more, thinking of Hensel and his mallet plugging the logs of this cottage into place, decades ago. The same *thump, thump.* My husband had built this *Hütte,* and our own son's wife had locked its door against me.

2

They take the unguent, which, as we have said,
they make at the devil's instruction from the limbs of children . . .
whereupon they are immediately carried up into the air, either by
day or by night, and either visibly or, if they wish, invisibly.

— MALLEUS MALEFICARUM

I turned my back to the wind and saw Jost's footprints. Although it made my bones ache to climb the hill behind the granary, I did so to follow him. Those with candles were lighting them now, and the village was spread before me, beginning to glow, with the tavern lit brightest. I looked across to Künne's cottage yard, where in the fading light I saw someone, far too short to be my Jost, milking her goat for her. I shivered and pulled the cloak tightly around me so that the garment was doubled across my front. I remembered a time when my girth was such that the stitches strained to keep me covered. How long was I to wander?

Had Hensel crested the hill, he'd never have recognized me. The man who'd known my skin better than I did, who'd taken such pleasure in the rut that I stopped in the snow now to think of it—he'd have passed by me with only a nod. And now I could barely see my hands in front of me from the steadfastness of the snowfall. It was a storm and nothing an old woman should be out in. "Jost!" I cried into the wind. "I can no longer see where you've stepped!"

I could not bear the thought of the door fastened against me, so I descended the hill on the other side, the side that led to the forest.

As I walked, it began to trouble me that someone other than Jost was milking Künne's goat. He would milk for her sometimes, as she was old and stooping to sit upon the milking stool was hard work for her bones. But what other man would do that task for her? I was disturbed also at Irmeltrud's statement that the Töpfers thought her responsible for their hen's dry womb. Künne did not know such spells. She knew how to combine plants and other substances to help cure sicknesses—all but the plague, which no human seemingly could cure—but she surely did not know how to make an animal behave any other way than its nature dictated. And even if she had such knowledge, she would never apply it. The only type of person who could cast such a spell came with a very particular name, one that I hoped would never be spoken in the same sentence as Künne's.

Hexe: witch.

———

The friar had hinted strongly about *Hexen* but not used the word. The Sunday our priest first introduced us to him, everyone stared. We couldn't help ourselves. We had never seen such grandeur before. He wore a great black robe of such voluminous folds and length that it flowed down to the ground like a pitch-black alpine waterfall. Underneath, his tunic was so purely white that I thought he must have dressed in the very church itself, pulling the garment from a protective casket as he knelt before the altar, for it bore no signs of mud or wear.

"We have a new guest to our village," the priest had said. "This is Friar Johannes Fuchs. He is here to help us."

The friar then stood and took the priest's place at the pulpit. The robes so consumed his body that as he walked I saw no sign of legs moving beneath. He glided. I closed my eyes to remove the rapture of that magnificence. And when I opened them again, I struggled to look beyond the robes, to see the face of the man bold enough to wear such opulence. He was young and his chin bore no hair. His mouth was small, a mere smudge in his face, and he looked as if he had never known a day of lightness. But he was not thin; it shocked me that his cheeks were rounded as all of ours had been in times of plenty. He had shaved his pate, forming a circlet of hair like Christ's crown of thorns.

"I come from a monastery many days' journey away, founded by those who follow in Saint Dominic's footsteps," he announced. "You have no doubt heard of our large fortress surging to the sky, blessed by God and Rome."

I marveled at the booming voice that came from one so young. He was not afraid to rise and address us, all strangers.

"Here in your tiny burg of Tierkinddorf, the woods are thick on all sides. You are nestled snugly out of harm's way. But my city sits on the edge of a wide river and enemies sail to our banks, ready to steal our goods and all that we cherish.

We have built a wall around our city to fortify it, and none may come or go without a gatekeeper's consent. We could not imagine the liberty you have to wander your fields without always looking behind you. You are truly blessed to be so insignificant and tiny."

Did he wish now to live with us? I wondered. *He wanted our freedom as well?*

"But there is one thing that you are not blessed with, and that is a profitable harvest. I received a piteous letter from your lord, summoning me. Lord Obermann told me of your seedless fields."

I looked at the back of Lord Obermann's head. He was seated in the front on a handsome carved chair, the only chair in the church. Even the priest sat on a rough bench, and most of us stood.

"Yours is not the only village that is suffering. All across this land, people are hungry. Even in my city, we are counting the cakes in the larder. And that is why I have set off on this miraculous journey, with Christ's hands governing me, to find out why the land is cursed. I am here to help you, people of Tierkinddorf."

I could not concentrate on anything after he said the word *cakes*. In his city, they still had cakes? We had not made sweets for years now. Not even for fests. Sweets required flour.

"There is a reason for every circumstance we face. A reason why the flower droops, why the clouds bloat and thin and drift away. An explanation for the dropping of a kettle, for the goodwill of your neighbor, for the five fingers upon each hand. And God alone knows these reasons," he said. "I am seeking God's counsel for why the fields do not bear grain. I am journeying our countryside so that he may guide me and usher me to understanding, and then, perhaps, to remedy."

I felt a surge of relief within me, and judging by the respectful but obvious clamor his speech created, I was not the only one. He was going to find out why the harvest was withheld! Thank God in heaven! And more than that, he would fix the problem! He was better than prayer, better than sacrifice. He was an actual man, gliding across our snow-covered hamlets, doing the work of God.

"What is God's reason for punishing you? Why do you not have fullness upon your tables and in your bellies? You are desperate to know why, and I am here to move the questions from your tongues to Christ's ear. We of the Holy Roman Church believe that just as God punished the world with a flood, he is now punishing you with famine. If we can discover the particular people who cause all to be blamed, you can again gain God's mercy."

Women and men made the sign of the cross and then kissed their clasped hands in pure joy. I felt my stomach shift within my body, as if my very organs were calling out to the friar for help to fill them.

"And so, neighbors, maybe you already know whom God is angry with, but you have not been able to think the thought. But I urge you to give in to it. It is of no advantage to protect those who make your children cry with hunger. Pay attention to those around you. I am here now. You may seek me out to whisper into my ear."

I was so happy, my fingers clenched in my lap. I knew he would find no one in this village whom God wanted to punish, but surely he would move on and find the true offender in another village. He would rearrange our lives back to the way they had been. He was a good man. *Thank you, thank you, God!* I mouthed.

"And now then, let us hold the mass," he concluded.

The priest continued sitting in the background as the man in black and white led us through the calls and responses, as he poured the tiny measure of Christ's blood into the goblet, as he held aloft the small loaf that we would all nick with our teeth for a crumb.

Yes, we all suffered from hunger in our homes, but the church had reserved bread so that we might still hold communion and call Christ into our bodies.

As I knelt before the long robes and sipped from the goblet and bit at the rock-hard loaf, I felt an infusion of blessing. It was like a wedding day, or the first day of true warmth after a long winter. The friar was like an altar carving come to life, one of the old saints surging forward with Christ's power in his gait and a Christian fire in his eyes. I could have kissed his robes, lifted the hem to my lips and inhaled the dust and incense that clung to it. I didn't, though. I returned to stand with my family, rosy and uplifted.

———

As the brightness of the friar's robes faded in my mind, I could not feel my feet. It was dark now, and the snow was a layer upon me—I carried its weight as well as my own. I stopped walking and listened. I heard no other stepping in the wood, saw no sign of Jost or anyone else. I was utterly alone. And then I felt a tingling at each knob of my back: the fear of the woods.

All my life I'd heard tell of the beasts that skulked in the forest after nightfall. A man who by day gathered kindling would by night crouch down until his fingertips scratched the dirt. His jaw would lengthen and the sinews of his arms and legs would knot and twist. His body would hair itself coarsely. Lifting his face, he'd stare at the tops of the pines until claws dug into the ground beneath him and a tail sprouted from him, and he'd open his mouth to sing the howl that curdled the soul, that made lovers turn in bed and touch each other's faces to confirm the smoothness. Owls would lully their cry too, in tandem with the wolf, calling out to all creatures that death was only a bound and a bite away.

Into this wood I plunged, witless. I began singing a tune to keep me moving. "I Must Go Walk the Wood" was its name, and 'twas a song of love and forlorn wandering:

> *Thus am I banished from my bliss*
> *By craft and false pretense,*
> *Faultless, without offense,*
> *As of return, nothing certain is,*
> *And all for fear of one.*

I sang it with a ragged laugh, and after "and all for fear of one" I could remember no more. Some days my mind was like a sprawling tatter of twigs left behind by a summer bird. *Evergreen tree, evergreen tree . . . My bed shall be under the evergreen tree!* Wasn't that the way the song continued? I suppose I sang partly for Jost to hear, would that he might. Otherwise, I would walk to the crisp yawl of the owl until snow or wolf brought me down. The snow diminished, became little drift-

ing thoughts about my head. I had been here too many years.
The only one my age was Künne. All else gone. All sleeping
with their name scratched in wood above them. A moon lent
some light, what little it could pass me through the disap-
proving shadows of the trees. I wondered if Hensel watched
my movements from above. Did he wish anything to do with
me now? I was no winsome lass. My breath clouded the air in
front of me and I stopped finally, flesh cold as any a butcher
put to ice. I had not kept track of my path. I did not know
which way home might be, or if the door would even be
opened to me if I could find my way back.

Perhaps the friar could bring harvest back to our fields, but
I was lost and in darkness. How could I benefit from his work?
I did not expect to leave the forest. "Hensel, I will join you this
night," I said, sinking to my knees in the snow. "The door of
the house you built is barred to me. Our son is abroad wandering, with no ken that I do the same. And she who hunches by
the fire . . . Oh, Hensel, you see what she has wrought!"

And then a voice spake into my ear: "By craft and false pretense!"

I whirled around with my hand clutching my throat.

No one was there.

I lunged to my feet and heaved myself through the trees,
running as fast as I could.

Above me, as if spoken from a high bough, came the voice
again: "As of return, nothing certain is!" I turned and ran the
other way. I feared to look up to see her, for it was certainly a
woman, and only willed myself God's speed. Suddenly the
snow felt like a kitchenful of women pressing their knife tips
into my skin. Above me, she whistled the song. She was

keeping pace. What creature was she? She used the air as verily as earth, and soundlessly. "Jost!" I screamed. And then, because I was confused, "Hensel!"

She laughed at that, a sound so evil that I stopped myself, as one transfixed, to hear it. She used her wickedness to draw my eyes up, up, until I saw she dangled in the air, her dark, uncovered hair coiling and uncoiling around her head in the wind.

"We will feed you," she said. On her forehead was an impurity above her left eyebrow. She carried the mark of the devil, a kiss from fetid lips that stained her skin red.

I took one step backward, and then a second, and then her hand was on my shoulder and she was behind me, turning me to face her. Oh, the heavy iron weight and iciness of that hand! It froze down through my cloak and into the very chambers of my heart.

I stared into her wicked face. She was comely and her lips full and lush, yet I could not admire what Satan had kissed. Her eyes shone with unholy interest in me, and my spine hunched further to lower me from her gaze. This horror traveled the air! She stepped upon mere wind! I tried to run, but she held me in thrall. And then I saw that I knew her. She was from a different village and I had seen her at Michaelmas, as all the townships gathered to share our feast.

"Old Güde," said she, "the famine ends here in the forest. I trust you are ready."

She showed me her palm, crusted with blood. With a cry, I pulled it to my mouth and tasted. Animal blood. Meat. With that taste in my mouth, I no longer wished to run from her.

"Come and eat," she said.

I followed her into a clearing where six women scratched designs in the snow with their fingers, bent intent on that purpose. I did not understand the chanting. All I saw was the fire and the pig on the spit above it.

They ceased their movements, fingers dangling, eyes hooded, and watched me approach.

"Do you give yourself to him?" she asked.

I faltered. The smell of the pig was strong. I knew its skin was crispy with hot fat. I knew the succulence would drench my fingers.

"Old Güde," said one of the women, "it is only a simple agreement. To sign the devil's book and then to eat."

I walked closer to the fire. I was surrounded by crows and the women all gone.

"Faultless, without offense," sang the air.

Behind the glow of the fire, I saw him. The cloven hooves to match those on the spit. The unearthly sound as he walked to me in the snow. He had a strong body, haired like an animal, and held a book. *God has forsaken me,* I thought. For he had the face of Hensel, my husband of years past, the most gentle being I had ever known. This beast had his eyes, the ones that rollicked me into bed and through and into his hands.

"Güde," he said, and his voice too was Hensel's, hushed. "I cannot bear to see you starve."

My lips parted and tears came to my eyes. Sweet Hensel! No matter that he came to me amidst all manner of depravity, with cloven hoofs and women in a circle becoming jet-black birds. It was he, my one true love.

He never let go of the book, but somehow both hands were caressing me, pushing off the hood to stroke my hair. I threw my head back, careless as a girl, to feel those hands again. I pressed against him—madness, and devilment; surely it was a trick.

"I love you still," he said.

And although I could not see them behind me, I knew all the crows nodded and looked at each other sideways, cocking their heads to position their eyes.

He pressed hard against me, and I jumped to the side instantly, eyes wide. It was true what the tales told. The devil has an ice-cold prick. I felt it even through all the layers of wool I wore. I fell to the ground and sobbed, staring at his cloven feet. This wasn't Hensel after all! I sank into the snow, deeper and deeper, until I felt it would completely swallow me. My hands shifted in the snow to push me back up, but it was as if I pressed them against well water.

A crow walked to me, black claws carefully treading in the snow. It was the woman from the air, from Michaelmas. She lifted one wing, as large as my arm, and used her beak to pry loose a feather. She offered it to me. A pool of blood appeared in the snow.

Suddenly I was sitting up and the book was in my lap. The snow was solid beneath me.

"Sign and you may sup," said Hensel.

I was at eye level with the pig on the spit. It stared at me wildly. I could sense nothing now but the agonizing aroma of its crackling fat. And then I felt as if I tipped backward, but it wasn't me, it was the pig, spinning on his spit. Both of us rolled our eyes. The forest flickered, completely black for a moment and then lit by the fire again.

In despair, I dipped the quill in the pool of blood. He

pushed a kiss into my mouth. With their wings, the crows stroked me. The pages of the book fluttered impatiently. A drop of blood landed on the page.

"She's as good as signed," said Hensel, and I realized anew who these creatures of the forest were.

"No," I shouted. "I know how to write my name, and I have not signed!"

Yet, as I stared down, the blot lengthened and thinned. Soon it was a *G.* And then the *ü,* and the *d.* It was spelling out my name.

"No!" I shouted, and slammed the book closed.

Everything vanished. It was pure darkness without the pig's fire. I held my breath and listened but no one moved in the dark. I was profoundly alone. Then I saw a basket in front of me, loaded with meat. I stood up. I was unsure if I had signed or not. "Hensel," I whispered to the forest. I knelt and dipped both hands and fed myself, keeping my mouth close to the basket, gorging as fast as I could. The meat was hot and filled with juice. I fed with frenzy, in disbelief of the taste that was so extreme and so *good.* I closed my eyes to better savor the fibers mashing between my teeth, threading into the spaces where teeth used to be. The meat was so succulent, it was as if I could drink it; grease filmed my lips.

I cared not what the book said.

It was not as real as the taste of pig in my mouth.

———

I had been wrong thinking that my life would end that night, by design of wind or beast. I walked hardly a child's tread before I emerged back into the meadow. I climbed again the hill, saw the drowsing lights of my village, and descended to my home.

The door was open a crack and Jost ran to me in alarm when I pushed it further.

"Mutter! You're frozen to the core!" He dragged me to the fire and saw for the first time my basket. "Drop that," he commanded, and rubbed my hands to warm them. I looked across the room and saw that everyone was in bed. Irmeltrud had her back to me although I believed she was yet awake.

"You can eat of it, Jost," I said. "I kept some for you."

I smiled and pointed to the basket.

His face had the expression I've seen only in the last few years—the one that says I've said something odd, or called Matern by Jost's name or forgotten my own.

"'Twill spark the fire a moment only," he said. "But I cannot eat of it."

It was a decayed bit of basketry, splotched with weather and missing several reeds.

There was no meat in it.

3

It is useless to argue that any result of witchcraft may
be a phantasy and unreal, because such a phantasy cannot
be procured without resort to the power of the devil.

— MALLEUS MALEFICARUM

Jost unwound the scarf from my head, spreading it to dry. Then he fetched my blanket from my straw pallet and put it over my shoulders. As my shivering ceased, I became aware of a new smell. Although Jost's departure had brought disaster for me, it had brought a filling dinner for the family. Walking his traps, he had found a rabbit, which Irmeltrud stewed. Only a bit remained for me, and Jost ladled it into the bowl that earlier had held only carrot broth.

"It was such a sight, Mutter," said he. "A pure white rabbit I never would have seen against the snow, but for one black stripe against its pelt as if a fire had scorched it. It was passing strange."

"He tastes well enough," I said, my fingers pushing the soft flesh off the bone. His previous bones, sucked and cleaned, were piled on the hearth.

A rare smile lit Jost's face. "Alke is tanning it for a wrap. It will fit around her neck." He pointed to it hanging from the rafter, salt rubbed into its nether side. The pelt was lovely, even with the ghostly holes where the bright eyes had been. The rabbit had a host of soft bristles in a measure, while a lesser-nourished creature might have had scant. It would toast Alke's neck through the coldest of winds.

"Thank you for your flesh, beast of the wood," I said. I made the ancient sign of the meat blessing, four fingers downcast to mirror the legs of the still-living beast, and then upturned them to show its felling, and finally pressed them to my lips to prove I honored the eating. I then made the sign of the cross. I put the final bone into my mouth and pursed my lips around it, like Hensel with his pipe of yore. Then I placed it with the others in the cock.

Jost spake in a whisper. "Why did you go out in such weather, Mutter?"

I looked into his kind face, where I saw evidence of my own gray eyes and cheekbones. "She said I chose it?"

"I searched for you," he said. "I called and called your name. There were no footprints in the snow."

"Jost, I did not choose it!" I knew full well the tale that had been told. Old Güde, who has no mind anymore, who forgets her own name, had flung herself into the storm. *We tried to stop her, but she would listen to naught,* Irmeltrud likely had told him.

"I'm no fool to cast myself away from the warmth of the hearth in the dark of night. The snow was falling fast! I could not see my hand though it be a spoon's length from my face! Do you think I wished this? She pushed me out."

He blinked. Then Jost lowered his voice even further. "You are getting older, Mutter. Sometimes the things you do seem . . . out of sense."

I whispered my next words also, for I saw that Irmeltrud's back was too rigid for her mind to be relaxed and dreaming. "Have you not seen the hatred in her, Jost? I have been kindly to her all these years, and yet she hates me. She cast me out and then barred the door. I pounded and cried such that Matern cried out as well, but her heart was a thorn!"

He looked at the basket I had brought home with me.

"Jost!" I hissed. "Do not judge me by that folly."

"You said it had meat in it and it had none."

"Ask the children about her barring the door! The door that Hensel made!" I stood up in a fury and moved to the bed where Irmeltrud and the children lay.

"Mutter! Thank God you are back!" Irmeltrud sat up and encased me in a hug so seemingly true that I was confused. "Have you known how many hours Jost plogged the wood for you? We went to bed sore affrighted." She pressed a fervent kiss upon my cheek and I struggled not to wrap my arms about her, I was so needy for such a touch. "Alke! Matern!" I said their names loudly to rouse them. Blushed with sleep they were, and glad for me. Alke buried her face into my chest while Matern snaked his arm to my waist.

"Großmutter, I dreamed you were back, and you are!" said Matern.

"Tell your father in what manner I left," I commanded.

"Mutter asked you to get food," said the boy. "And we waited and waited for you to come, but it was Vater who came with the rabbit."

"Tell him how I pounded at the door to be let in, how I did not wish to go. She kept the door closed to me," I said.

Irmeltrud gasped and her blue, blue eyes opened wide. "Oh, Mutter! Mutter . . . Jost, surely you know I have no heartless way like this! Güde was pounding at the door but as a game for the children. They rapped back and laughed, and she laughed too!"

"If cries be laughter, then betides the bee will kiss us next spring rather than sting," I said bitterly.

"Großmutter, were you not playing?" asked Alke.

"No! She asked me to get food, Matern said. Would a daughter-in-law ask that of such a time-tried old woman? At that hour? She cast me out!" I cried.

Above Alke's golden head, Irmeltrud exchanged a look with Jost. I felt like a child; I held no sway. She had convinced the children it was a playful jest as I begged for my life on the cold side of the door. And now Jost was persuaded too. Any protestation would only mire me further. "I want to sleep now," I said, pushing Alke and Matern from me. I rose, tired past belief suddenly, my body remembering the ordeal it had been through. I accepted a kiss from Jost without looking at him. I trundled to my cold straw and curled up on it.

I looked across the room with its solitary table and benches at the remains of the fire. In the corner of my vision I saw the shadow of Jost as he pulled back the bedclothes and moved his big body into them. I prayed he would not rut with Irmeltrud this night; I could not bear the sounds of that further betrayal.

From the height of the rafter, the little rabbit stared down at me through the blank holes of its pelt. One solid black stripe where the devil raked his finger.

———

The next morn when Jost opened the door, a cloud of snow fell into the room. He had to dig for nigh onto an hour to free the door of its wall of snow. Then he set out again, whistling, to see what else might have wedged a paw in his traps.

We had nothing for breakfast but water, and Irmeltrud and the children left to gather branches for our fire, moving outside through the tunnel Jost had prepared. As I closed the door behind them, I saw the rich fold of whiteness that blanketed everything, white as ever Mary's soul was. I sat by the fire, mending Alke's nightgown. Irmeltrud had already threaded the needle for my shaky hands with a piece of thread unraveled from a burned pot cloth. The room seemed very dim compared with the brilliance outside. The needle flashed its own small light, yet I had to bring the gown close to my face to see my uneven stitches. Alke tended to toss in her sleeping, and the weight of her own hip had wrenched the fabric. I heard a scratching at the door and straightened a bit to listen. 'Twas a small sound. It came again and I rose to open the door. A cat was there, its paw still raised in the motion of grinding its claws against our wood.

"Feh! Shoo!" I shouted, and slammed the door.

It wasn't a black cat, which the Pope had warned against, but any cat is known to be trafficking with the powers of evil. I made the sign of the cross, accidentally dragging the sharp needle along my forehead as I did so. I cried out in pain, and brought my other hand up to the wound. My fingers came back red. At the fire, I pressed the burned pot cloth to my head. It made no difference if it was spoiled. The cat scratched again.

And again.

And again.

Then the thick wool that covered the window moved. The beast was batting the cloth from the other side, sitting on the small sill. "Pursue me not," I whispered, dropping the needle and pot cloth. I watched one paw make its way through. The cat clawed at the edge of the wool until it was able to push it to the side and stare in at me. A gust of cold wind came with it.

It was a gray tabby, with stripes like the shadows trees throw on the ground. Its eyes were green, I could tell even from across the room. Its mouth opened and it gave a distant meow, its tiny, sharp teeth grimacing at me.

"I did not sign," I said. "And if the book signed for me, I am not beholden to it."

The cat sat down on its back legs, its shoulder still pressing the window cloth to the side. My heart was pounding. I made the sign of the cross again, and then, beginning to feel the sweat pressing out all over my body, walked to pick up the broom from the corner. I was terrified the beast would leave the sill and leap into the room. But did I have the daring to swat it with the broom, to push it backward into the snow?

"Be gone, you devil!" I said.

I took two steps forward, the broom braced in front of me. So close now to the animal, I saw that the eyes were golden-flecked, and that a black slit ran up them vertically. Like the stripe on the rabbit pelt. Whose eyes were these?

Our eyes fixed. The slits in the cat's widened until there were two black pools in the middle of the green. 'Twas a transformation. It took the evil from the cat and made it the soft thing women kept in their laps years ago, gamboling after thread. Once these were not hated but loved. They spake their mews sweetly and drank the stream that issued from the cow, sitting there by the bucket, milk dripping from their whiskers. And making all laugh from the furiousness of the pounce on a poor mouse. Of course, in the granary we had to have cats to keep down the rats. But Künne's family had had one that would come into the house, to sit by the fire with the family; this was how I knew the feel of the fur. They even named it, calling it Flüstern, since its soft step in the cottage was like a secret whisper between hushed voices.

The cat stayed on the sill until my eyes went blind from the blaze of white behind it.

"Is your fur soft?" I asked it.

The eyes remained round bowls for me, and it was this that caused my ease. "You are naught but a beast of the barn," I told it. "Go there now to warm yourself."

Its back haunches sat in the layer of snow left on our windowsill. As the animal rose again to standing, I heard the smush of snow pressing under its weight. It issued another meow, so like to the tender mewling of a babe that I repeated it in my own quaver.

The cat leaped down, brushing my skirts as it dashed inside. The window cloth flew back down to cover the light from outside.

The cat knew just where to go and jumped onto the hearth. It curled its tail around its body and tucked it under its chin.

The marvelous eyes closed. It would sleep, as slumberous as me in my straw.

I sat on the edge of my chair and looked all along its length. Pleasing stripes, and the flesh padded firmly against the bones. This beast looked as though it ate better than Jost's family.

Leaning to pick up the needle, I ran my finger along it to rid it of its blood and then wiped my finger on the pot cloth. The cat dozed, no companion but for the rising of its skin with each breath. I picked up Alke's nightgown again to finish my task.

———

When I awoke, the shadows were different. Alke's gown had slid to the ground and I picked it up, snapping it in the air to rid it of dust. At this, the cat awoke. The eyes were once again slits, and I dragged in a quick breath of alarm.

It stood and pressed its back up to the ceiling, as coiled as the snake Eve had trusted. I stepped to the back of my chair, thinking to keep the wood between us.

Then the cat's body sank while the hind parts remained in air, and I saw this posture for what it was: a stretch upon waking. I had seen Jost do the same to prepare for a hard day grooving the millstones. It jumped down from the hearth and came to my skirts, stepping lightly. It pressed against my legs, making a buzzing sound like a muffled bee that instantly brought me back to Künne's cottage as a girl, playing with Flüstern to get a purr. Without thinking, I crouched down and touched the cat's head, between the ears.

I groaned in a faltering sort of joy and tears came to my eyes.

Not since Hensel died had I felt such a thing under my hands. Warmth, softness, *life*. Matern and Alke gave swift hugs, but to linger with my hands reveling in such warmth . . .

Soon I was heaving with my weep, both hands passing over the cat's fur, plunging into the thicker pelt at the neck and smoothing down across the ribs. Underneath, the belly pelt was the softest of all, and the cat cared not that my tears landed on it. My hands became clogged with its fur, for it came out with my pressuring, and I scattered the hairs on the ground, continuing the stroking that was bringing such pleasure to both of us. The cat began a sort of prance under my hands, with only its front paws dancing.

I leaned back a bit and looked at its motion. It stepped on, a single-minded look in its eye. I laughed in surprised amaze. "Why, 'tis like you're kneading your own bread," I said.

Had its paws been hands, the resemblance would have been uncanny. Its muscular arms pressed down into the ground, as women drive themselves into dough, then picked up quickly to renew the force pressing down. "If only our granary had the flour for you," I said, "You'd make a fine dough to rise, I see that."

It gazed up at me, the eyes again rounded like black fruit. "Why do you ever have the slits?" I asked it. "It makes the folk affrighted. You'd fare better were your eyes always innocent."

It lifted its chin in response, and I scraped my fingernails along the fineness of the jawbone, while it stamped out its delight.

"O cat," said I in satisfaction, "I wish that——"

I heard the latch lift and felt the cold air blustering into the cottage. "Güde!" screamed Irmeltrud. "What are you doing? What are you *doing*?"

The cat darted out almost before my hands knew it was gone, running outside. Irmeltrud screamed a curse after it, and the children came into the cottage, looking frightened.

"Güde, you fool, why were you tarrying with the devil's handmaiden?" Irmeltrud grasped my hands and pulled on them to get me to rise. She got a good look at me and screamed again. "The blood upon your forehead!" she said, her mouth remaining open in a horrified gape after she spake.

"I'm not hurt," I said. "I pricked myself with the needle."

"'Tis the sign the devil leaves to mark his own," she whispered. She used her skirts to shoo Alke and Matern into the corner, away from me. "You wend your way to hellfire, Güde."

I stared at her, frightened at the fear she showed. "'Twas not a black cat, only a gray striped one. I was mending Alke's nightgown and the needle slipped on me. I pricked myself."

Irmeltrud grabbed the nightgown from the chair and threw it into the fire. Alke began to cry. "It burns blue," Irmeltrud said. "Devilment!"

Then she picked up the pot cloth. "What be this?"

"The blood from my head," I said.

"And the blood of others?"

"No!"

"What did the cat bring you?"

"Naught! It is only a cat, like those that run the granary clean of rats. Irmeltrud, I beseech you, cease this! I am no more a lover of the devil than—"

"Children, see you the blood here?" She held up the pot

cloth and in the corner the children silently nodded. "I shall burn it, but the children shall remember, Güde, should we ever be asked what we have seen."

She cast it into the fire and again watched the color of the blaze.

"You must be careful," she said, folding her arms and staring at me, more unnerving than when the cat had done so on the sill. "Künne faces the inquisitors tomorrow. She may name you."

"How have you become so cruel?" I asked. "You know I am nothing but an old woman."

She turned her back on me and went to the door, opening it to pick up a bundle she had dropped at the sight of the cat. "We traded today with Herr Hahn," she said. "While you stroked the devil's beast, we dragged a week's worth of wood to his door in return for a ham hock. It's not large. Were there only four of us eating, it should suffice. But with a fifth, we shall all still be hungered."

I turned and looked at the children. Had they understood what she had said, and what was lying underneath, like a snake coiled in a rock's shadow?

4

It is probable that the devil favours the number three more than any other, for it represents an effective denial of the Holy Trinity.

— MALLEUS MALEFICARUM

The next morning, I woke with a dread heart. It was the day Künne must defend herself. Irmeltrud was in a rare, high mood, laughing as she dressed the children. Jost was more sober, for he knew Künne as a kindly woman who had oft supped with us when he was young. We walked to the church, feet crunching in the heavy snow. The air was yet dim as we walked, and I heard the scant birds of winter make their morning calls. We walked in a single line, I in the rear, stepping in the large footprints Jost made at the front of the line.

The hall was cold, even with the bodies gathered to hear Künne's trial. Two tile stoves, one at each side of the hall, worked to dispel the chill. They were the pride of our village, given to the church when the first of our lord's lineage became a Christian. We all kept on the clothing we had worn in the snow; perhaps we'd shed it if the room warmed. Jost guided us close to one of the stoves, knowing the wee ones felt the cold most. There were only a few benches here. We sat on one and the rest of the people stood.

Künne sat at the front of the room, on a high stool evidently built for this purpose. She hovered above all of us, even those standing. She seemed witchly in her height. The stool was unfair; it made a natural woman look unnatural. Künne had watched everyone file in, and when she saw me, her face twisted into a sort of a smile, what little she could offer on such a grim day. I looked at her gray knotted hair slipping from her cap and fingers like crow's claws resting on her thin thighs, thinking of who Künne once had been, fleet on her feet, beating even the boys at the races in May, hair shiny and cheeks ruddy like a trout's breast. When I could bear her face no longer, I looked down.

And saw my own hands on my thighs, as clawlike as hers.

Friar Fuchs, in his magnificent robes, stood up and by raising his hands brought silence into the church. "Good people of Tierkinddorf, I travel our land charged with the duty of ending the devil's work begun in the hearts and souls of womenfolk. They are doing his bidding, as chilling an army as ever fought behind shield and armor. I have been instructed how to descry these women and test them. My purpose is to find such a woman here in your village and administer the punishment that will release you all from paying for her crimes. For who would want to pay another's debt? If one among us here today is a *Hexe,* we shall find her out and punish her."

There. He had said it. The word I feared: *Hexe.* Witch.

He held a book up. It was thick, a solemn black with golden lettering. "This is the *Malleus Maleficarum,* written by the great Heinrich Kramer and his apprentice Jakob Sprenger. I had the honor of traveling throughout southern Germany with this most dedicated of inquisitors, learning from his fine example to ferret out the worst in women, to steadfastly question them and deliver them into the vengeful hands of God. A man must have a strong spine to face the devil's servants.

"No one in this village knows Latin," he continued, "which is the language of God's messengers, the holy men of the church. The name of the book, translated for you, is *The Witches' Hammer.* And this device—seemingly only paper and ink—is a hammer. With it I will hammer the *Hexe* out of this woman. Think of the smith who stands by the forge all day, hammering the bend from iron, straightening it to its proper use. If this woman should be found guilty of witchcraft, I will straighten her to her proper use."

He lowered the book down and held it by his side.

"Let us pray," said the friar.

I stared wildly around the sanctuary, seeing all heads bowed to that litany of monstrous requests to God, even Künne's. Did they not see? She was already tried in the friar's mind—tried and condemned.

"Who shall provide the first testimony against this woman?" the friar asked.

Frau Zweig stepped forward. I knew her to be a troubled young woman. Though she and her husband had both survived the Black Death, she had never been able to bear a child. She questioned why they had been spared, if their sparing had no further utility.

"I want to speak against this woman," said Frau Zweig.

"She has kept my womb empty although three times I have felt a child quicken there."

"How has she done this?"

"I sought her for advice to keep the child safe—the first time. She told me I was wrong, that there was no child. I should have known then, when I saw her wicked smile, that she was working magic to destroy the life inside me."

"How do you know she worked this magic?"

"It was all in her face. She gave the evil eye to that child, and it left my womb as snow melts on hot skin."

The friar nodded. I saw Künne look over at Herr Zweig—his head was bowed still from the prayer.

"It took some years to again bear fruit. I asked Frau Vogler for an herbal poultice to help me get with child."

The friar frowned. "An herbal poultice? Why did you not seek help through prayer?"

"I cannot say," she faltered. "This has always been the village custom. The very day I applied the poultice I felt the heartbeat in me. I listened to the beating, so fast, so beautiful!" Here she paused and looked up at Künne. All of a sudden she gasped. "And here she now continues her devilment, casting her eye upon my husband! You wicked animal! You lost your husband to the plague and now you covet mine! Do you not see, Friar? She is covetous of all I have and that is why she tortures me!"

The friar looked sternly at Künne, whose face was the truest picture of bafflement I have ever seen.

"Cover her eyes so that she may do no harm," instructed the friar. "I wear a sachet of consecrated salt around my neck for protection. The *Malleus Maleficarum* instructs that a witch is powerless to harm those who seek justice against her. But cover them nonetheless."

Our priest, Father Luft, took a scarf from a woman in front and used it to cover Künne's eyes. I began to cry, silent tears running down my face. I imagined the same was happening, hidden, behind the scarf.

"Pray continue with your testimony," said the friar.

"I listened to the beating of my babe's heart. But as I smelled the reek of the poultice, the beats began to slow; soon there was immense space between them, and then they stopped altogether."

"Are you accusing Frau Vogler, who gave you the poultice?" asked the Friar.

"No. I accuse Künne Himmelmann, who gave the herbs to Frau Vogler."

"Frau Vogler, do you confirm this to be true?"

Frau Vogler, in the center of the congregation, nodded vigorously. Irmeltrud leaned across Alke and Matern to look at me.

"You have a third instance of this woman bewitching you?" said the friar.

"Yes. This time I hid the news of the quickening from all, even my husband, because I knew Künne wished me wrong. Yet somehow she knew. I saw her pick a berry from a bush and gnash it in her teeth, looking straight at me. It was like her teeth seized on my babe. That instant, my stomach spasmed and the life in me ceased."

"We have duly noted your testimony," said the friar. He pointed to a man scribbling furiously in the corner. "My notary transcribes each interrogation so that there may later be no question that we carefully sought justice."

"And God willing, may that justice come down upon her head," said Frau Zweig. "Maybe then I shall see issue from my marriage." She walked to her husband.

"May we hear from others who accuse this woman?" asked the friar.

Jost stood. "May I come to speak?"

"You may."

My body froze. Not Jost! I watched, disbelieving, as he walked to the front. He moved slowly, and with each step I bit my tongue to keep from calling him back. I was aware what peril I was in; all here knew me to be a friend to Künne.

"Künne Himmelmann is no more a witch than I am," said Jost. "And we all know that men cannot be such."

I clenched Alke's hand in pure sudden joy. Irmeltrud rustled her skirts.

"You are wrong on that account," said the friar. "Although the seductive nature of women, harking back even to Eve, leads them more frequently into the devil's path, there are men I have seen burned to death for the same crime."

Jost swallowed. "I had heard that only women were witches."

"Since your logic fails, perhaps you ought to sit down."

"There is more I wish to say," Jost pressed on. I saw the fear in his eyes. He had not thought that speaking on Künne's behalf could bring him under suspicion.

"You may say it."

"Everyone knows that Künne is no witch. All but one, a

vindictive woman who needs someone to blame for her own barren womb. The rest of us know Künne as the one who has cured our fevers, given us poultices and drinks that brought relief to us when we were sick. She alone in our village possesses the herb knowledge, and she freely shares its avails with us. She is a healer."

"Who is she, a common peasant, to heal sickness?" the friar replied. "That is for learned men."

"Learned or not, she has healed us. I ask of you in this room, whoever has found release from pain due to Künne's kindness, step forward and be counted, that we may in turn release her from this horrible accusation."

I stamped my feet on the ground, ready to stand and straighten my knees for Künne. I pressed my hand, the one not holding Alke's, onto the wooden bench to help me rise. But when I was halfway, I realized I was the only one doing so. Everyone else was standing in place, staring at the friar's face. And when I looked too, I subsided onto the bench. There was danger in the room; had Jost been facing the friar rather than us as he spake, he would have said something different indeed.

This man was here to build a fire. And he cared not who burned in it.

Jost walked over to Künne and kissed her hand. "No one moved," he told her softly, since she had not been able to see.

She gave a single sob.

That was too much. "I do," I said. I faltered up to standing. "She is my friend. She is kind and full of goodness. She does not care whether you bear a child or not, Frau Zweig!"

"Write down the names of these two," commanded the

friar. The notary looked confused; he was not from our village and didn't know our names.

"I am Jost Müller of the granary. The one who stood was Güde, my *Mutter*." With that, Jost came back to our bench and sat down. His hands were shaking.

"We find this in the villages," said the friar. "Petty jealousies. Arguments that have continued between families for many decades. To ensure that we are properly accusing this woman, are there any others who wish to speak?"

I held my breath. I was squeezing Alke's hand so hard she let out a little whimper, and I released it. Künne sat as still as the stone the Töpfer family had said she sat upon to curse their hen. I craned my neck to see where they were. Would they speak or yet stay silent?

"I have a report of witchery," said the familiar voice of Herr Töpfer. He stood directly behind me. I felt Jost's shoulders sag beside me.

"Approach," said the friar.

"We have a hen," said Herr Töpfer. "Each day for years we collected her eggs. We ate of them and bartered them for other goods. We relied on the eggs. One day we noticed Frau Himmelmann come to sit and rest on a stone near our door. We thought nothing of it, as she is old and needed to rest before continuing on. But after that day, the hen lay no more."

"Ah," said the friar. "Christ permits me to see a symbolic link between the two accusations. Künne Himmelmann wreaks havoc with fertility. As one who can no longer partake in the cycle of birth, she takes vengeance on those who can, even so slight a creature as a hen."

"Frau Himmelmann passed by me one day without offering me a greeting and as her shadow fell across my face the image arose in my mind of my dead *Mutter*," cried another woman across the room.

"Yes," said the friar. "She purposely reminds you of the sorrow of your interrupted lineage."

"We want our hen to lay again," said Herr Töpfer.

"And so it shall," said the friar. "And so it shall."

———

On May Day, years past, we had donned our gowns of white and put on the bright girdle at our waists to show we were ready for marriage, should any village lad be thinking of taking a wife. Künne had been a beauty, braids thicker than any other girl's. "Güde, will you kiss a lad today?" she asked me, her eyes shining. I plucked up her braid and weighed its mass in my palm before answering.

"I may," I said.

"And will you let him touch you?"

"I may," I laughed.

"And show to him your rosy, rosy skin?"

"No!" I yelled, and spun away from her in a delirium of laughter, running the length of the hill beyond her *Hütte,* my girdle spinning out behind me until it dropped from my waist. She plunged to get it before I could.

"You will become betrothed!" she said. "You will give all of yourself. Güde, we are almost women!"

I grabbed the loose end of the girdle and pulled. Standing a-kilter on the hill as she was, she was knocked off balance and fell into the tall, sweet-smelling grass. I sat down next to her and tickled her fine neck with a long grass frond. "Almost women," I repeated.

"Promise me we will still race," she commanded.

"Only girls race," I laughed. "We'll be stooped from serving our husbands and our feet will hardly hasten."

"I wish I could roll this day into a ball and keep it in my hand forever. The sun, the smell of this grass . . ."

"The fact you are faster than anyone," I teased.

"My legs carrying me so fast, yes, I want to keep that too." She wriggled her body over until she could lay her head in my lap. She plucked a tiny flower at her side and held it up to me. "Do you know this flower?"

"No."

"It's the five-fingers blossom. Mutter tells me it takes away fever."

"Will she tell you all the flower lore?"

"Yes, as soon as I am a woman. Then it will be *me* people come to when they are ill."

———

Although the testimony was very damning, the friar told us the inquisition would allow a final test of innocence. He ordered a large kettle of water to be boiled on the stove at the end of the hall where I sat. No one spake as the water heated. When I heard the bubbles violently moving the kettle on the stove, I shuddered.

The friar took off Künne's blindfold and helped her down from her perch. Though he clearly believed her to be in concert with the devil, he offered her the bracing arm any man might give to an old woman. Taking a box in the shape of the cross that the notary gave him, he walked her to the side of the room, slowly and with pomp. They stopped in front of the boiling kettle. He opened the box and took out three pebbles.

"This is for the Father," he said, dropping one into the boiling water. "And this is for the Son, and this for the Holy Ghost." All three stones sank into the hissing water.

"Künne Himmelmann, if you are able to retrieve these three pebbles and the holiness of the Trinity keeps your skin from burning, you shall be released from the accusations facing you today," he said.

My own hands clenched in prayer. I believed strongly in the goodness of the Father who sent his Son to earth, and in the sanctity of the Son whose very soul was a dove beating its wings inside his skin, but I had never seen a woman fight boiling water and win.

Künne's hand hovered over the water. The water danced up to meet it, spitting playfully. She withdrew her hand. "Before I do such a deed, I beg the Father to assist me. May I pray?"

The friar tightened his lips. "We shall soon find out if your plea is heard. Go on."

Künne looked around wildly. "I hardly have words in front of all these eyes."

"It can be difficult to perform a righteous act that one has mocked."

Künne reached out and touched the friar. I winced as she did it. Künne was always one to put the kisses on any cheek, to reach out intimately to a traveler who only asked the road. "I have never, Friar, never mocked the act of prayer. In the dark times, I beseeched our Father. When the Black Death was upon us, my lips were always moving in an endless prayer. And though the prayers did not keep my husband on this earth, nor my children, nor the loved ones of any of us in this room, I still believe in the goodness of our God. I trust that we must endure travails on earth to earn a place in paradise."

The friar examined the place on his arm that she had touched.

"Will you not extend mercy to me, Friar?" she asked. Since he did not look at her, she put a hand to his cheek, and he jerked back as if her hand was a leper's.

"You are bold," said the friar in a low tone. "Sinfully bold. I know what the water will tell us. *Go then!*" He yelled the last part and seized her hand, pushing it into the kettle.

She screamed and pulled it out instantly.

"Have you the pebbles?" he asked.

"You know I have not!"

"They would have sprung to your hand if you were innocent!"

Künne made a keening sound, then plunged her hand in again. She threw her head back and the sound became a scream, her face a horrible rictus of pain as her hand plumbed the depths of the tall kettle, seeking for the stones. She came up with two and threw them at the friar. Her hand and arm, up to nearly her elbow, were an angry red. "You will find me guilty even if Jesus Christ should stand here at my shoulder and sing praise of me!"

"The third stone, Frau Himmelmann?" asked the friar.

She blew upon her arm as if it were a hot spoon about to go into her mouth, and waved it around with a cringe that made me gather up my skirts tight in both hands. I wanted to run to her and usher her to her own pots of salve, waiting in her cottage.

She bit her lip so hard her entire jaw went white, and held her hand over the kettle. Even the steam hurt her, I saw. And then she tried. She darted in but didn't go far before she screamed and pulled it out again. She shook her arm wildly, gasping and shrieking, droplets of water spraying around her. And then her hand went in again, as if she tried to trick it, like a boy might jump into the river before giving himself time to be afraid.

She could not conquer the boiling water. She looked at all around her in despair, her eyes piteous. And then she fastened her gaze again upon the kettle. "My skin is burning," she said simply. "I have already failed."

She had not said her prayer before making the test.

—————

On the way home, I stepped into the large snowdrifts, wanting to suffer. My leathern boots were soon wet and ice panged its way into my feet. Jost walked quickest of all of us and soon disappeared.

They had wrapped Künne's hand in bandages, and would unwrap it at the end of three days to see if it had been spared. In the meantime, she would wait in the stone tower that had always been the prison but now was coming to be called the Witch's Tower.

Frau Töpfer scurried to catch up with Irmeltrud, nearly knocking me over as she flew by.

"What think you of the day's events?" she asked excitedly.

"That didn't put soup in my mouth, but it filled me somehow," said Irmeltrud.

I watched their stolid backs, not believing what I'd heard. It filled her somehow? Künne's suffering was soup in her mouth? I ceased walking and remained frozen. They walked on, a babble of bright spite. "I knew it of her, old hag. Jealous of our hen. She'll be clucking soon enough, with fire at the hem of her gown!"

"That one is fearful for her," said Irmeltrud, nodding back at me.

"Fearful she'll get the evil eye too?"

"No. Not fearful *of* her, but *for* her. Because they are friends."

"Then she had best stay off my stone!" laughed Frau Töpfer. She reached out and patted it, for they were now nearing her dooryard. "Keep in good health, then," she said to Irmeltrud and the children, then walked to her own door.

I finally roused myself to walk again. As I approached the Töpfer yard, Frau Töpfer came outside again, hatred in her eyes. "My bread has fallen," she said. "The first we've had in weeks, and it's flat as a leaf."

I stared at her, thinking of the cat kneading, its paws working in replica of a woman's dough-pressing hands.

"You had better not be part of this," she said.

5

An example was brought to our notice as Inquisitors . . .
a certain buried woman was gradually eating the
shroud in which she had been buried.

— MALLEUS MALEFICARUM

We had no dinner that night.

The children went and sat at the table at the proper hour. "Mutter, I'm hungry," said Matern.

"I have nothing for you, *Lieblinge,*" said Irmeltrud. She went outside with two bowls and filled them with snow. She set them in front of the children. "It's the fairies' food," she said. "Light as air."

Alke began to cry.

Jost had not looked at me all afternoon, consumed with building up the fire so that we would at least all be warm, then sharpening his knife. "I'll go milk Künne's goat for her," he said. He took the bucket and a knife with him.

"Alke, I'll mend your nightgown for you," I said. "Even if you're hungry, you can sleep well with tight stitches in your garment."

Alke let snow fall out of her hand onto her lap, and all heads twitched to look at me.

"Can I not do such a simple task to please you?" I asked.

"You're dazed, Güde," said Irmeltrud. "The gown is naught but ashes today."

"How is this so?" I asked.

"I threw it in the fire yesterday, and the pot cloth too, for the animal here with you had brought blood to them both."

I remembered somewhat, then truly remembered. I had been petting the cat that had rested on the sill to stare in at me. I touched the mark upon my forehead.

"Well might you touch it," said Irmeltrud. "That cat has transfixed your mind, be it black or yellow or gray or striped."

But she knew my mind had been similarly vexed even before the cat came. In recent years, I had forgotten the most basic things, such as Jost's name—and one time, a horrible day in the forest, who he was. He was a stranger, holding a pheasant by its neck, and I struggled with the thought that perhaps I ought to know him. After he removed his hat and spake some words with me, I fixed my head and did. "What shall I sew, then?" I asked simply.

Irmeltrud shook her head and put branches onto the fire, then went to sit with the children. I took the iron fire prod and poked through the ashes, wondering which of them was the nightgown Alke used to dream in.

I hoped Künne's dreams in the Witch's Tower were of May and brilliantly colored flowers.

When Jost returned, he had meat. His face was grim and to my look of wonderment he answered, "Künne's goat."

Irmeltrud readied a pot for the chunks of hindquarter, and

the children ran deliriously around her skirts. It was frightening to see how excitedly they danced, because it showed how desperately hungry they were.

"But Jost, this is surely not even a tenth of what that goat had to give," said Irmeltrud. "Did you leave the carcass at her barn?"

"I was not the only one with the idea of killing it," he said. "Many men were at Künne's tonight, sifting through her larder and casting a murderous eye on the goat."

I let out a cry of alarm. "Do they not think these things still belong to her?"

"She'll not return for them," grunted Irmeltrud.

I looked at Jost. "No, no. She may pass the test."

"I think she will not return," said Jost to me, in as gentle a tone as possible. "So many spake against her, and her arm was red with boils already before they wrapped it."

"So how was the goat divvied?" asked Irmeltrud angrily, now that she had a better look at what he had brought home. "We are the closest neighbors and ought to have the largest share. This is lacking, Jost!"

"I was lucky to get what I got," said Jost. "There were many men there. The entire village is as hungry as we are."

"The Töpfers had bread to bake today," said Irmeltrud bitterly.

"But you went only to milk the goat," I said. "How did it happen that the goat was killed?"

"Ah, God, your mind gone and your eyes too!" said Irmeltrud. "He took a knife with him, clattering in the bucket."

I was ashamed for him, until I remembered that he had spoken up for Künne in front of the friar.

"So the bucket is empty, I see," said Irmeltrud.

"They drank straight from her udder before gashing her throat," said Jost.

"And was there anything in the larder for the taking? Where's our share of that?"

"Gone too quickly," said Jost.

"And why didn't you press the men to give you what was rightly yours? You let them leave with hands full?"

"Curb your tongue, woman. There were wild eyes there and knives still wet. Enjoy what we have and be silent," he said.

"And why weren't your eyes wild then as well? Your children sat down to eat snow tonight!"

"You would have been frighted at the scene, wife. Had Künne herself showed up, she would have been torn limb from limb. Things were broken and thrown across the room, her bedding savaged to see if coins were buried there. I'd not be surprised if they hack the walls down to feed their fires."

An aroma drifted from the cooking goat meat, and Irmeltrud fell silent to inhale. Tears sprang to her eyes. "We lived through the plague, a time when you saw someone and thought, *I may never look upon you again, so good tidings.* We lived through it and bore children and to what end? To starve in our homes?"

"God will provide for us. All we need is a good spring to plant again," said Jost.

Irmeltrud gave a low laugh and I knew what she thought

of the idea of a good spring. Did such a thing even exist anymore?

"Step back, children," said Jost, for Alke and Matern were so near to the meat that they could easily fall in the fire.

We all sat and waited as the meat cooked. Then finally Irmeltrud pulled the pot from the shelf and we all hastened to the table. She distributed the chunks by size: the largest to Jost and herself, then middling-sized to the children, and a tiny piece to me. It scorched my mouth, as it did all of us, but we were too famished to care and ate through our tongues' pain. The meat was tough since the goat was stringy and as ill-fed as the rest of the village. Nevertheless, red juice oozed from it and my teeth joyfully mashed the fibers as I tasted the salt of it. I reached for Alke's bowl of snow, now melted into water, and drank it.

Afterward, we all sat looking at the empty board, shocked that the feast had ended so soon. Irmeltrud brought over the cooled pot and we ran our fingers in the grease and licked them.

And then the cat jumped onto the table and tried to oil its paw as well.

"Fie!" screamed Irmeltrud. She sprang to her feet, upsetting the trencher, which smashed to the ground. The cat yowled and dashed into the shadows at the other end of the room.

"Are you keeping it, Güde?" she asked.

"May it please God, I never opened the door to it!" I protested. My heart was beating rapidly from the clash, and I wondered how many more pulses it had left before ceasing its work.

"Did it not spring onto the table from your pallet?" she demanded.

"When did I have a chance to bring in the beast?"

"It must have come in as I did," said Jost. "And tame yourself. 'Tis easy to rid ourselves of a cat." He stood and walked to the corner.

"Cross yourself, Jost! Perhaps 'tis Künne here to visit Güde. Look at the animal's leg. Is it red and sore?"

"Be silent," said Jost. "It is no more Künne than the fat in the pan."

"I wager the jail keeper sees her no longer in the tower. She made herself invisible and slipped through the door, then cast herself as a cat so that she may visit Güde—"

"Silence!" roared Jost.

Matern, predictably, began to cry. His sister simply looked on with alarmed eyes. Irmeltrud pressed her lips together and stared at me. As angry as she was at Jost for bellowing, she blamed me.

"Künne is a good woman who bound herbs to ease us all," said Jost. "We have her to thank for the good health of these two, and I don't remember you thinking ill of her when you were straining in childbirth! She's dear to Mutter, and thereby dear to me. If we see her burned at the stake for the foolishness of that woman who is barren and can't believe it, it'll be a sorry day for our village."

Jost leaned over and easily picked up the cat. Carrying it to the door, his face bent into its fur, he pressed the latch, opened the door, and silently tossed the cat into the snow.

"Won't it be cold?" asked Alke.

"It can shelter in the granary," said Jost. "And it's wearing its own coat, as thick as the pelt we're drying for you." He pointed to the rabbit hide hanging above the fire.

"Vater, was that Künne?" asked Matern.

"It was a cat only," said Jost firmly. "Poor Künne is less comfortable tonight than that cat could ever be. Now let's get ourselves to bed so that we may be ready for what befalls us tomorrow."

"I don't have a nightgown, and there wasn't enough dinner," said Alke.

"You'll sleep in your shift, as you have been," said Irmeltrud.

"What happened to her gown?" asked Jost.

"It had blood on it from the devil that marked your mother. I burned it."

"No, son, I scraped myself with the needle while mending it," I cried. "Any woman can have a needle slip."

"I'll hear no more about witches and devils," said Jost sternly. "Your own daughter will shiver tonight since you burned her nightgown for a simple stain."

"Mutter told us to remember the blood," offered Matern.

"I am worried full sore for our children, Jost," said Irmeltrud. "Signs are everywhere around us: cats appearing out of nowhere, bloody marks on foreheads. Are you not concerned that Matern and Alke are in danger?"

"I am not," he said. "Witchcraft is no more in our house than it was in Künne's. You're doing nothing but scaring them."

Tears brimmed in Irmeltrud's eyes and she put a protective arm around Matern's shoulders, reaching across to grasp Alke's hand. "Children, get onto your knees," she whispered.

We all of us knelt and made the sign of the cross. "Our Father, save us from the women who ride at night, cast to the wind by the force of their own evil," prayed Irmeltrud. "Keep our door free from beasts that hide the form of witches. Rid our village of evil. Bring us food, Father, that we may sup in fortitude as at your table. May meat load our board to groaning, and purity reign in our hearts. Amen."

Even for this short prayer, my knees were aching from balancing on the dirt.

"No more talk of witches," Jost instructed as we all rose. "Let's go to sleep and dream with our stomachs full."

With relief, I lay myself onto my tick and drew the blankets up to my neck. I always was grateful for the straw receiving me, but now that my body worked more slowly, the repose was more beloved. Sometimes as I sank in, I half wished I would not rise again.

"My nightgown was warmer than my shift," Alke sniffled across the room.

"Then blame Güde's shaking hands while you shake," said Irmeltrud.

6

All witchcraft comes from carnal lust,
which is in women insatiable.

— MALLEUS MALEFICARUM

In the middle of the night, it put two paws onto my chest, bold as an incubus. In the light from the waning fire, I saw the cat was back. I shuddered in fear and made to push it from me. But it licked the hand that came at it, and then licked at its own paw, and the industry of its motion was so like to that of a child that I stopped, entranced.

Hesitantly, I held my hand up, and it butted against it like a baby calf seeking the nipple. I petted it and was lost again in the softness. Why did fur feel so much finer than skin? And heat pumped from its body too, better than any blanket. It settled its entire body onto my chest and I relaxed under the warm weight. I peered about the room to see how it might have gotten in. Had it dug under the door or prised up the window cloth? The instant its purr began, the singing began.

Thus am I banished from my bliss
By craft and false pretense . . .

It was a high, reedy woman's voice, singing from the other side of the wall. I stiffened, waiting to see if Jost and the others would wake from it. The cat continued its purr, even as my hand slackened on its fur from my sudden fear. For who would stand facing the wall of this cottage and sing, if not one of the women who rides out at night? *Faultless, without offense,* sang the voice, but I heard the smile that belied the words. There *was* fault, there *was* offense.

It was the woman who had walked the air above me the night Irmeltrud put me out.

"Off me!" I whispered harshly to the cat, knocking it with the side of my arm. Without a sound, it was gone. "Why do you seek me out?" I whispered to the air. "I am a child of Christ. Use me not in your twisted design!"

After a long pause, the voice began singing again. This time the singer was inside the house, next to my straw bed. All I could see of her was her dark shadow. She had left her corporeal body abed and sent her shadow whistling through the night. She leaned over me, still singing, and I saw she was a perfect reversal of what she ought to be. Her dark hair was white as edelweiss and her skin black as scorch. Her teeth were black too, and her eyes, except the very centers, which blazed white. Her loose hair unfurled and lengthened, stretching like a sheet being unfolded, until I lay beneath the canopy of her motionless, hovering white hair.

I closed my eyes to this hideous spectacle and willed my lips to speak their prayers. But they would not rustle for this task. I was clenched in bewitchment, unable to move.

Lightly, softly, I felt her hair descend upon me, covering every bit of my skin and the tick too, as careful as a death shroud. My skin prickled in sheer terror, but I could do nothing. She was now pressed against me like a lover, her face upon my face. She sang into my mouth. Then each hair from her head, acting on its own, curled under my body and lifted me. We floated through the wall and I felt the bitter wind.

She sang and I kept my eyes closed fast. She sang me into the forest, where the crows unwrapped her hair and she released me. I finally opened my eyes and gasped to see the same women crowded around me.

"Güde, welcome," they spake at different pitches, sounding like a ghastly, wronged choir.

One held out a piece of meat, and as much as I tried to keep my hand at my side, hunger won out and I accepted the offered flesh into my palm. As they watched, fascinated, I lifted the chunk to my lips and pushed it in, entire. It was succulent but nothing I had tasted in my life.

Juice coating my tongue, I watched as the witch's stark black and white faded and her cheeks gained the bloom of living skin, her lips the stain of berries.

There were four dogs outside the circle, each with its tail tied to a string attached to a lamp set in the snow. These small lamps gave all the light available to me as I stared into each of the women's faces, wondering if any was Künne in false guise. None of them was of my village.

"The villagers all ate of Künne's goat," said one women. "But we gave the beast the obscene kiss, so they have tarnished themselves with that flesh!"

They all laughed, hands full of the unknown meat. There was no beast on the spit.

"What do we sup on?" I asked. "The leavings of the goat?"

"No, the child that Frau Zweig forgets she bore!" said one.

"It is easy to cloud a mind with snake paste and demon-wort," added another.

"She complains of an empty womb but she has borne children to us, spidery and malformed, which we put to our mouths and ate of. We have eaten of all of them," she concluded with glee.

I spat the flesh out onto the snow and spun around, stumbling, to race away. But I had taken no more than a step or two before a tree root, invisible beneath the snow, caught my foot and brought me down.

"When famine keeps the fields empty, what else are we to eat?" asked the one who had brought me there.

"I am not seeing this! My eyes are tricking me!" I screamed.

"And your tongue!" laughed one wickedly. "You spit into the snow but cannot bring up what you have already swallowed."

I tried to retch then, as sickened as I ever was when carrying Jost inside my body, but nothing came. I spat and gagged, on my hands and knees in the snow.

"Tell me it was not the Zweigs' child!" I wept in between the efforts of my throat. "Tell me I am sleeping in my bed! I do not want to live in this world!"

"You are but a child of pleasure, Güde. You love the fur of the cat; you love the pelt of the rabbit. You are earthly and rutted like a sow with Hensel. You pulled his face to yours to feel the prickling slaver of his tongue. Of course you want this world!"

"I want to die now!" I said, my face pressed into the snow.

"Why not see as we do first? We only offer pleasure."

A hand pressed against my back, firm and kind. "Rise, Güde." It was the voice of the woman who brought me. "You did not eat of the child."

I made myself sit up, wanting desperately to believe her. "What was the meat, then?"

"Künne's goat."

"But it was passing strange."

"It was the goat," she insisted. She had such red lips, the color of flowers, of the brightest May Day ribbon. "Color too," she said to the women behind her. "To pleasure the eye of Güde. Fur and skin and color: all these we number as tools to bring Güde to us."

"But we know what she *truly* wants," said one.

"The ice-cold prick!" said another.

I saw for the first time that behind the semicircle of women waited another group; these were men. Among them stepped a goat, the very vision of Künne's goat, even with the tan spot on its rump. Its bell clanged eerily in the dark forest.

"But I know her to be slaughtered!" I protested, panicking again. "And did we not just eat of her?"

"You will see what we wish you to see," said the women in unison. They all knelt and the men behind knelt as well. They spoke in unison with broken tones, like a death rattle.

"Am I not in my bed dreaming?" I whispered to myself. "Are there not fleas a-biting and bringing me to wakefulness?"

My skin was numb now from the snow, and my bones beginning to ache, as if I had set them to carry far more weight than they could.

The goat muttered the chant too, his horns glinting as they moved with the motion. He walked to me and I stared at the flanks that narrowed to the knife-thin ankles and then the sharp hooves.

"We now pray," said the women. And I saw that they arranged their hands in prayer, not with the fingertips pointing up as we do each Sabbath, but with the fingertips pointing down.

I shuffled backward in the snow, and the beast similarly stepped forward, maintaining the scant distance between us.

Was this Künne's goat, that I had seen her milk a hundred times, her forehead nestling against its side? The goat impatiently shook itself and the bell rang out.

"I will not do this," I said. "You may drag me from my bed and I cannot stop you. But I shall not pray to your unholy master nor chant your wicked words!"

The goat bounded off and in the midst of its leap vanished.

"Hensel could make her pray!" called one of the men. I stared into the dimness to see which man had known the name of my love.

"Douse the lamps then."

One by one, each of the dogs was spanked on its ass, causing it to run in startlement. As they ran, the strings attached to their tails pulled the lamps over, until the flames met snow and died. We were in darkness.

And in darkness, the moans and low laughter began. Although I could see nothing, I knew there was much commotion happening. Then, in a moment's time, I saw him there before me: the kind, rough face.

It was like the days when Jost was first born, when he

would cry in the night with no candle burning, and I'd see my husband's yawning face in the half-light left by our dying fire. He'd wake faster than me, have brought the babe to my breast before I scarce heard his weep. "Suckle your son," Hensel would say gently, and in darkness I would do so.

It was the same now, but with no crying child. Just the kind face I could barely see.

"Güde, how you have lacked to me," he said.

Tears trickled down my face in blessed amaze. Hensel! Back to me as handsome and strong-voiced as before I put him in the ground. I stepped closer to him and laid my head against his chest. Inside his heart was beating the same skipping rhythm that his mother had given him when she dropped a crock on his foot when he was a child. His arms crept around my waist and I burrowed into his heart's sound, trying to suppress my own tears and the murmurs around us so that I could hear only that richness. How long had he lain in his grave with his chest pulsing?

"Your hair still smells sweet as hay," he said. He pulled me away to stare into my eyes. I nearly swooned. It was him! It was truly no trick. Whatever bargain he had made, whatever black words he had uttered to make it, I cared not.

And as my man had always done, he hitched up my skirt.

I cried out to the wind and sagged into his hands, into his mouth. I returned his fervor and willingly spun as he turned me around. My skin began to feel like that of a woman's again—no longer loose but taut with blood and desire, muscles underneath the skin clenching. His hands tightened on my waist as he pressed me forward against a tree. My fingers seized on the bark and I bent down, as eager for the rut as a maid half my years. I spread my legs, balancing my feet on the uneven surges of the roots that spread from the tree.

"You signed," he whispered into my ear. "You signed the book."

"I never did, my love," I protested, but I didn't care if I had or not. All that mattered was feeling *this* again, the heat of my husband, those familiar hands cupping my breasts. His rhythm, how he rutted and how his heart skipped to its own odd devising.

They were still murmuring around us. I only listened to Hensel's ardent breathing. My fingers clawed the tree bark, thanking the tree spirit for bracing me.

Upon my foot, I noticed a tiny pressing, side to side. I did not have to look to know that it was the cat, kneading bread there.

I was overcome by his kisses and his hands and his gusts of breath and, surrounding us, the cries of pleasure between the trees, everyone clasping someone in the darkness, everyone slaking themselves, a carnal passion that made the snow heated.

To my left, forehead against the tree, I saw the dark dog shapes return to their upset lamps and sit patiently in the snow. I couldn't count the incredible number of shadows I saw from the corners of my eyes, embracing and bending. It was like a wind shook all the trees and we were boughs, swaying and tossing with its power.

"Ah, God!" I cried, and then I timed my breath to the grunt from behind and he and I strove together at this act, and I thought of nothing but the hot slide of him in me.

The dogs howled for the wonder of it, and the crows made a

mockery of the sky, and I thought my body would burst for all the pleasure it had had. I ran my hand down Hensel's thigh and wept, but without caring, when I found his leg ended in a hoof.

And then I was alone.

And the snow was untouched but for my own footprints, staggered as they were.

The cat led me home, always a gray shape delicately lifting its paws a few steps ahead of me. The door was locked and so I sank against it, while the beast meowed on the windowsill for Jost to awake.

———

I woke to the sound of Alke and Matern playing a hand-slapping game. I opened my eyes to see their hands in the air, their faces in concentration. The sound of skin on skin, the slap of the game, was rhythmic and brought me back to the nighttime forest and the layers of hushed voices.

I was in my bed. The straw beneath me was warm enough for me to have lain there for hours. The fire was already built and Jost gone. I ran a hand down my stomach. My nightgown was dry. I wiggled to the edge of the bed, feeling the dizzy tilt of sitting up too quickly from a deep sleep.

As I stood, I lifted my skirts to see if there were marks on my skin.

"Please spare us the sight of those old shanks," remarked Irmeltrud. "My stomach is already off from the lack of break-fast."

I dropped my skirts. She was right. I hated to see my legs myself: angular, crossed with knobbed veins. When I was younger, a fine layer of muscle had sat beneath the skin, show-ing itself with my every move, as plump and firm as sausages.

"Good morning, Großmutter," the children chorused, tim-ing it with their slaps.

I smiled feebly and hovered over them, nodding at their game in encouragement.

"It stings," said Alke. "You can hit less hard."

"If you play with a boy, you should expect stings," said Matern.

She smiled an older sister's smile at him. He mirrored her, and there they sat, heads gamboled like quizzical chickens'.

It would seem the night had never happened. I had thought all the ardor of my husband's kisses would surely have rough-ened my skin, but looking at my arms and legs, I saw that I was pale and untouched as ever. I went to the pan on the hearthstone and washed my face and hands with its warmed water. My skin smelled as always. It was a dream I'd had, that Hensel returned. I pulled at the skin of my forearm and saw the true outline of my bone as clearly defined as any saint's relic. I should already be buried in the churchyard.

He who chops wood is the cause of the actual fire.

—MALLEUS MALEFICARUM

Hensel and I had wed in the year of the mute wolf, on a
June day. He milled in the morning, but the men all
converged upon him at once and dumped their grain upon his
head for merriment, and so as I stood next to him for the troth-
ing I smelled the wheaty odor. He winked at me throughout
the ceremony, so much so that I giggled and earned a frown
from the priest. I had remained a virgin for him, although
Künne had told me I was foolish to wait so long since I already had his promise. The night I made love for the first
time was the first night I'd spent in this cottage; our marriage
bed was the one now used by Jost, Irmeltrud, and the two
children.

All the wedding party gathered at the window, pushing
each other aside to lift the cloth and peer inside. They jostled
for space, shouting lewdly, "Open your legs wide then,
Güde!" and "You'll have to press through the briars to find
the cuckoo's nest, Hensel!"

Künne's face appeared. She made no call but simply grinned and winked in at me.

"Can we not pin down the cloth?" I pleaded.

"Aw, give them their pleasure too," said Hensel, smiling gently. "It's summertime! We are all lovers now." He positioned his body so his head blocked the view of the window for me. Such a handsome face! The eyes that wrestled with a gentian for the best kind of blue, and the strong jaw with soft whiskers. Hensel's eyelashes were longer than a broom's straw and I sank into his kiss until I didn't care who saw my legs wrapped around him, and eventually giggled at the thought of his arse pumping away to their amusement.

Afterward, I pulled my gown back down—clean white it was, embroidered with tiny bluebells by my steady hand— and we invited everyone in to sit at the table and eat with us. They crowded in, the entire village practically, except for Ottilie Shuster, who'd set her cap on Hensel and spent our wedding day crying in the forest. They were so many that they sat upon the bed—making great sport of avoiding the wet area where Hensel's seed had leaked—and upon the ground and leaned against the wall . . . and there was so much food back then! We had nary a thought of not sharing what we had; there was so much. Hensel's mill was going all the day to grind the meal and oft he had to tell the men to return the next day; he had all he could do to grind what he had. There was a flock of sheep on the hill that was his, and he traded for whatever else we needed. That day we offered our guests bread, and lard cakes, and lamp chops with fat sizzling around the edges of the meat, and a profusion of radishes.

Everyone ate to satisfaction, making the sign of the meat, the women coming to kiss my belly for the life that might be in it already and the men pinching my cheeks to retain the redness Hensel's romping had brought to them. I had thought the cottage would burst for all the life in it, for the merry songs that would end in laughter, the milky puddle that embarrassed me and still clung to my thighs, and the women calling out the names of the animals who assist fertility. And the gurgle of the tankards being filled, my own arm aching from the filling and refilling of the pitcher, but minding not, for I couldn't stop smiling and every time I walked past Hensel he would grab my waist and pull me onto his lap to make everyone cheer, and how many times I was kissed that day! And how I too ate, my fingers darting like crows onto the trenchers to grab a bite here and there, thinking perhaps a child was inside me needing its first bite of lamb—and there *was* a child. It was Jost, hearing the cries of the villagers' good time too, and the song about the alewife's bosom.

They didn't leave until the next morning, and the next time Hensel took himself inside me it was only us two. And thereafter, in bed, on the table, on the hillside, or on the granary floor as the mill ground the grain, it was only us two, no spies at the window. I loved what Hensel did, how he could push himself so deeply into me. I loved all the words he whispered to me, how he bit his lip in agony, how I was all the time pressing a cloth between my legs to catch the drippings as they came. There had been one more child, a little body sleeping in the cradle, but she was crafted of air and only stayed a moon's cycle. Only Jost survived, the one who'd benefited from the neighbors hooting and whistling him into life.

When Hensel sickened from the plague, I never believed it could take him. He was so loud, so rough! What could ever defeat him? And yet his skin purpled and blackened and he writhed under the weight of those hideous bubbles. Künne and I used compresses upon his skin, and they did bring him easement and his moaning did abate. But they could not save that man whose soul was a very bear, grinning its way through all the honey and his large paws knocking away the bees. After we buried him, I remember thinking that I would never have a man inside me again.

———

"What are you dreaming on?" asked Irmeltrud.

"My wedding day with Hensel," I replied.

"Oh. I wondered if you might be casting your mind to Künne," she said. "Preparing your way to farewell."

It took me a moment, blinking, to think of what she meant. My mind was now caught in the image of her wedding day. I had waited outside the cottage with the others, not hooting at the window, but nevertheless with a broad smile. Irmeltrud was sweet back then. She wanted to be the miller's wife. And I thought too of how I'd given them the bed and let Jost prepare for me a mattress of clean hay in the corner, for I knew my days of producing children were long over. How Jost seemed to love the rut as much as his father, and brought Irmeltrud to the bed often. I tried not to hear but the cottage was tiny. And I remembered the first season when the grain had been ruined. *Künne . . . Preparing your way to farewell . . .* What gown would Alke wear for her husband on their wedding day? The fire had taken her nightgown. Who would embroider the tiny flowers when my fingers were so cramped and old? Were there flowers in the fire? My back was hot from sitting on the hearth. My skin prickled; my own gown was too close to the fire, might burst into flame.

Why would I need to say farewell to Künne?

I had given my body to someone who wasn't Hensel. I had freely moaned with him and never fought him off. I had welcomed him as a bride. It wasn't wrong if it was only a dream. The dogs had watched us. The lamps had plunged us into darkness, but I still felt the lamps at my back. All the heat of the lamps in the snow. It was hot, and the man was back there too. Not Hensel. Not even pretending to be Hensel. A different voice growling into my hair. A hot voice pressed into my back, ready to burst into flame. And what had he said? My gray curls falling into my face while he bucked into me. While he spake into my curls. While my curls singed. They were witches, and what had he said?

Preparing your way to farewell . . .

Was my back on fire from the heat of him? Or the dogs' lamps?

You signed the book, he said. But I never did, I never did, I never did, I never did.

Irmeltrud was slapping me. "Would that you don't awake," she was muttering. She pressed a wet cloth to my forehead and grunted. I was on the ground. I could reach out and touch the closest leg of the table's bench. "Are you all right then?" she asked.

"My head hurts. . . ."

"You were in a stupor and fell to the ground. Your head hit first."

"Is there blood?" I asked.

"No. Simply a tumble as a child would take. You shouldn't have sat so close to the fire; it made you dizzy." She sat me up and made me drink some water. "It's not even dented," she said as she pushed off my cap to run her hands through my hair. "What looks worse is the mark upon your forehead."

"The one you termed the devil's mark," I said.

"Which you denied," she said. She took away the wet cloth and stared hard into my face. "I can't believe the number of wrinkles that have beset your face," she said. "I hope to die before my face is that of an apple fallen from the tree and left to shrink and tighten."

"For all the frowning that you do, your wrinkles will be a hundredfold."

She slapped me.

I pulled away from her arms and rose to my feet. How bleak this day was, compared to the delicious, secretive dream I had had!

"I want to sleep again," I said.

"Might as well. You sleep until I rouse you for Künne's unbinding," she said.

I slumped onto my straw and began to weep. *That* was what she had meant by preparing my farewell. It had been three days, and today they would unbind Künne's arm to see if she had been burned. Everything I touched was harsh. The fronds of the hay poking me, the roughness of my linens, my own skin. I wept silently, wishing something in my life were soft.

———

Jost came home with no food. The traps were empty.

He came over to my bed. "Why are you yet sleeping, Mutter?" he asked.

"I cannot bear this day," I said.

He nodded. "I wish I had some food to offer you in your sorrow. Do you wish to stay home when we go to the church?"

I closed my eyes to consider that possibility. How wonderful to drift along on this hay, to try to forget what mischief the day held for such a good woman. "I cannot," I said. "Mine will be the only kind face she sees. Mine and yours. I must go."

"You will do her some small bit of good," he said. "Where is Irmeltrud?"

———

The church was full to brimming. Those who hadn't come to Künne's inquisition had heard of the boiling kettle trial and came with frank eagerness to see what lay under her bandages. When Jost and I arrived, Irmeltrud and the children were already there, standing in front.

Frau Zweig's eyes glowed as if her waist were thick with child instead of her heart with hatred. She twisted her hands with excitement. Next to her, Herr Zweig looked miserable.

Künne sat again on the lofty stool, like a thin bird on the worst branch. Her eyes were uncovered, yet no one could accuse her of casting the evil eye, for she only looked down into her own lap. Her bandages were dingy and browned. Her quarters in the tower must have been foul to so quickly taint the pure white. The kettle was yet on the stove. I did not need to peer into its depths to know there was one spiteful pebble still sitting on the bottom. The door opened, and in the swirl of snow the friar appeared. He paused like the queen of May Day accepting all the lovers' admiration, then strode to the foot of Künne's chair.

"Good people," he said, "today we see if the test was passed. Frau Himmelmann was not able to gather the three stones of the Trinity, but if God sees a soul worthy of salvaging within her, he will keep her flesh unblistered. If, however, he detects in her the promise she made to the Prince of Darkness to serve him and abandon all that is holy, we shall see the ugly burns upon her skin. For just as her fetid heart is ruined with boils and pus and black sores, so shall her skin show the same rudeness."

I shuddered when he said "black sores." Hensel's face flashed before my eyes, and I remembered that one horrible mouse-sized sore that burgeoned in his neck, that was purple as a cabbage and caused him such torment. And the horrid surprise of the treacle within it, when it finally burst and fluid seeped forth.

"Shall we pray?" asked the friar.

All heads quickly bowed, though Frau Zweig still wore a secular grin.

"Our Father in the remotest height of heaven, who observeth our every deed and passeth judgment, we beg your hand to guide us today in rooting out evil and restoring piety to this village. Your Son died for our sins, and in sure confoundment of his purpose, we find sin increasing and spreading. We see that women are become wicked and in love with wrongdoing, that when they can no longer bring children to the earth they instead bring malevolence. We ask your guidance in breaking the spell that has kept Frau Zweig's womb empty when it was many times clearly filled. We beg you to return sense to the hen, that she may give the eggs that are her earthly duty. If we have wronged Künne Himmelmann in our accusations, leave her flesh as untouched as the snow that drives outside. But if we are right in our surmise that she traffics with the devil and his demons, let the flesh speak for itself. We proceed upon your blessing. Amen."

The friar stepped onto a block so that he could reach Künne's arm. He lifted it out of her lap, and it was so limp it was as if she were fever-struck or lay in the plague cart.

How I longed to see unburned skin beneath! What joy it would be to laugh in the Töpfers' faces and to shoot Frau Zweig a shaming look. Künne would climb down from that stool and Jost would carry her home, where I'd feed her . . . I didn't know what I could feed her.

I would press a kiss to that smooth skin and thank God for saving her. All day I would rub that stretch of arm and marvel.

Künne made no grimace as the friar unwound the cloths, and the hope began in my heart. Should she not be twisting in pain if blisters were beneath the bandages? Yet she calmly sat as if no further sensation came than that of a housefly crawling her arm.

The Lord is merciful, I thought. *He knows she has not bewitched anyone and he will set her free.*

I grasped Jost's hand. The friar continued pulling on the cloth. And then, suddenly, his efforts were curtailed. The cloth was stuck. He pulled harder and Künne shrieked and tried to pull her arm away. We could all hear the tearing of the flesh as it clung to the cloth. Künne writhed and bit her lips to keep from screaming. The friar did not try gently, but ruthlessly yanked with all his strength, pulling his arm out to full length like a woman measuring cloth for a garment.

I could see the mottled pink of her burned skin and the trickles of blood arising from the torn flesh. Künne whimpered, and thankfully the friar was soon finished. The bandage was a ghastly sight, brown with dirt on one side and stained with blood and mess on the other. The friar held it in the air, dangling, like an important scroll.

Künne tried to set her arm back down onto her lap, but it was too painful. She held it hovering in midair, staring at the cloth in the friar's hands as if she hated it.

"The spot of murderer is upon you," said the friar. "You have killed young babes who were not yet of this world."

"Murderer!" screamed Frau Zweig, and she stood up to point at Künne. "You owe me for the souls of three!"

And all was suddenly mayhem, with the few benches knocked over as people jumped to their feet and pulsed forward, everyone shouting, all in a frenzy to denounce Künne. They advanced upon her giant stool and would have torn her from it if the friar hadn't stopped them.

"We will not abuse so crudely," he said in a low voice that

somehow still penetrated through the clamor. "We will send Künne to a higher judge in a goodly manner, not like pups attacking the runt. Step away from her."

It was done. His words had as much power as a prince's. There was a respectful ring of space around Künne.

"To cleanse this soul to return it to God, we must burn the malefaction from it."

I heard an intense wail of anguish, which was abruptly stopped when Jost clamped a hand across my mouth. The rest of the villagers moved from foot to foot, restless, barely containing themselves from seizing Künne. She sat as a stone, the burned arm still hovering, too painful to rest on any surface.

"We must make a holy fire," said the friar. "A parishioner today gathered the wood and received bread for her sacred task. I have blessed the pyre and the stake, hewn from the tallest tree found in an hour's walk, and carefully stripped of its bark and made smooth for its task."

My saliva went bitter at the thought of who might've cut such wood. Which of us had been such a Judas?

The friar turned his back to us and addressed Künne. "Are you prepared to purify your soul to return it to God?"

She made no reply.

"It will be a joy to you, Künne Himmelmann, to feel the heat of forgiveness cleaning your bones. Renounce your promise to the devil and you shall be relieved of that obligation to the Lord of Darkness."

"When?" she asked. Her voice was a mere croak.

"Now."

A half-suppressed chortle came from Frau Zweig. She had her revenge.

"Sir," whispered Künne. Her voice was but a reed. I saw her swallow and try to gain power. "I renounce the devil now. I am sore ashamed for my deeds." She paused. Her blue eyes fixed on the friar's face. She was earnest, her eyebrows raised and her hands clenched in fists. She swallowed again, dropping her gaze, and continued. "I wish I had never, out of jealousy, kept the babes from Frau Zweig. I renounce that and beg her forgiveness. Can I not prostrate myself before you and God and keep my place on earth, to toil in humble servitude to those I have wronged?"

"The best toil you can make now is to give God your base self," replied the friar.

"I will never forgive you!" shrieked Frau Zweig.

Künne looked down at her arm, the betrayer of her entire body. "Our mighty God has blessed me with herb knowledge," she said. "I look at my own arm and know I may pack it with herbs and in a moon's phase heal it. I know too that I may make a pessary for Frau Zweig that will help fasten her husband's seed in her and later ease her in childbirth. I will remove the hex from the hen and she will lay again. I will make my potions that everyone in the village relies on, to lessen a fever or bring the humors to their proper balance. I will be a slave to this good village, devoting all my labor to undoing my treachery."

"She never will!" screamed Frau Zweig.

"God has given *you* herb knowledge?" asked the friar. "We all live and die according to his mandate. It is his will that we burn in fever or rise from the sickbed. You are blasphemous to think you have such power!"

"But you say my herbs had the power to cause Frau Zweig to expel her babes. Is that not blasphemous as well?" She faltered through this short speech, and I groaned as I heard it. I knew what she had just spoken had sealed her fate. Silence reigned, then Künne began to cry. I sank onto my knees and Jost put his hand on the crown of my head. The friar adjusted his robes and when he raised his head again his face was filled with fury. He reached over and, incredibly, used his fingers to prise open Künne's mouth.

"Is there not a forked tongue in here, flickering behind your teeth, to speak such vile lies? I would bind your mouth, but for the fact that fire will silence you far more profitably!"

I heard the strange gags as his fingers plied her throat.

"I command you to silence," he said. "Let that besmirched speech ring for all eternity as your final words."

"Every prisoner that is condemned deserves to say their last farewells," spake Jost loudly.

"Who has interest in what farewells a *Hexe* may give?" the friar replied.

"She has the right," maintained Jost.

"Approach," said the friar.

Jost's hand moved to my elbow to guide me. I walked like a newborn goat, my legs crumpling beneath me, staggering under the weight of movement. The top of my head reached her knees. I stared at her skirt, black with filth. What had they done to her in the tower?

"We have never believed this of you," said Jost.

I heard a commotion behind us in response.

"Did you not just hear me confess?" she asked.

"You spake to bend his charity but held no sway. Your last words should be to claim your innocence," he said. "Do not let this false testimony stand."

"He will build the fire higher if I let it stand," she said. "I want to die quickly, not feel the flames halfway licking my feet."

I could not believe her boldness in speaking of this, with everyone breathing softly to catch our every word.

"Mutter, you should say your last to Künne," Jost said.

I had no idea what I could say. I raised my eyes from the blackness of her skirt up to the raw meat of her boiled arm, crooked in midair as if she held a basket on her forearm, up the sturdy cast of her bodice to the face I knew better than my own, for I had only seen mine reflected in still water, and water was never still in our village. I gazed up at her as if I were a child begging for the comfort of a lap. And her face did comfort me, all the kindliness of the wrinkles earned by living, the broad cheeks I had kissed endlessly over the years.

"Güde, my dearest friend," she said. "My dearest and most beloved friend. My heart wrenches to think of how sweet has been the life I lived with you."

I clenched her skirts in one hand and pressed my forehead against her knee.

"I remember well," she continued loudly, "how you counseled me against the witchcraft. How I wish I had listened to you! I scorned your concern and did as I pleased. Had I only listened to the pure words of Güde, who despises any device that turns a soul against God! Güde, who pulled me to my knees and prayed with me, all for naught."

Her leg was quivering. The cloth scratched against my forehead. I listened to these words and marveled at them, in great consternation. Had I counseled her? I could not remember such a thing.

"With your great affection for Frau Zweig, you urged me to cease my unsavory craft, but I was too hateful to stop. I hope Frau Zweig knows the travails you went through, to try to move me otherwise."

I heard her voice change a bit. "Jost, your *Mutter* is a wondrous, humble soul. Be ever grateful that she and Hensel had instruction of your morality as you grew, for they are truly those whom God favors for their service."

"Hensel Müller died with crusted sores on his body!" called Herr Töpfer. "Is that how God favored him?"

"We know good and wrong perished equally in that scourge," said Künne. "Lift your head, Güde, and give me one final kiss."

I was dazed with grief. Could I not find words to succor her? Would I sob rather than speak, dumb when I most needed speech? I attempted to say something, but there was no breath in my throat.

"It's all right, Güde," she said. "Don't think for a moment that I went to my death not knowing the love that has sustained us through all life's misery."

I did lift my head and she leaned down to kiss me, bent almost double. She held the burned arm to the side to keep it away from contact. As my lips pressed the soft dough of her lined cheek, she whispered urgently into my ear, "Bring me the herb that hangs on the back of my door. It will deaden my suffering."

Then, too soon, she was straightening again and my lips pressed only air.

"We have long counted you as family," said Jost, and Künne nodded. He pulled me away.

"Your time of humility commences," said the friar. "We will strip you, to see that no amulets for protection have been fastened to your skin."

The friar's notary stepped forward to help Künne down. She stood unevenly, as if she would faint. I noted again the rustling of the congregation, as if the merest bit of caution kept them from rushing to Künne and burying their teeth in her flesh. First, he took off her cap. He undid the ribbons of her bodice and pulled it from her shoulders. She screamed once, briefly, as he pulled the fabric off over her arm. Then he undid her skirt and it toppled to the ground, stiff with whatever filth she'd endured during her imprisonment, and removed her kirtle. She stood now only in her chemise. Everyone stared at the looseness of her flesh visible through the sheer cloth. He pulled it down over her breasts, as a lover would, but this was no ravishment.

Her breasts were as loose as pigs' bladders deflated on slaughter day. The nipples were like pendants hanging on a thin necklace. She was gaunt, as all of us were during these years of crop ruin, but her stomach protruded to show the surfeit of food she had once had.

I look like this, I thought. *Her breasts are my breasts.*

He wasn't finished with her. He pushed the chemise down past her hips and now she was naked but for her woolen socks and stout leather shoes. I sensed that everyone was horrified. They all thought of the rosiness of their own skin and hoped it might remain so forever. Then even her feet were bared.

This was the sight in the holy house of God: a woman stripped of everything, shivering in the cold, depraved as Eve.

Everything about her was gray but the bright red of her arm.

"Don't shiver," said the friar. "God's love will soon warm you."

He turned and walked out the side door of the church, and the notary gestured for Künne to follow. Her buttocks were so sunk from hunger that I saw the bones under them as she walked.

I knew I had to slip away to Künne's cottage to search for the herb she asked for. If the boiling water had caused her such torment, what would bare flames do to her?

Everyone was filing through the small side door, and I waited until Jost was attending to Matern's tears to move as quickly as I could to the front entrance. I was going the wrong way, fighting the forward thrust of everyone else. "The stake is in yonder yard," said Irmeltrud.

"Can't bear to see it, old Güde?" the baker asked me with a wink.

"It'll be a tremendous thing to see her cured of her evil," said his wife. "For that one it's been a long time God was waiting to punish her."

I sobbed and pushed past them. I looked to the sky for snow. If it fell heavily enough, they wouldn't be able to start the fire. But all I saw was the impenetrable gray of a skillet. I hurried along as fast as my body would allow, afraid someone would call out and deter me. Although I traveled at a mild enough pace, considering how slowly my feet found purchase in the snow, I was soon winded. A cloud issued from my mouth with every breath. Behind me I heard the voices of the villagers; the commotion had all the laughter of a feast day. My neighbors had forgotten the goodness of Künne. They saw nothing in her but wrinkles and a quavery voice, and had not more feeling for her than one has for a beetle that has plumbed its way through your flour. None of her family yet lived to defend her. I was lucky I had Jost.

As I neared her cottage I saw underneath the most recent layer of snow the tracks of many men. The snow had been volleyed about—some had run, some had kicked in fury or dragged objects through it. Her *Hütte* was the size of ours, but Künne's husband had cut decorative panels that hung from the roofline, so rather than being straight it had a pleasing curve to it. I saw the now pink puddle of blood where they had slaughtered her goat. I stood over it for a moment, thinking of the meat I'd eaten in the forest. My fingers clutched at my skirts, then I forced them to pull her latch. I had no time for mulling over my strange thoughts.

But inside, I found myself still again. It was amazing what they'd done the night the goat was killed—they had knocked every crock off her board and made tiny shards of them, torn down her herb bundles and garlic strings that had hung from the rafters, overturned all the furniture and scattered her bed. There not a stretch of ground without straw upon it. They had even pawed through her garments, no doubt hoping for a buried coin, and these lay tossed asunder, as if Künne herself had been wearing them and strewn them as she stripped.

I would not allow myself to cry. It was cruel, I reasoned, but she never saw it. And wouldn't, I thought with a pang.

I rubbed my head and tried to remember why I was in Künne's cottage. Was I to milk her goat? I righted her bench and then sat upon it. I stood again to brush off the straw. Had Jost sent me on a task? The goat had made a fair mess of the cottage. Amazing what ill handiwork such a small body can do. I looked around me at the clutter but saw no pail for milking. It was odd that Jost had sent me out like this. He should have milked the goat himself. I wondered where Künne was. She would be sore distressed at the state of her worldly goods. Well, there was nothing to do but look for the goat. I went outside. Foul weather, the kind of cold that is like a shout. Not three steps from the door, I saw blood in the snow and I remembered. Why was my mind such a traitor? Künne had asked me for an herb to ease her suffering and I must deliver it! I hastened back inside. She had said it was hanging on the back of the door.

But there was nothing there now.

The pillaging men had spilled it on the floor with all of her bounty. I looked about wildly. How might I recognize the herb? I had oft sat with Künne as she bundled plants for drying but had not bothered to learn their names or properties. They likely had her tied to the stake by now. There would be one long, final prayer, but I too had a long walk ahead of me to return to the church. I stooped and picked up one bundle of a yellowish dried plant with tubelike blossoms. Could this have been on the back of the door? I sniffed it. It was mildewy-smelling. I picked up five more plants from the floor, distinct from each other. They were all I saw. My arms full of them, I ran through the door and into winter again.

I cried out at the foolishness of the task. Would I stand there in front of the village and one at a time hold up the bundles until she nodded at the right one? And somehow secretively place it in her mouth without anyone stopping me?

And I was not unaware of the danger to myself if I was observed helping her foil the punishment. *I must choose,* I thought. *I must decide which is most likely and crumble its blossoms into my hand and roll them into a* Pille *that I might slip to her unseen.*

I retraced my steps back to the cottage. I flung down the plants and sought a crock to prepare the paste in. There was one in the corner, broken, but still with its base intact. I lit a candle to heat the wax and went to regard the plants again.

Perhaps they had already lit the tinder under her feet.

As I looked closer, I saw that one bundle was nothing more than flowers chosen for their comeliness. I flung it behind me. The remaining four plants were very similar; in fact, three were exactly the same. I tossed the replicas away. Now there were two.

"Ah, God, guide me," I beseeched. I knew of no way he could show me other than by making the herb jump into my hand, so I closed my eyes and prayed. "God, let my right hand fall upon the proper herb. Let me bring succor to Künne, for she has in no way betrayed you."

I let my hand fall as it would, and it seized upon the herb with bell-shaped flowers and dark, dried berries.

But perhaps I had betrayed God, and he would punish me through Künne?

They said in the forest that I had signed the devil's book

and I could not say if I had or not. Perhaps God would send me to the wrong bundle in vengeance?

Why had she not sent word from the Witch's Tower prior to this day, so that I might gather the herb before the men threw it from the door? I had to make a decision.

"Lord, I honor you and your unending goodness," I said. I tore off the heads of the plant God had urged me to select and put them in the crock. My fingers flaked them until they drifted like ash to the bottom. Then I held the candle side-wise over the crock until a few drops of wax fell in. I quickly rolled a hot ball of the blossom dust and the wax. I made three of these, which were easily hidden in my palm.

Then, scarcely bothering to blow the candle out, I hied my way back to the church.

———

When we gather wood for our home fires, we stack twigs and branches. We are not permitted full logs: those belong to Lord Obermann. I have heard some tell how much hotter the lord's fire is, with the thick logs burning for hours in his great hall. Yet here, for the village's use, were logs.

They were arranged in a circle in the yard of the church. They had a pattern to them, as they met of equal lengths and turned the corner, as if someone truly cared how the pile pleased the eye. In the center was a tall post, the height of a May Day pole. As I approached the grouping of my villagers and kin, I saw Künne lying on the ground. The notary was slapping her.

"She's dead," I heard someone murmur. "The devil already took her soul. She would have woken up by now."

Jostling up behind me came Frau Traugott with a bucket of melted snow.

"About time!" said the friar's notary, who took it from her and dashed the contents over Künne's chest, to make her heart feel the iciness.

I held my breath. Would that she did not wake up!

But in a few moments, Künne sputtered and sat up. Water dripped off her into the snow. "You fainted," said the notary. "Your connivance was merely a delay, however." He pulled her up to standing. As horrible as it had been to see her stripped in the church, her nakedness was even more disturbing here, open to the elements and to the cold sunlight, which allowed not a single modest shadow. Her arm was a bright red against the mossy white of the rest of her body. As he escorted her to the pyre, all eyes were on her, so I dared not approach. She walked up the row of logs carefully, for they did shift a bit, and she grasped the notary's arm to keep from falling. He tied her hands at the wrist, crossed, and ran the rope around her waist and above her breasts to the back of the pole. He then knelt to tie her ankles. This posture, bent with his head near the gray pocket of her sex, made the young men hoot.

"What a whore, her last thoughts being of the face in her thighs!" one called.

The notary, his task completed, walked backward down the pyre as if down a ladder. My bowels uncoiled within me and I cramped so terribly that I sank to my knees in the snow.

"All pray," commanded the friar.

Obediently, they all turned to the west, the direction where we last see the sun's iron slip. For generations, villagers have faced so while offering up beasts for sacrifice. The friar did not notice this, for he had already bowed his head. They all knelt and closed their eyes in piety. I saw what wondrous fortune this was, for now their bodies faced away from Künne. This was my moment.

"Vengeful Father, who seeketh purity and is askance not to find it, we beg your hand to come down upon the frail body before you and smite the evil from it. Strengthen Künne Himmelmann with your fierce and holy love. . . ."

I staggered to my feet. The snow was the icy crystalline kind, which permitted me a bit of silence if I stepped carefully.

"Burn the devil's influence from her and lighten her soul. . . ."

I hoped the friar would pray at length, for I was still quite far from Künne.

"As her soul shrieks out the anguish of repentance, let us be filled not with terror but rather with joy, dear Lord, for your will shall cleanse. . . ."

As I passed by Herr Fuhrmann, my skirts brushed his back and he twitched. I watched his neck, alarmed, as it halfway rose. I bent down, ready to plunge to my knees and behave as if I had always been so, but he lowered his head again. I continued.

"We seek mercy only when it is merciful. But were we to leave this child unchastened, her soul would further degrade. . . ."

I looked up at Künne. Her eyes were wide with horror, and she soundlessly screamed at me to hurry. She pushed against the limits of her ropes, which made the post creak. She ceased instantly. She put her teeth together as I have only seen wolves do, and showed me the face of a beast keening for itself.

The friar paused. I froze.

He cleared his throat.

Please, do not let this be the end of the prayer! My palms tightened around the chilling balls of wax.

I took another step, though the friar's silence endured. Why had I not brought *Pillen* from both plants so that she could take both and be assured of the right one? What if I had brought her a mundane plant for fever ease? I stepped again. Surely he would speak amen or continue on. If I was caught bringing surcease to her, I would wish to swallow the *Pillen* myself, for I'd be standing atop a pile of wood soon as well.

"We are sobered at the sight of our wicked sister," continued the friar.

Now it was only an expanse of snow between me and Künne. Her eyes looked like what might fit in the eyeholes of Alke's pelt. I placed my foot on the first log and began tottering. Would I be able to climb up there? I *had* to. I leaned over and used my hands to climb like a four-legged beast, one hand clenched around the *Pillen.* I clambered clumsily, until I caught a glimpse of Künne's feet. There was something so unearthly about the sight of bare feet against raw wood that I surged with wondrous power to the top of the pyre.

"So it is with joyful hearts, full of the love of our God who is so true, that we offer up our sister. . . ."

It sounded as though he was coming to the end. It was strange to press against Künne, naked and shivering, with myself garmented. I thrust all three *Pillen* into her mouth and watched as she struggled to swallow. Her terror had left her mouth dry. I rubbed my palm down her throat. This was a way we had made sick lambs swallow bitter treatments, by rubbing their throats in a downward motion.

Her throat worked.

She swallowed.

We would never be able to discuss whether my choice was one of folly. "Dear Künne," I whispered. "I want you to know—"

"Even one *Pille* would have been enough. I will be away from my body before the flames touch me. Güde, be very careful. Hunger has made enemies of all."

These were no words of love, but I shouldn't have expected them. Her mind was not on young girls in a meadow with flowers in their laps. Her reality was an entire village gathered in scorn, to watch her naked body erupt in flame. I kissed her dried lips and tumbled off the pile of logs as fast as I could. I only cared now that I had chosen well for my friend.

"In this, as in all things, we praise you. Amen."

I was about to assume a kneeling position as the heads came up, but I was facing the wrong direction. I saw a few faces frown in surprise, so I quickly turned.

The friar made a sound of disgust. "You face west like your ignorant forebears. Do you not see that God is enveloping you, in all directions? Rise, people of Tierkinddorf."

The villagers all stood, wiping snow off their knees, and turned around again to see the woman perched atop the pile of wood.

"Did you pray with us?" he asked Künne.

"I prayed of my own devising, sir," she answered.

He nodded grimly and motioned to his notary, who held aloft a torch carrying a yellow ball of flame at its tip.

"Praise be to God," said the friar.

The man touched the torch to a bit of kindling in the lowest tier of the pile. He walked a few steps, then bent to light again. He circled Künne, lighting her wood three more times. I studied her face, hoping to see her eyes drift closed in a sweet dream rendered by the herb.

The fire crackled and began sending up smoke.

"Better this than hellfire!" jeered the cobbler.

"Burn, *Hexe*!" This was from a female voice. I did not have to turn to know that it was Frau Zweig. I could now feel the heat from the fire and knew it must be twicefold for Künne. Her eyes, rather than watching me, fastened on some spot in the distance. Clouds of smoke kept blocking our vision of her. A spasm crossed her face and I held my breath. Was it the herb working? Or the heat becoming unbearable?

"What are you looking for?" screamed someone. "The devil to fly on horseback and deliver you?"

The fire had crept up the log pile but had still not reached her feet.

I clasped my hands together and prayed, not an elaborate prayer like the friar's, and not even specifically addressed to God, but a simple, crude prayer, of three words only, over and over: *Ease her quick. Ease her quick.*

The crackling sound was enormously loud. I thought, in between the repetitions of my prayer, that I would never be able to cook over a fire or sit by one again for warmth without thinking of this fire. *Ease her quick. Ease her by craft and false pretense.* I wailed in distress at the witch's song intruding on my prayer for Künne. I had to keep my mind pure for her. *Ease her quick. Ease her quick.*

The flames would be at her in another moment.

Why had I not grabbed all the plants and simply stuffed them into her mouth? Why had I taken the time to melt the wax and create tiny *Pillen?* I was desperate to see her face become lax under the herb's spell. I could have crept faster, given the plant a longer time to take its effect in her body. I had been no friend. Why, I had even stood still in her cottage for long moments I'd had no right to waste, as my idiot mind tried to regather the purpose of my mission! My hands fell out of prayer and I raised them to batter at my temples. Why had my mind failed me on this most important of days? *Ease her quick. Ease her quick.* The heat was unbearable. I knew my own face must be red as the sex of a sheep pushing out her lambs. *Ease her quick.* I watched one flame, the tallest, flicker near Künne's right foot. If I had failed, we were about to watch death in the most dire way, writhing through intense pain. *Please, God.* I watched her bite her lip as a second spasm crossed her face. I knew not how to interpret it until she laughed.

And then I was full glad, for I knew the herb had control of her.

It wasn't one to loosen her muscles but instead clenched them.

She spasmed again and again and tears rolled down my face as she painlessly twisted in the herb's influence. She leaned forward, as if falling, but the ropes kept her in place. She continued bending, over and over, like she was in the river doing her washing. Her hands and fingers moved, and if they hadn't been tied they would have flown up into the air like startled birds. And then her hair, her gray hair in flustered waves around her face, a profusion falling onto her thin shoulders, suddenly snapped with white light and burst into flames.

We all cried out; how could we know the fire would not consume her from the bottom up but would instead select the most combustible part of her, like a starting fire chooses the smallest kindling? The flames moved her head around, made it seem someone stood behind her manipulating it, front to back, side to side, as if she wildly agreed with someone and then vehemently changed her mind. Her mouth opened wide, but no scream came. Her eyes glared at nobody. She was already gone.

I gagged at the smell, which clogged my throat. I backed up, bumped into someone.

Künne's feet were burning now, releasing a sour, fumid smoke that seemed monstrous, from hell. And her face began to disappear in the bright red flames. The fire did strange things to her expression: cocked her eyes, curled her lip. I could hear chants behind me.

"Burn, witch!"

I wondered how they could open their mouths to speak in this cloud of stench. I wondered if goats, sheep, and other beasts that stood in the yard as the smell of their kind's cooking flesh drifted from the chimney were equally nauseated.

How long would this fire burn? There was certainly more than enough fuel to keep it going into the small hours of the morning. But I did not want Künne's fire to go on so long, couldn't bear the thought of her ashes drifting in the wind unheeded, after people lost interest and went home. I would tend this fire until every ember gave up.

———

She did not stand upright for long. The rope burned, releasing from the stake, and her body slumped onto the pile of wood. This brought more jeers. As she landed, her arm stretched out toward me, and I watched the flesh and muscle jerk in the flames, but by the time I saw the whiteness of the bone appear, no one stood with me. Künne was no longer distinguishable in this burning mass; except for the smell, this spectacle was now the same as any hunter's fire. Since there was no woman to hate within the flames, everyone had made their way home. Even the friar had considered the duty rendered and was probably back studying his book to prepare for his next journey. I hoped he would soon leave our village. It was a desperate and terrible thing to kill Künne, but perhaps everyone felt it had cleared our curse. I knew, though, that my sweet friend had had nothing to do with the fields lying barren.

I waited through all the sounds of the evening coming on while the fire yet burned. The owls took their turns over the light that surprised them, and the wolves howled far away. Darkness fell and I crept closer to the fire for warmth. I would not abandon her bones here, where the wolves could find them and drag them into the forest. Snow fell, a light, flaky snow that I brushed from my shoulders without leaving any true wetness. It wasn't until the blaze was the size of a small kitchen fire that I felt Jost's arms around me. "You must come home, Mutter," he said. "You can be of no help to her now."

"I won't leave her bones," I protested.

"You must," he said. "How will it seem for you to bring them with you? The friar is a hard man, and he already wonders about you and me."

"I will wrap them in my cloak and tend them in the night. In the morning, you will help me bury her as she should be buried, next to her husband."

"You know as I do, Mutter, she can never be buried in holy ground."

"Then I shall bury her in her cottage yard," I said. "With a cross above."

"The villagers would think that blasphemy, to be burned for a witch and then buried under a cross," said Jost.

"What do you think they mean to do with her bones, then?" I cried.

He was silent a long time. "A hole," he said finally. "A simple pit in the ground."

"With no spot marked for God to find her? Jost, we will bury her ourselves, deep in the woods where they won't see the cross."

"We can't, Mutter. It is too dangerous. Künne would not want us to do that. We must leave her bones here, for them to do with as they wish."

"But if the wolves drag them off?"

"Then the wolves drag them off."

He wrapped his arms around me and hugged me, and my nose was filled with the warm, sweaty scent of his body, a relief from the ash-clogged smell of Künne. I inhaled deeply, burying my nose in his woolen cloak.

"Mutter, remember what Künne told the friar, that you

had tried to sway her from the witchcraft ways? She wanted you to be safe. She would not want you to risk your life for the sake of bones she cannot now use."

"Will you say a prayer for me?" I asked.

He let me go and we together stood facing the small fire and its pile of cluttered bones. "Father, we pray that you allow Künne into your kingdom. You have the truth in heaven and we hope that you accept your falsely accused daughter into your merciful, all-knowing hands."

"Amen," I said.

I walked to the fire to look one last time at what remained of my dearest friend on earth. The fine rigging of her fingers still clenched at the coals, and the longer shards connected them with the rods that I thought were her shoulders, or her ribs, a confusing jumble. A broad expanse of white was her pate, buried facedown in the ashes. I was glad not to be able to see the hollows of her eyes and the strangeness that a nose becomes: I had seen a few skulls in my lifetime and did not like the face that lies under our living faces.

Jost had come to fetch me not only because it was dark and time to be climbing into our beds but because he wanted me to eat. I stared in dumb wonder at the plate waiting for me on the board: three slices of ham, each thick as my thumb. The children were asleep already, and Irmeltrud was sitting at the table with a nearly empty tankard of ale. "We drank it all," she said flatly, "but saved you some meat."

Ale in the house? How? And three thick, thick pieces of meat, each larger than what I'd expect to eat in any meal this year. I thought with sudden terror of the child's flesh offered me in the forest. "Where does it come from?" I asked.

"The friar arranged it to reward the gathering of the wood," said Irmeltrud.

Jost winced.

"Your son here wouldn't do it," said Irmeltrud, "wouldn't put food in front of his children. But I'm their *Mutter* and I will do as I must to put food in their bellies."

"Did the children help as well?" I asked, remembering that they had been gone much of the morning.

"They did indeed! It was good, warm work for them and look at how we feasted."

"Someone had to do it, after all," said Jost uneasily. "At least it was not gathered in spite."

"Yes, we honored Künne with our morning's work," said Irmeltrud. "We blessed the wood as we cut it and used Lord Obermann's sled to pull it."

"Did she know?" I whispered. I had missed the beginning of the ceremony while I prepared the *Pillen* at Künne's cottage. Had the friar made a grand announcement of which family had made the burning possible?

"I think she did not know," said Jost. He sighed, a long sound that made Irmeltrud stop in mid-drink. "Mutter, you should eat. We can't undo anything that is done."

I walked myself to the bench and sat. I looked a long while at the pink cuts of ham. Heard the sound of Irmeltrud greedily swallowing the last of her ale, then heavily setting down the tankard. I touched the meat. It was warm still, slightly greasy. The skin was rough under my fingers. Then I cupped the first slice in my fist and drove my few teeth into it.

Hunger has turned me into an animal, I thought.

8

They used the phantasm of a cat, an animal which is,
in the Scriptures, an appropriate symbol of the perfidious,
for cats are always setting snares for each other.

— MALLEUS MALEFICARUM

In the morning, Jost woke me early so we could go back to the fire site and watch the raking of the ashes. The friar stood guarding the laborers; Jost and I stood behind and to the side of him so that he would not notice us. I had slept heavily, with dreams of my own hair bursting into flames.

The men moved their rakes as if they were in the fields preparing the soil for planting. How I wished this were so! That they had labor that warmed their bones and that the dirt heeded the lessons of the tines and nourished the seeds the men would next drop! But this was a field that could bear no crop. We had sown the soil with ashes. Setting aside the large bones, they pushed snow over the gray remnants of my friend, and she was instantly vanished. One gave a whistle, and I wished the skies were full of birds and their cries. Birds were here when the air was warm, when the fields issued buds of grain they stole with wicked abandon.

As I watched the men gather up the bones and roll them into cloth, I felt little emotion. I had already released Künne last night with the prayer Jost offered. I shed no tear and felt almost as if I were still dreaming as we trailed one man with a shovel. He chose a spot at the base of a pine tree not far from the churchyard, but definitely outside its holy realm.

"This tree then shall mark it?" he asked, checking with the friar.

"No landmark for such as these. As their lives were unfit in God's eyes, these *Hexen* must lie in anonymous ground," replied the friar.

The man threw his shovel and where it landed, he began digging as best he could in the cold ground. I would have laughed at the action if he were digging a different sort of hole.

"God be praised," said the friar directly to me.

I stiffened. I had not known he noticed us. I was scared to look into his eyes and so studied his shoes. They were not coarse and softened with use, but made of fresh and tough leather.

"God be praised," I echoed.

Our priest emerged from the church then and walked across the churchyard to the friar. He glanced at me and Jost, and we both took several steps backward and half turned away to watch the man continue to dig.

"You can feel the strength of God's work here," said the priest.

The friar nodded thoughtfully. "I am filled with holy light at moments like this. It is an honor to be Christ's servant."

"Our village is indebted to you."

"Not to me, to God," corrected the friar. "I am only an earthly hand to do his divine will." He held up his right hand in front of his face, as if he scarce believed it was his. "*My* body does *God's* bidding. And it is such a fierce and wild sensation to do so!"

"Were you always pledged to do his work?" asked the priest.

"I heard his call when I was but a child. God spake to me in a dream, and I quit my father's house to join the Dominican brothers. They were more of a family to me than my own brothers ever were. And fate brought Herr Kramer to me, who infused me with his brilliance. I am truly blessed among men."

"We are the true nobility," agreed the priest. "Our meals here on earth may be meager, but in heaven we shall feast."

The man with the shovel walked away, and the friar and priest followed him. He had not had to dig deeply. There was little to bury. I listened to the wind until Jost pulled at my sleeve.

We went home, and because I had been wakened so early, I returned to my straw. But it was strange to be lying there while the rest of the household moved. Irmeltrud swept, although no crumbs had had a chance to sully the ground, nor beasts to move across it since our empty larder offered no scents to entice them. Jost sharpened a knife though there was nothing to cut. "Is there naught I can help with, Jost?" I called out finally, sleepless.

"Rest and sleep," he said. "The air is brisk, so snuggle down into your straw."

This time my sleep was dreamless. For a while, Matern came and slept next to me, burrowing against my back for warmth. This child was the tenderest of all of us, and I had paid him no heed yesterday. I was certain he must have sobbed all throughout Künne's burning. He swung an arm over me and I kissed the small hand, tucking it into mine, grateful. His stomach rumbled from last night's rich meal, making my spine quiver as well. "You're a good lad," I whispered.

I drifted back into sleep.

But this was not to last.

"For God's sake, Matern, are you lazing while the rest of us are doing the work of the house?" came Irmeltrud's brittle call.

"Vater said I could rest like Großmutter," he answered into my back, barely moving.

"And by what honor have you earned this?"

"Because I was so sad," he said. "I tried to help Vater, but I couldn't see because my eyes were full of the weep."

"It's enough we have one useless body in this house," said Irmeltrud. "I'm damned if we will have another. Get up and find your *Vater.*"

The small hand slipped out of mine and the forehead left my back. I was instantly cold. He got out of bed without a word and did as she bade. I pulled the blanket up so it covered me to the ears. Irmeltrud's cruelty was growing, and I wondered that even this day she would keep comfort from me.

The door opened as the poor boy went out, and soon after I felt the straw shift as something pounced up on it. Of course:

the cat again. I lowered the blanket and peered over its striped body at Irmeltrud, busy with Alke at some task, and unwitting of the new visitor. I lifted the blanket to show the cat a space it might choose to hide, and indeed it quickly stepped into the hot void by my belly, turned twice, and lay down nestled against me. Ah! Warmer than Matern, even! And such fur. I cupped one hand into the warmest part of it, between the four legs, and stroked its tiny head with the other. The cat commenced the strange, guttural shaking of its body, the purr of its pleasure. And I drifted off to sleep yet again, my fingers drowsily moving and my body basking in the heat from this small oven. It was past noonday when I awoke again.

Jost had returned and it was his stamping his boots to rid them of snow that wakened me.

"Nothing in the traps?" Irmeltrud inquired.

"It seems all beasts know these forsaken woods have no food for them and they have moved to better prospects."

"Well, you'll go again and there'll be a fat rabbit there, its leg caught."

Jost moved to the fire and warmed his hands. "All of us men see the same thing. No tracks in the snow but our own. No beasts are moving."

"But surely if you walk farther . . . ," protested Irmeltrud.

"We have all searched the length and breadth of these woods," said Jost. "Künne's goat is gone, the sheep herd is gone; we were lucky enough to get the pig meat yesterday."

"Lucky," grunted Irmeltrud. "The luck of my sweat."

"We gathered to speak just now with Ramwold. He read the runes again, and the truth is the same. We must form a hunting party and journey far from here to find the beasts that have scattered."

I propped myself up on my elbows to see Irmeltrud's response. She folded her arms and approached him at the fire. "Let the others go. You're so thin! Let the young ones go and fetch for us."

"Don't tell me you're scared to stay alone?" asked Jost in a rare, teasing voice I hadn't heard him use in years.

"I can't bear the thought of you not coming back," she said, ignoring his playfulness.

"We all take that risk alike," said he. "The runes told of deer in the forests south of here, a large herd. Would you not like venison after so much air that we've eaten?"

"How long a journey?"

"The runes didn't say. A week? A fortnight?"

The cat now reacted to my shifting and stood up. I held the blanket down to contain it.

"Will we be yet living when you return?" asked Irmeltrud.

"What else would you have me do? I cannot ask animals that don't exist to step into my traps." He put his hands on her shoulders and pulled her into a hug, even though her arms were still crossed. Such uncommon tenderness! It was as if he didn't think he'd return.

"When does the party leave?" she asked.

"Tomorrow at first light. We see no need to delay, we are all so terribly hungry."

The cat squirmed, upset at being confined, and finally yowled. Everyone turned to look at me. I released the beast, and it leaped to the foot of my pallet, where it yowled again. Irmeltrud grabbed the broom from the corner and advanced upon the cat. "I see something we can eat," she said grimly. "I'll cook it up and we can defeat its evil in that manner."

"Mutter, no!" cried Alke. "Wait for Vater to come home with venison. We don't want to eat evil!"

The cat batted at the broom, and Irmeltrud smacked its flank. Behind her, Jost moved to open the door. "There's not enough meat to bother," he said. "It's a wee beast." The cat ran a diagonal path away from Irmeltrud as she continued trying to hit it with the broom. I got out of bed, barely noticing the cold, and tried to grab the broom away. The cat darted to the open door, running through Jost's legs, and was gone. Jost closed the door and Irmeltrud stopped fighting and let me have the broom.

"There, then!" she said. "You won't lift it for an instant to rid this cottage of dirt, but you have all kinds of vigor when it comes to protecting one of the devil's own!"

"Stop, wife, it was only a cat!" said Jost. "You were glad enough of them when there was grain in the mill and the cats kept the rats from it."

"That cat is uncanny," murmured Irmeltrud. "It came from Güde's bed, as shameless as an incubus. . . ."

"It's merely a thing to keep an old woman happy," said Jost.

"No one in this household listens to me," said Irmeltrud.

That night, Jost and Irmeltrud said goodbye in the way that lovers do. They grunted and panted and made such revel that I knew the children were awake next to them, hoping it would soon cease. *Should they make another child,* I thought bitterly, *so there is another mouth that is hungry?*

Long after things became quiet, I could not sleep.

I heard scratching at the door and this time did not hesitate. There was no bad in that cat. It was simply a mouser, and one that would cuddle against me, the only one in this household that had to sleep apart from the others. I opened the door to it and raced it back to the straw. I held up the blanket again, so that it might crawl under, but this time it perched on my chest and simply stared at me. Irmeltrud's words chimed again in my ear. This was how the incubi came to women in the night, sitting atop their bodies with eyes shining. I stared back at those eyes, riveted. The cat was a dark shape outlined by the remnants of the kitchen fire behind it. Its ears were alert and triangular, making me think of the pagan shapes we had been told to no longer think of. I breathed uncomfortably under its weight, wondering if this was friend or foe. Then, on an eerie pivot, its head slowly moved, and as its eyes caught the last glow from the fire, the face became alive with a demon's malevolence. The green eyes shone through the dark like lanterns, and I felt the palpable beat of evil in the room. These eyes were the brightest light in the dark cottage.

"The cat is Satan's apprentice!" I screamed, and tossed my bedclothes from me, hearing the thud as the cat hit the ground. Jost was instantly at my side. I screamed again, pointing to where I last saw it. "Oh, Jost, its eyes!"

Irmeltrud joined me in screaming, and I clung to her, terrified. She had been right! How I wished she had pounded it with her broom until its wrong heart stopped beating. To think I had slept with it nestled at my breast! I shuddered to think how its eyes must have glowed beneath the blankets.

Jost scooped it up and tossed it out into the night.

"Lock the door!" I cried. The children were on my straw now too, hugging the mass that was Irmeltrud and myself.

"What did you see?" asked Jost.

"Its eyes shone in the darkness bright as any candle," I said. "I have never seen such a fright!" But just the day before I had seen innocent Künne Himmelmann burned at the stake. Was the cat's gleaming face truly worse? "It was pure evil," I continued, subdued. "The wildness of its gaze . . . I saw how much harm it meant me."

"I know not what to say," said Jost. "I believe you, Mutter, but I also . . ." His voice trailed off.

I let go of Irmeltrud. My own son did not believe me.

Jost left in the morning as planned. We all kissed him at the door and then stood there in the cold, watching him gather with the other men and then disappear.

9

The days passed. At each meal hour, I watched Irmeltrud hesitate and wonder whether to call the children to the board for the mere ceremony of it or to hope that they forgot this family ritual. She began an endless accounting of what food had once been in our larder: the berries in profusion, the meat that softly bled into the cloth we wrapped it in, the breads, the carrots, and the cabbages all lined up like children on a bench. She wouldn't stop. Onions whose outer film we discarded—"Just tossed away, because we had so much!" she mourned—the oily meat of a goose, the jelly inside a cow's hoof, the cheeses of various colors and thicknesses, the knife one might choose to attack a particular cheese.

This afternoon, as we sat with the wind blowing open the window cloth and sending in little sniffets of snow, she spake of her father's sheep herd. These were hardy creatures that never minded the snow, even if it came to the height of their woolly heads. They tramped through it and bleated their happy cries across all the hillsides. In summertime, they were a gorgeous sight, like clouds come to rest upon a green sky. The sheep gave so much: their thick wool was carded and spun into strong thread, their mutton was juicy and renowned across this land. But when her family fell ill to the plague, the only untouched ones were too young to know how to care for the sheep. Irmeltrud remembered her mother saying, "Go and gather them and bring them to the barn for their meal," and she went so far as to go outside and walk toward the sheep, but being so young, she only tried to drag one to the barn by its feet. It resisted and sprang out of her grasp. "The sheep died of starvation, Güde," she told me. "They all tried to come to the barn eventually, but I was so young I couldn't understand what they wanted. A week later, a neighbor man came. He had been ill himself and, remembering the sheep upon recovering, came to see if he could help. The sheep were all on their sides, dead as trapped houseflies. We did our best to salt the meat and store it, but so many had already begun to rot that we had to simply leave them for the birds that could eat around the worms. Such an incredible waste, I can't bear to think of it!" And with her head on her arms, Irmeltrud began to cry.

I was filled with amaze: these sheep had been dead nearly twenty years! Did she think we'd still be eating of their salted flesh had she and the neighbor been more painstaking?

After she cried awhile, she propped her chin on her folded arms and proceeded to wonder aloud what food others in the village had. The Webers had five chickens but ten children; they would not be likely to share. Across town, the Brauers had a cow, but she knew it had been sickly; probably they had already slaughtered it while flesh still clung to its bones. The cheese maker had been slowly selling all her goods, but surely she kept back a few wheels for herself. Would she be willing to trade, and if so, what could Irmeltrud give her?

She went on and on, her eyes squeezed to the size of juniper berries in contemplation. She looked like an old miser in a fairy tale counting out his money.

"Ha ha!" she said, her head rising. "The Töpfers' hen must be laying again, now that Künne's spell has been broken! I will run over there now and see if they will let us have an egg or two. What shall I bring? What shall I bring?" She walked up and down the length of the cottage. "We have nothing. Güde, have you hidden away anything?"

I shook my head.

"A bit of embroidery? A pinch of salt? I'll bring them some salt." She poured a spoon's worth into a napkin and tied it up. "Watch the children, Güde. I'll be back soon, hopefully with some eggs."

I did not stir from the table the entire time she was gone. Matern and Alke played a slow game of yarn. I knew none of us had energy to move, for we had last eaten on the ham earned with Künne's wood many days ago.

Irmeltrud returned with a scowl, but she did have a bundle under her arm. The children ran to her with wide eyes. "Sit down, then, and we'll eat, no matter the hour," she said briskly. The children obediently took their places on the bench. Alke pushed me a bit, her small hands on my hip, for I had sat too close to her spot. They folded their hands and bent their heads, in a blur of motion, for they wanted to pray and eat.

"Thank you, Lord, for this," said Irmeltrud. "We ask that

you multiply it, even as you multiplied the fish for the fisher-men, for this is scarcely enough for one to eat. We thank you for your mercy."

I opened my eyes when she said "scarcely enough for one to eat" and saw the snarl on her face. This was a prayer made in anger.

She unwrapped the bundle. It was old bread, with a rime of green around the edge. She took a knife to it, biting out words as she did so. "The hen is still enchanted and will not lay. Or at least that's what they say. I poked my head in and saw her looking pert as could be. But who would want to share in these evil times? They took my precious salt and gave me this horrendous loaf in return. Not fit to feed a dog. I wonder that they didn't blush as they handed it over. I was of half a mind to spill the salt on the ground and sow its bitter seeds with my spit. But I held back. Maybe they will soften and share the eggs later."

She gave the first hunk to Matern, who eagerly brought it to his mouth and began scraping it with his teeth. She struggled with the knife. "Should use an axe, for it's wood more than bread. How did they dare give it? It's something, though. Here you be, Alke." Alke's piece had the most green on it and she sniffed it for long moments before bringing it to her mouth.

"Don't grieve on it, child, just manage it," said Irmeltrud. The remaining bit was the size of Matern's and we both stared at it.

"I'll cut that in half, then," she said. But she made no move.

Her eyes lifted to mine in a blaze of hunger. The children

ate the bread, sounding like rats cutting their teeth on a table leg. Even though the bread was green and hard I wanted it. Fiercely. My head began to ache, a sharp, piercing pain as if someone had taken the fireplace poker and gone in through my eyes.

And I saw that pain in Irmeltrud's eyes too.

But as much as I hungered, a part of me began reasoning. *Jost is gone. Irmeltrud is free to practice her cruelty without rebuff. We are frighteningly low on food. She cut wood, and made the children help her, to put an old family friend to death. All for want of food.* I thought, *Maybe this is one time I should go without.* I realized my hands were hovering in the air, ready to receive the cut of bread. I pulled them down into my lap and clutched my thighs through my skirt. "Irmeltrud," I began, and it was but a whisper. I inhaled and made myself louder. "I am not hungry. You eat it all." She turned her back on me, still sitting on the bench but now facing the fire. I watched her cap bob up and down as she ate the bread.

————

Later, I was fetching snow in the bucket to melt for water when I realized I hadn't seen Jost for a while. I carried the bucket inside and used my hand to move the snow into the hanging kettle over the fire. It was thick snow and not easy to move. Irmeltrud sewed by the hearth. Alke and Matern played with the shavings of wood Jost had been whittling days ago.

"Where's Jost?" I asked.

All three of them stopped their toil to look at me.

"Don't you know?" I asked.

"Güde, the things you forget!" said Irmeltrud. "Your own son is out there in the cold, doing his best to find food for us!"

"In the woods?"

"No, silly old woman, far from here. He's with a hunting party gone several days now, and you have been told all this before!"

I settled the rest of the snow and went back outside for more, disturbed. It sounded untrue, that Jost would leave us for so long. A hunting party? Why, our woods were full of stags and bears; why should he travel further? I looked out over the land, snow glistening under a dark sky. It was as if the dimness of the forest was spreading. Even the meadow looked close and small and tucked up against the sky.

———

Frau Zweig came to visit, she of the thrice-quickened womb.

"Would you have any more salt?" she asked. "Frau Töpfer traded some with me. It makes things taste so fine."

Irmeltrud's eyes narrowed. "And what do you put it on?"

"Eggs. Our hen was not cursed," she said.

"You have a hen?"

"Yes. Have you not known of this? 'Twas hardly a secret." Frau Zweig reached out to Alke, to touch her cheek. All smiles she was, and she bent to kiss the young girl atop her head.

"I knew not," said Irmeltrud stiffly.

"You're so fair, my dear," said Frau Zweig to Alke. "Your lips are darling blooms of roses. Are you not a joyous, beauteous sight?"

Alke, in return for the compliment, curtseyed and kissed Frau Zweig's skirt hem.

"So you are wanting salt to better fasten the eggs' flavor? I'm eager then to help you improve your meals, while my children and I sit here with naught to eat," Irmeltrud said.

"Don't be bitter. Look, I've brought you eggs."

We all inhaled, our breaths loud. Irmeltrud's face showed a full smile, and I saw again the handsomeness that had once led Jost to her favor. Frau Zweig showed her basket. It contained three eggs, nestled with cloth to cushion them. I reached out and picked one up, felt the slump of the thing inside. "Three eggs," said Irmeltrud. Her smile faded.

"I know you are four with Jost gone," said Frau Zweig, "But this is all I can spare. Surely you and Güde can share?"

"You want the salt only to flavor your eggs?" Irmeltrud asked. Her meaning was clear: *What other food do you have?*

"You look like a wolf!" said Frau Zweig. But I thought she was more the wolf, with her wispy face and sharp chin. "Believe me, we are not hiding food from you. I would give all I had to keep the young sweetings happy." She opened her arms to Alke and Matern, and they went to embrace her. I saw Matern's eyes, however, focused not on her face but on the basket. He hugged carefully so as not to rock the fragile eggs inside.

I put a second hand around my egg, to make sure it didn't drop.

Irmeltrud's face did not shift out of suspicion, but she nodded. She went to the salt cellar and spooned a palmful, wrapping it up in the cloth from the basket.

"Your hen lays daily?" she asked.

"Oh, no, we are not as lucky as that. She lays when she wishes. Herr Zweig and I wanted to gobble them up but saved carefully these many days so we'd be able to trade."

I had to turn away so that Frau Zweig would not see my face. She lied! No one as hungry as we were would've been able to set the eggs aside; they would have been eaten raw and instantly, as I now craved to do with the one I held. Yellow yolk would have run down her chin and maybe her haste would have been such that she ate some shell too. The Zweigs must have food.

"Thanks for the trade then," said Irmeltrud, emptying the basket. "We'll do it again. Tomorrow, if she lays. You haven't made agreement with anyone else, have you?"

"Oh, no, I thought only of you with two small ones," she said. "But I think this salt will last us for a while. Perhaps we can trade again in a week."

Irmeltrud pressed her lips together until the entire area around her mouth was white as snow. Frau Zweig didn't see, though, for she turned to give a huge smile to Alke and Matern. They shyly smiled back. "I brought something for you two especially," she said. She produced a puppet as long as her hand, dressed in miniature breeches and shirt.

Matern reached out and grabbed the doll and held it above his head. Alke laughed delightedly, since she was taller than he was and could easily pluck it from his hands. Then she darted past him and ran around the cottage with it, chortling her joy to have a reason to run. I could scarcely believe her legs still worked after so much listlessness. Matern's high-pitched voice joined hers and the ground shook with the slapping of their feet. Around and around they went, stirring the skirts of the three women watching.

I was first to give in to the infectiousness. I clamped my hands on either side of my jaw to feel the shaking as I laughed; it felt like my body had forgotten how to do it. Frau Zweig was soon after, with her loose bosoms rolling above her bodice. She shrieked with laughter when Alke grabbed her about the waist and hid behind her, the toy still clenched in her palm. Frau Zweig winked at me and grabbed the toy and threw it across the room to Matern, who crowed and again held it above his head as if in triumph. Alke lightly spanked Frau Zweig's rump and she jumped.

"Child! The adults do the spanking, not the children!" she laughed.

I watched Irmeltrud's face relax and the edges of her mouth slowly, slowly rise. But she didn't have a full smile until Matern stopped right in front of her, making Alke plow into his back in surprise, and handed the toy to his *Mutter.* Then it was as though she were ten years younger, with a whimsical smile touching her lips and her blue eyes opening wider: finally, something she cared to look at! She took the toy and gave Matern a kiss for it, then spun in a circle, intermittently holding out the toy and snatching it back as soon as the children reached for it. They circled her deliriously until somehow they all fell into a rhythm. 'Twas miraculous to see, like the mill wheel's gears catching the teeth of the face wheel, everything working in harmony.

It was Frau Zweig who ruined the rhythm. She reached out

and easily grabbed the toy, then threw it to me. It bounced off my outstretched fingers and fell to the ground. I bent to get it but felt a bolt of pain in my back and stopped. Matern dove for it and lay on his back holding it on his belly, laughing so hard his face reddened.

We almost, but not quite, had forgotten about the eggs.

"Well, that was a bright gift," said Frau Zweig. "I'll be off now. Enjoy it, children!"

"No," wailed Matern, getting up and running over to bury his face in her skirts.

"Stay, Frau Zweig," said Alke. "Won't you?"

"I must go but I'll return ere much time goes by," she said. She gave kisses to the children and ran a lingering hand over their two heads. She gave them a *Mutter*'s look: protective, proud, and grateful. She'd make a good *Mutter* if her stomach ever stopped being barren, for she had these qualities plus the ability to make merry. Irmeltrud was still smiling, but I saw that she was relieved to close the door behind our visitor, for it meant we could now eat.

The children ran to the board and Irmeltrud produced a bowl to break the eggs into.

"We'll cook them," she announced, "and that way we can divide them."

The sound of the shell cracking was like a cowbell clanking on the hillside, for it reminded me of a time of plenty. We had cracked eggs thoughtlessly once, moving without need through the sound of sheep rustling and bähhing, hearing the cows lowing and not realizing what a miraculous thing it was.

Into the bowl slid the egg's innards, the wholesome wide yolk that made us think of the sun at noontide, and the slippery matter that protected it. Three times she did this and we watched the liquids pool. Then she stirred them with a wooden spoon until the whites and yellows blurred. As the eggs cooked in the skillet, we all watched spellbound. Moisture collected in my mouth, sour and salty. How fluffy and bright they were! We had nothing else in the house of such a color. Finally, we moved back to the table and Irmeltrud doled out the portions. She gave me a sadly tiny amount. I put the egg into my mouth to taste the hen's gift. I made myself chew, and when I swallowed, a sob choked up to meet the egg.

How pitiless the world was. The hen might not lay every day, and Frau Zweig would share with us only if she needed something. I thought of Jost trudging through the snow, as wet and thick as it was, and wished that a thousand woodland animals came out to stare at him, let him approach them with his arrows, and drop down into the snow with howls and groans.

"Ah, God!" I cried out, and then my forehead sank to the empty plate and I sobbed outright. Matern put the toy in front of me, and when I didn't respond, he closed my fingers around it. Then he grabbed for it, making a sound that tried to be a laugh. I didn't resist and so he instantly had it. As I sobbed, he looked at the doll's jolly painted face. Then he set it down on the table. All three left me there while they cleaned the plates.

———

Irmeltrud was staring into the fire. "The Zweigs have food," she muttered to herself. "The friar too. He brought some store with him when he came. We have to please him." The children had fallen asleep on the hearth. I would have carried them to bed but was too frail to lift them. Irmeltrud could have managed but was lost in reverie. "Cut the wood for him," she whispered. In the half-light, her head moved not, but her eyes slid over, smoothly as the door creeping open, until she stared at me from the corners of her eyes.

10

And I have found a woman more bitter than death,

who is the hunter's snare, and her heart is a net,

and her hands are bands.

— MALLEUS MALEFICARUM

The next day I walked as far as I could, to see if I could catch sound of the hunters returning. I knew what the look Irmeltrud had given me by the fire meant.

I knew it, I knew it.

So I set out to find Jost. Only he could stop her from her cruel choice. The forest path was buried in snow, but the opening in the trees showed me where to walk. I walked until my feet were soaking wet and the shoes useless scraps of leather, until I could not feel my fingertips and had to look at my hands to be sure they were still there. The wind howled and moved through my clothing. I became panicked, thinking how long it would take to return the way I'd gone and that every step I continued away from the cottage meant that I might become too exhausted to make it home. But I couldn't stop myself. And what would I be returning to?

I passed the Lehnt Rock, a landmark men spake of, but which I had never seen before. I huddled against its face for a moment, to block the wind, but then my feet of their own device moved me forward and I continued on. The land rose and I was climbing a hill, and at one point looked down to see the cottages of another town, Steindorf, that sometimes joined us for fests. The last time we had gathered together was years ago. The image of the dark-haired woman rose in my mind. She was from here. She had eaten of our food at Michaelmas, with her bright red lips. I stared down, wondering which *Hütte* she lived in. With a pang, I remembered that she had food. She had fed me pig meat. She had helped me fly. She could feed me and then carry me through the woods to find Jost. I wouldn't mind her black hair draped over my body if it meant I could see my son again. I was plunging down the hillside now, falling to my knees in the thickened snow. The *Hütten* here were of stone, not wood, with mud chinking the gaps between. I had never seen such an oddity. In my village, only the Witch's Tower was made of stone. There was a certain coldness to Steindorf, as the gray of the stone echoed the white of the snow.

Smoke pumped from all the chimneys, and I saw not a single person out of doors. I moved as quickly as a young woman now, hungry to find her. I walked to the closest home and pounded on the door. A woman came to open it and her face registered no surprise, no emotion. She was gaunt, with slack skin hanging from her high cheekbones.

"I want to find the dark-haired woman," I said. "Know you such a neighbor?"

"When all are flaxen, I know whom you speak of. The sisters. You must mean Fronika, since the other one is dead. But you do not want to seek her."

"I have traveled all the way from Tierkinddorf. I want to speak with her."

"We don't know where she lives. She has no cottage. She and her sister . . . they lived in the woods. Do not seek her. She is strange, passing strange. Such that any woman should shun her."

Now her eyes did show something: fear.

"We have heard about your village," she continued. "Beset with witchery. If anyone should come to us and ask who of our people might be the same, there's no need to sit upon a bench and think. Fronika has always been odd, as was her sister. How can anyone live without a house? You shiver in this wind, and they *lived* in it. Please. Return to your village and speak her name no more."

I backed away from her.

"Go home," she said as she shut the door.

I climbed the hillside again, using my hands to help haul my body. My hands and feet were now entirely numb. I believed they were still there by the fact that I saw them, but in my mind I trod along on my ankles and my arms ended at my wrists. Back I went into the dark woods, away from the stone cottages, away from Jost, wherever he may be.

I walked back to Irmeltrud, toward the fire.

"Where were you?" she demanded as I walked in.

Although I was shaking with cold, I went straight to my tick in the corner and collapsed. I could not have walked another step if the dear Lord asked it of me.

"In the woods," I moaned into my bedding.

"All this day?"

"Aye."

"Whom did you meet with?"

"No one. I walked to look for Jost. I went as far as Steindorf."

"A foolish lie! You never walked that far."

"I walked to Steindorf and saw their stone cottages," I replied, although truly I didn't care if she believed me. I wanted to sleep.

"The only way you could have gotten there is if the devil put you on his back and flew there."

I stiffened.

"Who did you meet with, Güde?" she repeated.

"I spake only with a woman there, who answered my knock," I faltered. "I walked all day. Look at my shoes, worn away to nothing."

"You must have worn them away dancing," she said lightly. "I've heard of the dances. I thought they were at midnight, though, not in the very heart of the day. Did Künne teach you the steps?"

"No, Irmeltrud, no. Please. Jost will return soon and he'll have food. More than he can carry."

"What am I to think when you are gone all day? What shall I say if anyone asks me about your doings?" It was as if she was trying to convince herself.

"Irmeltrud, all this hunger will pass. We aren't being punished; we have to keep our faith."

"We aren't talking about hunger," she said. "We're talking about you disappearing for an entire day. What is an old woman up to for such a length?"

I saw where her reasoning led, and I spake as quickly as I could to deter her. "I gave birth to Jost," I said. "I brought him into this world and I am dear to him, if not to you. If he should return and find me gone, he—"

She arched her eyebrow at me. "You're babbling nonsense. What does it matter that you gave birth to Jost?"

"I don't know how you would repair such a fault with him," I said.

"What fault?" asked she.

I cringed, for if I spake it, it would make it true. I preferred that we speak in unknowns. "I hope that I will die soon," I said. "I want to be buried next to Hensel, and God willing, it will be soon."

"There are knives on the board and a cold outdoors," said she. "You can hasten God's willingness."

11

ONE WEEK SINCE KÜNNE BURNED

In church the next day the priest stepped aside and the friar gave the sermon. He spake of the great glorious fire and the intense love of Christ he felt as he watched the flames consume the wicked woman. "But one thing I found troubling," he said. "The woman made nary a sound. In town after town, I have heard women shriek out their vile souls, with the torrid sounds pouring from them as the fire undoes their malefaction. Never have I seen a woman burn with such silence. She never screamed."

He paused to watch the villagers nod, each of them, like him, puzzled.

"It makes me fear that she took pleasure knowing her ill work was still being carried out."

This time only Irmeltrud nodded.

"I have word that the hen is still enchanted, and we shall not know for a time whether Frau Zweig may bear children again. Perhaps Frau Himmelmann's instrument still works a spell upon this village."

Instrument?

"Perhaps another, equally tainted, has taken up the plow at that blasted field," he clarified.

I could not swallow. Had they talked already? Lord God, would it happen now, this minute?

"Love your neighbor as you always do," he said, "But watch your surroundings and be careful with your souls. It may be that we have not yet vanquished what we intended to."

I sucked in an unsteady breath. I had not been accused. Yet.

Before he finished, the murmuring began.

———

After the service ended, I stood in the snow, of many minds. Should I walk again, as I had done, with my aching body and ragged boots, this time not to return? Throw myself upon the mercy of the people of Steindorf? To manufacture a lie, say I had lost my way but had not the strength to return to my home? Or should I walk again, but with the purpose Irmeltrud suggested? Walk until I sank into the cold and give myself to the bitter winter, an offering to God? I would not touch the knives, but wouldn't it be easy to sink into the snow, to curl up under an evergreen tree? *My bed shall be under the evergreen tree. . . .*

Faultless, without offense . . .

I could settle my cloak under a tree and lay down with a prayer on my lips for Jost; I could shiver under the soft drift of pine needles, hearing the wind move the boughs and the snow. I could watch the light grow dim and hear the wolves moan, could let the snow build up on me, flake by flake, until the forest forgot I was there.

One other choice awaited me. It was a harder choice; it involved the risk of brutality, of seeing myself tied to a stake of wood cut by my son's wife, with flames under my feet. But if I chose this option, I might be able to see my son again. I made my excuse to Irmeltrud, seeing the blaze of interest in her gaze, knowing that she would use this against me.

"Where?" she asked.

"I'll be back soon," I mumbled. "An hour, perhaps less."

"But where?" Irmeltrud was smiling. She now had a second reason to go speak to the friar: disappeared for two days in a row, shortly after Künne was burned!

"I just have to go," I said. I looked down at Alke and Matern, wondering if I should take a kiss from each now. How would it work?

"Can I come?" asked Matern.

"No!" said Irmeltrud fiercely, and she threw him against her skirt.

I reached out and touched the blond curls on his head, then caressed the softness of Alke's cheek. "Beautiful children," I murmured. Their eyes looked up at me trustingly. Blue gentians in the snow. They walked off before I did, so I stood in the wind while those dear bodies walked from me, with Irmeltrud in the center like the hilt of a sword.

———

I worked quickly in Künne's cottage, plucking the leaves from the remaining plants and heating the wax again to create the *Pillen.* She had said one was enough, to assure me I had done well, but with what I had I was able to make two. Then

I crawled on my hands and knees, hunting for her needle. It was thrust into a blanket she was mending, with a line of wool still hooked through its eye. I used my front tooth and hands to tear a patch of the blanket off.

I pulled my skirt up, still sprawled on the ground, and sewed the *Pillen* behind the blanket patch. Hidden.

As I neared home, I looked at the tracks in the snow for signs of any visitors. With my hand on the door, for a brief moment I allowed myself to imagine that Jost had come home and there was a bloody hunk of stag meat hanging in the corner.

I pushed and went inside. He was already there.

"Where have you been?" asked Irmeltrud. She sat next to him, her hands folded in her lap. She was scared about what she was to do, but determined anyway.

I made no answer.

"That cat has been meowing for you," she continued. "The one you said had eyes that glowed in the dark? It was here again for you. It meowed almost as if it were trying to speak. Like it was asking for you."

I looked at the friar. In his lap was that book he had held up in front of the villagers the week before. All of a sudden my vision tilted and I blurted out, "I didn't sign the book."

"What book?" he asked, interrupting Irmeltrud as she spake further about the cat.

"I didn't sign my name, but it signed for me," I said. My hands were quivering. I tried to sit down, but instead lurched onto one knee, as if being knighted.

"When you passed by Herr Kueper's door, his milk went sour," Irmeltrud said.

"Who has milk?" I agonized from the ground. "No one drinks, no one eats."

"I'm ready to denounce you," said Irmeltrud. "The signs have been so apparent, I wonder that our cottage hasn't been lit from inside with a hellish fire color, signaling to everyone what is harbored here."

"The book of the devil?" asked the friar.

"I didn't sign," I said.

12

The tower was cold. The straw was not fresh like the tick Jost prepared for me each year, but was dusty and brittle and filled with fleas. I had a little fire in the fireplace, but there were large slits in the stone, high above my head, that let in air from outside. As much as I shivered, I was glad for the slits, because I thought in time they could air out the horrible earthy spice that reminded me of Künne's stay here.

I had been left alone in the tower for two days. I had done little else but kneel on the dirt and pray for Jost's return, either with meat or without. I closed my mind to the thought of Alke and Matern, because they had screamed and cried as the friar took me to such extent that I wondered if God would allow me to die right then. They were old enough to understand that Künne's fate could soon be mine. I wondered how Irmeltrud had steeled herself. Surely she had told herself she was doing this to help the children, but then to hear their absolute panic . . . wouldn't it have made her doubt herself? Little Alke sleeping without her nightgown, and Matern in his perpetual tears . . .

I went to the corner to relieve myself and swept dirt over the hole. This was how Künne's bandage and skirts had gotten so filthy. I pressed my forehead to the earth. My mind was whirling such that I couldn't linger on the memory of her thin frame surrounded by fire, it hurt too much. Thinking of Matern and Alke was too much to think about, too. And the thought that I might never see my son, Jost, again cut worse than anything. If the hunger never ended, would Irmeltrud feed Matern to Alke, weakest to strongest? Would she take a knife from the board and slice a thin rind of flesh to chew on? Would she venture into the night and steal the Töpfers' hen and cut Frau Töpfer's throat to catch the blood for a pudding? I wondered if the friar had already given her food or if I would have to go to the stake for that meal to be earned. I fingered the nub in my skirt where the herb *Pillen* were hidden. I would wait until the last moment possible, to see if Jost would return home.

Every time I let my mind fall to dreaming, I saw him stepping in the snow, weary. He was the only link I had to Hensel and the old days, the brightness, the larder full of food, the smiles of neighbors, the smell and stink of animals . . . And then I had to quickly wrench my mind somewhere else, for I couldn't give up on him. I had to believe he would return.

At noontide, the door would open and someone's quick hand would throw in a morsel of food and shove a bowl of water along the dirt. I never saw who it was, even though I would try to position myself and call out, but he opened the door only a crack and moved as fast as ever he could.

The first time food was thrown in, it was a large radish. I picked it up and brought it close to my nose, inhaling. In the autumn, someone from the friar's city had pried this from the earth. Their radish field had yielded harvest, as our village's had not. This very root had been in someone's hands; they had pulled the green stem with its frond-edged leaves until the plump body of the vegetable had appeared, with its tail moving from rose to white at the very tip, which we called the cold hound's tail. Perhaps in the friar's city they had some other name for it. Perhaps the bland-faced man who bent to pull this from the dirt, like a bird pulls a worm, thought of the tail as a cat's whisker or a crone's gray hair.

The leaves with their furred undersides, such that Hensel used to tickle me with them, pulling a leaf across my cheek, were gone now, already boiled in some other woman's pot and eaten, and the redness of the radish was now rusty. I ran my tongue along the smooth surface, tasting already the bitterness of its body. And then I bit and chewed. I had always loved this simple gift of the garden, because the triad of colors broke my heart. The lovely hazy green of the leaves, the bright red of the vegetable itself, and then the shade one must eat to find: the bright crisp white of the inside. Nothing was prettier upon a plate than the grace of the spreading profusion of leaves, and one bite taken from the whole. I looked upon my once-bit radish, devoid of greenery, and trembled. What right did I have to hold it, being so pale and undone in such a gray place as this? It was as if a butterfly had lit upon the butcher's leavings. I ate in a circle until the red wore a white girdle. I snipped the tail off with my front tooth. I gave the radish all the appreciation I could.

Thank you, radish, for your firm flesh and brightness. For giving yourself to me.

The tower's cold and rancid odor made me want to scream. Would that I were a woodland mouse, able to burrow down through the dirt and under the walls! I was tempted to take one of my *Pillen* now, simply to deaden the suffering of my mind, but I knew I would be wise to save them for the later suffering of my body. If only I could disappear, take myself into the woods and vanish against the grayness. Who cared what mischief I was up to, what thought I ever manufactured in my body? I was like seed fluff the wind takes: useless, of no import! Hensel had been the exact opposite, so alive. Even now, decades after his death, it was easy to see again the ruddy color of his cheeks and the impossible blueness of his eyes. I had had him for so brief a time. It seemed we barely put our hands together to dance before he was gasping some last wishes. . . .

That first time we'd danced, he took my hand in his, even though the piper was still leaning over in conversation with a slip of a child who wished to purse her lips to the pipe. We stood, linked by our hands, waiting, not looking at each other, and I trembled at this simple touch. And then when the music started, such a roar from everyone's throats, our hearts hammering at the rollicking of our steps, my braids loosening, ribbons flying, we women throwing back our heads and laughing at the impossible speed with which our men spun us. And in the space between songs, I clung to Hensel, feeling his heart and his sweat, already his, smiling up at his blue eyes smiling down, knowing his large hands at my waist would soon be knowing every part of me. To capture that again! To join the women in a circle taking off our caps and rebraiding our hair, making a grand show of spreading the locks over our shoulders for all the men to see, tucking edelweiss in and threading its stem in with our fair hair, to look across to see the men watched with half-lidded eyes, just waiting for the music to start again so we would stride toward each other, given permission by the dance to touch.

And when Hensel courted me, I already knew what he felt like, how his head would bend down to mine to hear what I said.

The sweetness of those days. I could bite into it, tear it like a dog.

I shifted my position on the dried straw, trying to get warm even though it wasn't fresh and capable of holding heat.

The day we buried Hensel, paying a man to dig since Jost was too young, was the day I'd needed Künne the most. She cried as sullenly as me, hating the priest whose words made it seem that this was a choice God made, that I should accept the divine reasoning I could not understand. And she was the one who suggested to her husband that he come and help me mill the grain, trading his plot of crops to another neighbor. Thus it was that Ortlouf Himmelmann became our village's miller and later taught Jost the trade that his own father should have taught him. And soon after Jost began milling the grain in earnest, Ortlouf too sickened with the plague and died. It was as if the mill wheel determined who lived and died. I wondered now, bleakly, if Matern was strong enough to take over the milling—should there ever be another harvest—if Jost did not return.

———

The next day it was radishes again, two this time, rock hard. But I sat on the ground as shameless as a babe and ate of them as if they were soft, buttery lamb. I brought my bowl of water close to the scant fire, for what was left from yesterday was a thin plate of ice. I knew they would never retrieve the bowls: who could ever drink from pottery touched by a witch's lips?

I had run my fingers over every stone in reach. It wasn't that I wished to find a loose one; I knew I had no real hope of escape. My trudge in the woods to the village of Steindorf showed me that no one would take me in; wherever I went, I would be suspect as an odd woman, a witch. And if I escaped and found a way to live elsewhere, what good would that do me? The only thing I cared about was seeing Jost again. I had my herbs from Künne and my steadfast hope of his return, which was all the pleasantry life could offer me. But I did number the stones with my fingers, just a way to pass the time. To run something over my fingertips that wasn't dirt. I would rest the hot flea bites against the cold stone to help ease them.

If I were a witch, I could move through the stones and fly through the woods to find Jost.

That would have been worth signing the book for.

———

I wondered when my trial would be, if I too would be tested by boiling water. I sat upon my tick and thought of how it would feel to put my hand into that pot, the pot we would warn children against in normal times. Perhaps if I prayed unceasingly, God would grant me flesh without sensation, so that I could put my hand in and gather the pebbles one by one.

I watched a flea bounce up onto my skirts, near the hem where the secret pocket was. I grabbed the flea and pressed it between two fingernails so that it popped open, flattened like a clove of garlic under the side of a knife, even while I thanked it for its choice of jumping. It had helped me remember that I already knew of something that took the sense out of flesh.

If I faced a trial, I could eat one *Pille,* easily pick up the three pebbles, and pass that part of the test. My flesh would no doubt burn, but perhaps gathering all three pebbles was the more important part? After all, they were representative of the Holy Trinity, and the sweet Lamb of God would know that I was innocent and guide my hands, as the friar had said to Künne. I could be proved innocent! But instantly my hopes plummeted. Irmeltrud would never allow that. Even if I passed a trial, she would think of more to charge me with. With my supply of two *Pillen,* I could only withstand one trial—and a burning.

———

I awoke to the cat's cries, far above me. At first I screamed, thinking it hovered in the air like a demon, but then through the moonlight I could see it rested on the sill. It had managed to press its body through one of the slits but was now stranded. The height was too severe for it.

I stood and walked over, groaning at what the cold night

air could do to a woman's bones, but feeling a small sense of comfort at the sight of the small, striped beast.

"Did you climb a tree on the other side then, *Liebling*?" I called up to it. "And thought a tree would be on the inside as well?"

It meowed just as I finished my question, which made me shudder. The cat was surely speaking to me. It paced the thin walkway of the sill. "Come down and warm me, kitty," I coaxed. "It's a leap you can make."

It meowed again.

As I stood there with my head tilted back, my neck began to hurt. The beast keened to me, showing its sharp, white teeth.

"If you have wings," I whispered up to it, "sprout them and come to me. I will accept any comfort now."

And then my head became too heavy for my neck and I walked back to my tick. For a long time, I lay looking at the arched shadow of the cat huddled above me.

———

It had made it down somehow, whether with wings or with claws digging into stone or a giant's leap, I knew not. But there it was, purring and pressing against me.

"How did you conjure yourself here?" I asked. I raised my hand halfway into the air, and as eager as a lusty boy, it rubbed itself against my arm, lifting its lip in pleasure to show me its teeth. I ran my hand over and over that fur, thinking of how animals had such a gift that they kept from human hands, the deer in the forest with its tawny hide, the boar with its bristles. I pressed my ear to its flank to hear the clamor inside, a steady rhythm as the beast breathed. I petted until it tired and paced to the end of the straw, then came back, revived for more, the way Hensel had once dozed and then turned to me for more rut.

It settled into the curve of my arm and then sprawled sideways as I touched the belly. Dogs will tease one another until one gives up in this way, displaying its stomach as a surrender. So the cat had surrendered to me. Alone and hungry in my dirty tower, I was victor over something.

I slept.

———

She crouched on the sill, her toes curled around the frost-covered stone. "Güde," she called to wake me. "Güde, Güde!"

I sat up with a shriek. Her black hair dangled past her feet.

"What will you say when they ask if you are a witch?" she asked.

I pressed my hands around me to feel for the cat, which made her laugh.

"Don't you know I am the cat?" she asked. "And since you have signed the book, you can take a form as well. What do you wish, Güde? An owl? Shall we sail into the night together?"

I voided into the straw, and the pungent smell of urine flared into my nose.

"Or perhaps a worm? You are so old and slow now, Güde; perhaps the worm is most like you."

I put my hands to my eyes, desperate to block out the sight.

"What would you have said to me, Güde, if you had found me the day you wandered to Steindorf? I saw you feeding Künne Himmelmann and I spake not a word to betray you.

Perhaps you came to ask for my silence? I freely give it. A sister does not betray a sister."

I heard the squeak of the straw as she sat down next to me. She uttered a word of a tongue I knew not, and suddenly I was sitting on wetness no longer and the stink of urine was gone. "Open your eyes, Güde. You are my sister."

"I didn't sign," I moaned behind my hands.

"Are you sure?" she asked.

I wasn't. I pictured again the book, how the writing had magically scrawled across the page while my fingers were idle. And more than the book, I remembered the pig meat, the sizzle of it against my fingers. "Do you have any food?" I whispered.

"Of course I have food," she whispered back. I withdrew my hands from my eyes and looked at her. Her face was so intense and dead pale that my heart leaped.

"I have food for those who have signed," she said. And instantly in her lap she held a cooked pig's head with its eyes closed and its ears singed. She tipped it a bit, so I could see the neck bone and the flesh that encircled it. "Dig your fingers in," she encouraged.

"Even if I have not signed?" I faltered.

"But you have, Güde."

My fingers weaseled over and dug into the pig's neck, pulling out a large hunk. As the meat went into my mouth, the pig's eyes opened and it looked at me with all the wisdom and recognition of Jost. The morsel fell from my mouth. "Whom do I eat?" I asked, horrified.

"The witches confused you with their talk of babes. It is

untrue, Güde. As one who lives in the forest, I know how to find the animals. It is only a pig."

"But it looked at me!"

"Have you seen the chicken quiver and run, even without its head? This is the body giving up its spirit reluctantly."

"But it's already cooked!" I stood up and ran to the other side of the small circular room. Her body's shadow hid the pig's face. "Leave me!"

"Jost would want you to eat," she said. "You will need to be strong for what will come next."

"Why do you speak of him? What do you know?"

"I know all," she said simply.

"Will Jost return to me?" I asked. The shape on her lap jerked and she laughed.

"I will only tell if you admit you signed the book."

I pressed back against the cold stones as best I could. She was no friend. She was evil. "You want my soul," I quavered. "You are no sister to me."

She laughed, a low sound to raise each hair on my body. "They'll burn you whichever way you answer, Güde. You saw what happened to Künne. You might as well agree and eat your fill tonight."

"Leave me!"

"What will you answer when they ask, Güde? But it doesn't really matter what you say, does it?"

"Go and never return," I said. My stomach was ice cold, and my legs trembled under me. I wished I might swoon or even die.

"What you've hidden in your skirts, Güde—who will

bring it to your mouth? Künne had you, but whom do you have?" She pointed to the hem, and I fell to my knees.

"Leave me!" I screeched with every morsel of breath I had, so loud that I myself cringed. The scream made its sound twice, as if I were in a cave. With my knees digging into the cold earth, I raised my hand and made the sign of the cross. Instantly, she vanished.

I fumbled at the sewn-up patch with the shape of the *Pillen* underneath. Why did she make me worry for that? It would be a matter of an instant to tear the rough stitches out; I could easily do it in my cell once I knew I had been sentenced to die. I sobbed until I fell asleep. The last thing I remembered before I closed my eyes was the feel of wet, cold dirt against my cheek.

13

The next step of the Judge should be that, if after being
fittingly tortured she refuses to confess the truth, he should have
other engines of torture brought before her, and tell her that
she will have to endure these if she does not confess.

— MALLEUS MALEFICARUM

He finally came, as I knew he would. His notary came behind him, with a carved chair and a small table. I recognized the chair, which had a heart and grouse carved into it, as
the handiwork of Künne's husband when he had yet lived.
The notary placed both in the center of the room and then
withdrew.

"There is a grave claim against you," the friar told me as
he sat.

I knew not whether to kneel before him or stand. "How
shall I . . . ?" I asked helplessly.

"Kneel," he said. I did so.

"You are accused of witchcraft," he said. "Do you deny the
charge?"

To be asked this so soon! *How will you answer?* the woman had taunted me. I could not lie before a man of God, but I didn't know what the truth was. I opened my mouth to speak, as I know he expected, but no words came.

"Your spirit is afflicted," he observed. "You wish to give the lie of denial, but God is holding your tongue to keep you from blaspheming."

I placed my hand on his knee, to beg a moment to gather myself, but he slapped it away. "You are a filthy trap in which sin has been caught," he said. "There is more dirt on your face than in this floor. You smell worse than Frau Himmelmann did."

I put the slapped hand back on the ground, to support my weight. Blood had dripped from the quill but I had not signed. If the devil tricked me into thinking I had done so, I would need to pull my mind together so that I could resist. My mind . . . I had once met Jost in the forest and not known him. My own son! My mind had wearied from all the thoughts of my long life; it didn't work properly. Like my hair going gray, my mind had weakened and gone stray. I pressed my hands hard into the dirt as I considered for the first time that perhaps my mind had made all. Perhaps there had been no rutting in the forest, no cat kneading, no flying through the air supported by a woman's black hair. No devil's book to sign.

"You are still mute," the Friar said. "The *Malleus Maleficarum* instructs on how to open the mouths of the cursed." He nestled his hand into the folds of his robes and came out with a small, roundish object that he set on the table to his side. I stared at it. I had never seen such a thing. Made of iron, it resembled a pear. It was rounded in two ways, with one swell and a larger swell at the bottom. There were spikes at its tip.

"This is a pear," he said. "After I show you its use, perhaps you will learn to speak."

He let it lie there and admired it for long moments in silence.

"It is constructed in Münster and used to great effect by those who wish women to speak about the foul intercourse they have had with the devil. Can you guess, Güde?"

I was confused and wanted time to ponder the thought that still had me reeling, the idea that perhaps my mind had betrayed me.

"Regard its mechanism." He picked up the pearlike object and twisted a pin at its bottom. As he twisted, the pear opened up, in strips of jagged iron. There was a slow beauty to this unfolding, like a flower blooming. A strange flower, one with petals made of knives. There was no softness to this bloom, only sharp tips. He continued to work the object, until finally it was nearly flat in his palm with the bladelike strips pointing outward.

"And now do you wish to speak?" he asked me.

I was sore confused. What was this?

"Touch it," he commanded.

I lifted my hand and ran my fingertips around it. The points were not so sharp that they hurt my fingers, so I puzzled at what torture this might inflict.

"And then we wind it back up," he continued. I kept my fingers on it to feel the petals pull back up into the body of the device. When it was closed up tight again, he released it and it sat in my palm like a heavy, heavy apple.

"Oppressively weighty, is it not?" he asked. "Can you guess its use?"

I wondered if I would be tied to a stake, while the villagers each armed themselves with one of these and hurled them at me. I dropped it and the thud rang out as if I had dropped it onto stone.

"Pick it up," he said.

I gave it to him and he returned it to the table. "The *Malleus Maleficarum* suggests showing the instruments of torture and then giving the witch a night to think about whether she will confess. So I am showing it to you."

I shook my head and tried to speak. How, how would this be used?

"Think about the part of your woman's body, Güde, that is most sensitive. The place where temptation and lust reside."

I dropped my eyes to the ground while a fierce blush blazed my cheeks.

"Yes. That place," he said.

I still hadn't completely understood. What would he do with this tool?

"It is easily pressed into that part of you, Güde, when it is closed up and solid. It is not much wider than a man's prick and certainly far smaller than a babe's body. We can push it up, up, until you think, you whore, that you are rutting again."

My mouth fell open. I understood.

"Yes, yes, now you are seeing. It is only uncomfortable when closed up tight, but when I twist the pin at the bottom, Frau, you will feel these blades press against the walls of your woman's chasm. And the walls shall resist, so far as they are able. And then, after a point, they will begin to tear. And I will continue to twist the pin. I will twist it until the device is completely flattened, as you held it in your hands a moment ago. Your whore's passage will be in shreds."

He picked it up and bounced it in his hand, as a man will dandle an apple he prepares to eat. He stood up and began to walk away.

"And then I will close it again, which I have been told is even more agonizing. And I will slide it out and present it to you, with the shreds of yourself clinging to it. So you will need to think about how to answer my question tomorrow," he said over his shoulder. He knocked at the wooden door and it was instantly opened. He stepped outside.

The notary, with a flint of pity in his eyes, came to quickly grab the chair and table.

I had seen two kinds of evil in a short space of time. The one that had urged me to pledge my soul away had seemed far kinder.

———

How would he position me? On my back on the straw? Standing with my arms tied?

Think of something else, Güde.

Would he do it, or the notary? Slowly, twisting the pin after long moments of hesitation, or quickly, so that before I understood it, my body was issuing blood again, after all these years of not seeing that color between my legs? Would he take pleasure in it?

Move your mind.

Would I be able to bear it?

Think of Hensel. This village when times were happy.

I stared at my arms, withered as they were, and fiercely pictured them grasped by two other arms. Suddenly, two men were on either side of me and holding my weight as I swung into the air, feckless and proud, my feet higher than my head and the skirts flouncing, the special skirts of Harvest Fest, and then returning to earth, my feet scampering to get my speed up as the men swung me again. And then Hensel winked as I spun out of the circle in his arms only, pressed as close to him as women and men ever get, feeling the sweat drenching his shirt and him spinning me so fast my feet were only on the ground in spurts, the world a blur . . .

How I loved dancing at harvest time! My favorite was the Miller's Dance, of course, since my husband was the miller. All the dancers outstretched their arms, interlocking, and moved in circles past each other like the gears of the mill wheel. Each one supported the others, and we trusted our weight to the interlocked arms, so that we could fearlessly spin and not fall. We trusted each other. Back when there was something to harvest.

The men faded against the gray stones of my prison, the lingering grins becoming the seams between the stones, the curve of an arm becoming a spidery crack.

I fought to keep this heady memory in my mind: the music, feeling Hensel's back muscles through his thin, wet shirt. I fought to keep the partners bowing to each other and Künne's red ribbons flouncing just past the limits of my vision. My braids flying through the air and then bouncing down with a heavy thwack on my spine, the stiffness of my hands, for I had clutched others' hands to preserve my very life as I spun in these dizzying circles . . .

But a thought intruded, that of a pear made of iron.

Had he given it to Künne? Had she undergone that shame before they stripped her in the church? But how could she have survived it? No woman could live through the tattering of her insides. I would be stripped like Künne. All the young boys would ridicule me because they had never seen me when my hair was flaxen and my cheeks full and ruddy. All the men had wanted to dance with Künne or me. We had been merry, but who remembered that of us?

After we danced, we would rest, our hearts beating. One of the villagers who hadn't danced, whose breath was still easy, would sing. That was the first time I'd heard the song about being betrayed by false pretense. I stood up to sing it now, and ran my fingers over the stones of the tower. I walked in a circle, stepping back as I passed the fireplace, stepping in again afterward, and doing the same for the straw bed. I circled the round interior, singing, as demented as any half-wit that staggered in the streets.

I must've passed the remainder of the day doing this.

If any watched, they would have concluded that I had lost my mind.

———

I woke to her pressing a slice of pear to my mouth. It was perfectly ripe and the thick grain of its texture released juice against my lips and chin.

I had slept where I had fallen in exhaustion from my circling, and so I called out in confusion at finding myself on the ground near the fireplace. As soon as my mouth opened in the shriek, she pressed the pear slice inside. I closed my eyes to savor the taste and block out the sight of the witch kneeling over me, her hair tumbling over her shoulders as black as a crow. I swallowed the fragrant pulp and ran my tongue over my lips and as far down as it could reach, to catch the last bits of juice. And then finally I opened my eyes. "Do you have any more?" I asked.

"Of course. We make food from dung and wine from piss, so there is always sup in a witch's kitchen." She smiled at my reaction. "Does it not taste as sweet?" she asked.

"It's an abomination," I said, "For it's an echo of Christ's miracle, changing his body to bread and his blood to wine."

She ran a finger over my lips and I recoiled at the touch. Then she put that finger in her mouth and suckled it as a babe would do. "It's sweeter for having been on your lips, Güde," she said. "Those once red lips."

I had no words to answer this. She spake like a lover.

"Have you experienced the holy rite of communion?" she asked.

"Of course," I said, after a pause.

"It is a witch's best sacrilege," she said. "For we will accept the bread and accept the wine, and keep it in our mouths. On the way home, we will find the most horrible dung heap, rotten and crawling with maggots and sloppy with stink, and we will spit everything the priest gave us out onto that pile."

I scrambled to my feet to get away from her, my palms digging painfully against the dirt floor for purchase.

"I would never do such a thing! The sacrament is holy and good. I would never commit such an act!"

"Ah, Güde, the sacrament is wicked, not holy. There are many forces that move the heavens, which operate in the most appalling darkness. Christ is false. Do you not recall how we used to harken to the calls of the birds in the wood and summon the blessings of the beasts? And Christ has taken the place of that."

"Christ is the true one," I answered. "We were fools to see sense in a beast."

"Fools today!" she snorted. "Packed into a wooden box, standing in the cold, to call down God's help. We used to do it ourselves over the flames of the fire."

"We were ignorant."

"Then why does everyone still make the sign of the meat as religiously as the sign of the cross? People still believe, Güde. And soon the priests will be exposed for the shameful men they are; we will return to the old ways."

My back was against the stones of the wall, I could retreat no further.

"I cannot offer you what you want," I said in a low, low voice, barely hearing myself. "I do not want to join the circle in the forest. I wish to bow my head in prayer to the true God and accept the sacrifice of his Son. Please, please *leave me.*"

"Even if it means you starve?"

"Yes," I said. "Stop coming to me. Leave an old woman to her hard thoughts."

"Even though those you think are telling the truth are the ones who will tie you to a stake and burn you?"

"They do tell the truth!"

"And my final question, Güde. Do you ask me to leave even though you have already signed my master's book?"

"I did not sign!" I cried out. "It signed on my behalf, although I said not a word nor made any signal to ask it to do so!"

"It saw what was in your heart. We told you we would feed you if you signed, and you did sup with us in the forest, did you not?"

I froze.

"That was the barter," she said. "As the pig spun on the spit, we offered its meat to you in exchange for your pledge. And you ate fully of that pig meat."

"No!" I said.

"No? By my troth, Güde, I saw you eat."

"I ate . . . but . . ."

"But?"

"I did not consent!"

"What manner of fickle barterer are you? To accept the goods and not deliver what you promised in return?"

"But the meat was simply in my hands!"

"After you signed."

"Noooooooooooo!" My hair was standing up on end and the air sizzled around me. Had I made such a disastrous mistake? Had I? "I was confused! I am only an old woman and you tricked me! My mind has not been my own these days! I was so hungry. I was confused! Oh, dear God and his Son, deliver me, Christ! A bargain is not to be held to when the maker has been deceived!"

"What was deceptive, Güde? We offered food for your signing and you ate."

"But I didn't understand! When meat was placed into my hands, I was so hungry there was scarcely reason in my head!"

"A poor defense."

I understood. I had been tricked. If this witch was not a figment ushered into my head by the forgetfulness of the elderly, I had indeed made a pact with the devil. I felt aware of the flatness of the world and the pit of eternal darkness that surrounded us on all sides. I had just now tipped off the edge. "Why, why did you ever come to me?" I asked in despair.

"Your son brought me into your life, Güde." Her eyes grew in luster, and I saw that she was angry. "I chose you because you remember the old ways. Your girlhood was not so very long ago, when hunters revered their prey."

"Jost has surely naught to do with you and your wicked band—"

"He bargained with me unwittingly," she said, and bent her body into a strange posture, a crouch, looking as if she were about to spring upon me. Her body was tense like those of the cats that used to live in the mill, preparing to pounce upon a mouse skittering amidst the grain.

I took exactly seven steps backward until once again my back was stiffened against the wall.

She stayed in her crouch. "Do you remember the rabbit?" she asked. "The one you all ate and Jost made a pelt of?"

I nodded.

"Its skin hangs above your fire, drying out. It is promised to Alke as a wrap."

"Yes," I whispered.

"A beautiful white pelt with only one black stripe."

"Yes."

"It is my sister," she said, and suddenly she leaped upon me. Her teeth were at my throat, biting through my skin, her breath hot and ragged. I pushed at her without success as she pressed her weight fully against me and yowled. Then she backed away and spat. I clamped my hand to my throat. "When he found her in his trap and broke her neck, you were wandering in another part of the forest, Güde. He is the one I hate, but we do not gather men to our fold. Only women. You bear the brunt of his punishment, Güde."

My blood glinted on her teeth.

"I went howling from my sister's killing ground, seeing her hanging from his belt upside down like a worthless rag, and came to find you, sunk to your knees in the driving snow. I gathered the witches and my master and we tempted you."

Behind me, hidden from her sight, my fingers clawed at the stones. Surely there was a way out. I ran to the door and pulled and battered on it. Just like the night Irmeltrud had pushed me out. That was the night! *That was the night!* It was Irmeltrud's blame the witches had found me in the wood! I pulled at the latch and kicked and hit the door. "Help me, someone! Friar! Please!"

"The friar is as angry at you as I am," she said. "You'll find no pity from either of us."

"Help me!" I yelled. "Please deliver me! Lord in heaven, send me deliverance!"

"We all take forms to honor our master," she said. "I take the cat form and my sister was a pure white rabbit, with a black stripe for her raven hair. And you could be anything you wish, Güde. An owl to hoot through the branches or a horse tossing its hooves to a gallop by moonlight. And perhaps no hunter will pierce your heart with an arrow. *Perhaps.*"

I screamed at the top of my lungs and kept the sound going to drown her out. I screamed with all my breath, thinking of

the years without grain, the curse that God had passed down
to us, and why it was that hunger had cost me my soul. No
one came to the door. I didn't know if anyone was even nearby
to hear. And when I finally turned around, exhausted and broken beyond repair, even she was gone.

14

They are not content with their own sins and perdition,
but draw countless others after them.

— MALLEUS MALEFICARUM

The friar returned in the morning and I was so relieved to see him that I bent and kissed his hand.

"Holy man of God," I said as I remained crouched, "I am much refreshed to see one who embraces the lightness of Christ. I have spent such a hard night, sir!"

"Sit, Güde. And confess to me what has plagued you in the nighttime." His notary opened the door, bringing the carved chair again for the friar and a large radish for me. I sat cross-legged on the ground at the friar's ankles, like a child awaiting a good fairy tale. I took one bite of the radish and shrank at the desperately loud sound it made. I chewed what was already in my mouth, swallowed, and buried the rest in my skirts.

"There is a woman from the village of Steindorf," I began. "Unlike us, she has raven-colored hair. I have seen her in years past, enjoying the merrymaking at our fests. She and her sister, also dark. One night, both Jost and I were out abroad, but in different parts of the forest. I had been put out by my daughter-in-law. I wandered up the hill—"

"Irmeltrud put you out?"

I flushed. "That isn't the important part."

He gave a significant look to the notary, who hovered behind his chair. "Pray continue."

"Well, sir, I was wandering fruitlessly, hoping my son would come for me and usher me home. But instead he was checking his traps, and he found a beautiful snow-white rabbit with one black stripe. That was the sister of Fronika of Steindorf. I know not if she struggled in the trap and he had to wring her neck . . . regardless, that night we later feasted on her. And Fronika, angered at the sight of the hunter gathering up the rabbit, flew through the forest until she found me, to wreak her revenge. She called out all the witches, and they gathered there and tempted me with pig meat."

"Can you name all the witches? Was Irmeltrud there?"

"No, not Irmeltrud! She is my accuser, sir. The one you spake with in my cottage!"

"I know well who Irmeltrud is," he said. "And the others?"

"I knew them not. They were shadows in the woods. I think they were not of our village."

"I am doubtful of that," he said. "This village seems to be the seat of all the evil."

"But Fronika and her sister were from Steindorf—"

"So it would seem to a simple peasant woman. But I have access to higher knowledge. I have read copiously upon this subject. The witches are full of trickery and games of perception. And you have been caught up in their games."

"Yes, sir!" I agreed breathlessly. "I was tricked! For the book that they had, of names of souls, I never signed it and yet my name appeared in it magically!"

"Did you see the devil, Güde?"

"Yes, sir, with full, wide hooves and a man's body. In fact, he . . ."

"Do not stop."

"He had the face of my dear Hensel, departed these many years ago from the plague."

"Was there fornication in the woods?"

"Yes, with all involved."

"And you?"

"Yes."

"That is grievous news indeed. For such is the seed of evil spread, through the wretched womb of woman."

"But I am past childbearing years, sir."

"It makes no matter!" he bellowed. "You carry the seeds within you, wicked woman!"

"But I repent most wholesomely, sir! I am glad to leave behind those women, for I never wished to be part of them. It was all trickery, to show me the face of the husband I loved. How could I resist?"

"Many have, Güde," he said sternly.

"I am weak, Friar. There is little flesh under this loose skin. For it was as much the offer of meat as the showing of my husband that caused me to become one of them."

"Hunger!" He laughed, a coarse sound that was hollowed in the small confines of the stone tower. "You blame the loss of your *soul* on hunger!"

I wanted to ask if he had ever been hungry—his fine, thick

form did not suggest it—but I knew he would take such a question as an insult.

"Güde, since you are making full confession, I have no need of the instrument I showed you yesterday. My notary will sit with you, writing down all you say, to gather the story of your lapse from goodness. Tomorrow you shall go before the tribunal to make a public confession, and then you will be sentenced."

My fingers clenched into fists in my lap. My neck was aching from staring up at him. *You will be sentenced. . . .* I shifted in the dirt and rallied my spirits to ask the question that made my heart pound only to think it. But I had to ask. I had to. I began in a whimper, and started over. "Is there . . . is there any pardon for one who makes a full confession?"

"Not for one whose soul no longer belongs to God. You said yourself, Güde, that your name appears in the devil's book. You are not one of ours any longer. I could not save you now if I wished to."

"But I'm unsure of whether my name appears there!" I rose to my feet, clutching at his hands. The radish fell to the ground. "I think that too is part of their trickery! It wasn't Hensel, sir; he's in heaven with our Holy Father. I saw only the *appearance* of Hensel. And likewise, perhaps only the *appearance* of my signature!"

"We cannot take that risk. If you did sign, you are a contagion like the plague, and you will spread your foulness to those around you. You did rut with the devil, Güde. You admit that. The seeds are festering within you."

"Maybe that too was an illusion! And I am an old woman. I have seen my own son and not known his name! I forget things. I cannot provide a good report of the doings of the world!"

"To ascertain that your soul is pure, we should cleanse you. Would you not prefer that to continuing your life and then burning in hell forevermore? I offer you a short amount of pain here on earth, and then release from eternal hellfire."

"Isn't there a way to prove I am not a witch, sir? The boiling water trial that Künne underwent? Or may I be relieved of my sins? Isn't that why our savior Jesus Christ was nailed to a cross?"

"He provides relief from mortal sins only; yours is an immortal sin, by which you have lost your soul. Fire is the only purifier."

I stepped backward in horror, twisting my ankle on the radish. I fell, shrieking in pain.

"See? That is the devil's work there, Güde. He is working on you, even here in my holy influence."

I panicked. What could I say? I knew I had the *Pillen* to make the burning painless, but I still feared to end my life that way, with all the townsfolk watching in hatred. I drew a trembling finger through the dirt, thinking. The friar remained silent, waiting. The sight of my finger made me think of how I numbered the stones by hand. And I had an idea.

"If I were a witch, truly," I said, "would I not be able to fly through these stones and make my escape?"

The friar blinked. "Witches do have the power to move through wood and stone."

"But Künne remained trapped here, as do I!"

"Are you saying to me that I condemned Künne in error?"

I sat up and hunched myself over to seem as humble as pos-

sible. "No, sir," I said, although it hurt my every inch to say so.
"I do believe Künne trafficked with the devil and his minions.
You were right to put her to death. But I am unlike Künne.
The spirits of the forest picked me for spiteful play. I am only
an old woman, sir, and I am God's faithful servant and—"

"Your case is most perplexing," he interrupted. "I will con-
sult my book and return. Tell my notary everything you saw
in the woods."

He got up and left, his robes moving like a pennant waving
in a slow wind. I picked up my dirty radish and ate it as I told
the notary of everything I had seen.

———

That night, a storm tore through the heavens. Shivering and
terrified, I put as many branches into the fire as I could. Soon
I would have none left. But I didn't care. I lit up my tower
until it was so bright that the lightning's flashes barely made
a difference. I became so warmed my face grew as rosy as in
the days of festival dancing, when it was men and their smiles
that brought the blush to my cheeks. I stared into the yellows, whites, and even blues of this fire, the curl of the flame
that unfurled and then was instantly gone. This too was like
magic. If a cat could stand upon my sill and vanish and be
named magical, why was this vanishing not understood the
same way? Perhaps this was a bit of evil we all kept in our
homes unwittingly? But this was a blasphemous thought.
Fire was reserved to torment those in hell, so it was a tool of
God's, not his fallen enemy. The stones of the tower took on a
glaze of yellow, nearly beautiful in the flickering haziness.

The dizzying crackle of a piece of wood giving itself up to

the fire . . . I stared and saw the reflection of each fire of my life: as I sat quiet in my girlhood carding wool and thinking whom I might become in womanhood, as I stoked it and built it with fallen tree branches I myself dragged to the hut, as I dried Jost's hair before it after a washing, as I dried my own and watched it graying, as I spread winter garments before it to dry, as I put a kettle to boil or snow to melt . . . as I always dreamed, as I always watched the sparks for aught to tell me. The fire never spake, but I dreamed with it all the same. I admired it. I knew nothing else that had such power.

I touched the hotness of my face and tried to become easy with the thought of my own death, as I knew Künne must've struggled to. I wished the Lord might take my sleeping body. Or that a fever would take me. Or a toothache spread into my brain, like old Jutte Fink three-odd years ago. The idea of quitting this life to see Hensel again, the *true* Hensel, was actually something I longed for. I would be sorely beset to say goodbye to Jost, but it would be a pleasure to leave behind this slow and spindly body and be again robust for Hensel.

Oh, to no longer feel the cold wind seep through my garments! To never feel the pangs of hunger again! But I knew I could not bear the pain or smell of my own flesh burning.

One of our men had once ridden his horse all the way to Frankfurt and he told us of a terrible custom he'd seen in the town square. A man had been accused of theft and would not admit it. The lawmen therefore put his feet to the flame. He sat there watching his own feet burn, unable to move them as his ankles were trapped in cuffs of iron. The entire town hooted at this man as he screamed unearthly screams. The man who told us this was highly agitated, and would have intervened to help the poor accused if he hadn't known that the mob, so gay at the man's torment, would surely have included him in whatever tortures might follow.

"If the pain didn't kill him," our villager said, "he would become sick later while tramping through the mud and slops of the town on his stumps."

I didn't know why this story should linger with me as I went to recline on the straw, thinking that this could be the last evening of my life. More useful for preparing my mind would be the thought of Künne and the fire *she* endured.

But there was something about the Frankfurt story that stuck in my mind. It was the idea of the man sitting there, as if at leisure, watching his feet burn. At least at the stake one is elevated, alert. One's legs are under one and ready to run, should the possibility arise.

I thought too of the cat who was a witch in beast guise. Were all cats so?

And why had I been punished for eating of Fronika's sister? Why hadn't she transformed herself once trapped, and used her hands to free herself? Or screamed to her sister for help? Everyone knew how hungry we all were. It was not Jost's fault he set out a trap. Every man had!

Just then the door opened and Irmeltrud was pushed inside. She was soaking wet. She ran right at me and shook a finger in my face. "What did you say to them?" she demanded.

For a moment I was speechless.

"Answer me, you useless old hag!"

I was trying to understand. Why had she been so rudely pushed into the chamber?

"I swear, Güde, you should have died in the snow the night

Jost caught the rabbit. It was horrible looking at the meat in the pan, just waiting for you. Ten different times I went to cut it up for Alke and Matern and your son stopped me. What for? *What for?*" She spat upon the ground. "And now you've said something to them," she continued.

I understood now. Irmeltrud was also accused. A slow pleasure began within me. The fate she created for me was now hers too. How wondrous fair.

"No one's watching the children! If they fall upon knives or into the fire, who will help them? And you know they're scared of thunder! But you have not a care for them, only hatred of me!" she said.

"I said nothing to accuse you, Irmeltrud. But well I might have wished to—you betrayed me first!"

"Oh, you said something all right, you slot of a pig's prick-hole!" She slapped me and flew to my tick, kicking and tearing it until the straw burst out and she was surrounded by a blond rain. She screamed as she kicked, "This place stinks of the piss and slops of an old woman!" Then she laughed bitterly. "Do you know what you've done, Güde? You've made orphans of your grandchildren."

"No," I said. "Jost will return."

She sneered. "The hunting party's been gone so long now, even if they turned around and came home this instant, they'd die in their steps from hunger and cold. It's been over a week."

"You assume they found no game," I said. "Maybe they are strengthened anew and walking quickly back to us."

"Alke and Matern will be orphans," she said firmly, exhausted. "The children will eat on donated scraps, if there are any to be had."

I leaned against the wall, thinking about the two scared children by themselves. Now that the tick was destroyed there was nowhere to sit.

"Someone will take them," I said. "Tomorrow, as soon as the word is given that you've been accused."

"Who? No one will take on two extra mouths to feed."

"They will be cared for, not abandoned. This village . . ." I trailed off and my heart lurched in horror. The kindness I was about to speak of didn't exist anymore. The only man with food to spare also had a device of torture he carried with him. Who *would* take the children?

"You have condemned them to a slow death. I hope they burn you first, Güde, so I can watch and laugh!"

I grasped onto her insult. It was easier to fight her than to think of woeful Alke and Matern trying to keep the fire going and begging food from neighbors. "I hope they *do* burn me first," I said, "for smelling the stink of your blackened heart afire would kill me five times over! You never believed me a witch! You accused me to remove one mouth from the table!"

She gasped. "Oh, I know you to be a witch! Petting the devil's own beast, suffering pricks from his marking on your forehead, all your wandering in the wood—"

"The mark on my head was from *your* sewing needle. Are you the devil?"

She tugged off her shoe to throw it at me. It landed with a dusty puff against my chest. "The crazy things you've said, Güde! Returning from the woods with a rotted basket and inviting us to eat from it!"

I had no reply.

"Admit that you consort with witches, Güde! You and Künne gave your souls to the devil!"

"No," I said.

"Where's the conviction in your voice?"

It was all too confusing. Was I a witch? Did Irmeltrud truly think I was, or had she accused me for Alke and Matern's sake? And who had accused her? The friar had asked me if Irmeltrud had been in the woods with the witches, but I'd denied it. "He has a pear, Irmeltrud, that he puts in your woman's channel and its spiked leaves will ruin that part of you."

"What do you mean?"

"It's an instrument of torture to make you confess."

"I'll not undergo that," she said. She put both hands against the wall, propping up her weight, and thought. "I am an influential woman in this village," she said slowly. "I will speak privately with the friar and he will let me go. I was, after all, the one who arranged for Künne's wood," she said. There was a note of hope in her voice and I was jealous to hear it.

"You live with a witch and someone has accused you," I said.

"Someone? Very clearly you!"

"Not I," I said, and something in my voice registered with her.

"Not you?"

"No."

"Then who?" She began gathering up the spilled straw, something to do with her hands while her mind worked. She shaped it back into the rough outlines of a bed. "Who would see me undone? No one hates me."

I went to the fire and added more branches. We were both as industrious as we could be in our tiny, dank tower.

"Maybe it's someone who doesn't hate me but envies what I have. Remember how Enede Fett was so in love with Jost? Maybe she has bided her time until she can have him?"

"Then you think Jost *will* return," I said.

"I have no idea! When he kissed me, it felt like he was saying goodbye forever. And these woods are so vast. What if they travel in circles without knowing the way home?" she glared at me. "It must be Enede. Who else? Jost was so handsome back when he picked me, remember?"

"I remember," I said.

"That spinster biddy!"

I smiled. "Enede was very comely. I don't know why Jost didn't pick her. I'm sure he regretted the selection he did make."

Irmeltrud sat on the newly regathered straw, put her fists on her knees, and screamed until she ran out of breath. I held my breath with her. How I hated what she had done to me, but I understood that scream. I relished it. She screamed again, and I sank onto the icy dirt floor, letting the sound enter me thoroughly. I would not share the straw with her.

"What did you tell the friar?" she asked at length.

"I hardly know," I said.

She expelled air from her nose in a quick, scornful burst.

"I confessed to him that I had seen witching in the woods, with a hoofed beast bearing Hensel's face. But I also confessed that I did not know if I could rely on what my eyes told me."

"You spake of the cat?"

"I know not." I paused. "You see my gray hair and the lines across my face like cracked ice over the river?"

"I have for years," she said coldly.

"The aging is not only in my body but also in my head. Many times I'm unsure if I have seen the things I thought I saw. Or what I said, or how old I am. My mind is wiry and gray, like my hair."

She stared at me.

"And it will happen to you too, Irmeltrud, should you live past this. And then you will regret your cruelty and what you said to the friar about me."

"I had to protect the children," she said.

"So you *do* admit it! You accused me so the children could eat my share!"

"No," she said. "I had to protect them from your *witchcraft*."

"I have no idea what to believe!" I wailed. "I want it all back the way it was. Food! Food for everyone. And Jost here milling everyone's grain, and you still respectful of me since I am his *Mutter*. And no one in robes! I want our old world back."

"There is a reason God is punishing us," she said. "He sent the plague as a warning and now he has despoiled the land of any food."

"And what is that reason?" I called, at the very heights of my voice's ability. I hoped somewhere the friar would hear and come to answer. He knew God and his reasoning better than any of us.

"I don't know God's plan, Güde. Did you think a simple countrywoman would?"

"Is there a plan?" I cried in despair.

She hissed and made the sign of the cross three times over. "How dare you question that?"

"Because I don't see why we are being punished! We

were never bad folk. We didn't murder or thieve or covet. We only danced and ate and rutted and greeted each day with gratitude!"

"We don't know what people did when the doors closed between us."

"I know what we did, and we deserve our daily bread. The prayer asks for it, but we shouldn't have to ask."

"You are blaspheming!" she said. "The fire will cure you, please God."

I looked at the terror on her face and was glad I felt only emptiness. "The fire will end all this, please God," I echoed.

———

Not long after the storm passed the friar came to Irmeltrud. He stood just inside the door, no chair or notary.

"Tomorrow Güde will make her public confession. And you will join her."

"But sir—" Irmeltrud ran to him and knelt, pulling his robes to her lips and kissing them. "I do not plan to confess! I was untainted by her devious craft. My children and I are pure, sir, and embrace as always the mercy and goodness of Christ!"

He pulled away coldly and detached his robe from her fingers.

"Your Grace," I said, "you were to think on my question, of whether my old eyes have tricked me into seeing things that were not there."

"It is all the devil's work," he said firmly. "If you have seen witchcraft or only thought that you saw it, it is all the devil's work."

"Am I to blame for the devil fooling me with my own eyes?"

"You allowed him into your life."

"What of me?" asked Irmeltrud. "I have not seen anything. My eyes still belong to Christ."

"You have been accused of several deliberate acts of witchcraft and must face your accuser tomorrow," he said.

"Who is it?" She pulled at his robes and he took a step backward, his eyes furious.

"Do not befoul my garments, woman."

"I beg your pardon. I am only desperate with fear! Do you not recall how I assisted you, in humble servitude? I gathered wood to help in the burning ceremony, I came to you when I knew of witchcraft in my own home, so that Güde's wickedness would *not* spread to me or my children!"

"But you have been guilty of your own wickedness."

"Who *says* so?" she shrieked.

"You will face your accuser tomorrow. If I were to tell you who it was, you could work malefaction on that person tonight."

She wailed; the friar spake as if she were guilty. There was no question in his voice.

I tried again my prior argument. "Sir, if we were truly witches and capable of performing malefaction, could we not tumble the stones of this tower and walk into the woods as free women?" I asked.

"The devil has his own rules," said the friar. "And Christ has his. If the sacrosanct walls of this tower keep you imprisoned, with the devil pacing outside in frustration, that is as it should be."

"I am not a witch!" cried Irmeltrud. "Don't you see? I accused Güde. Why would I accuse her if I were myself a witch?"

"I do not guess at the choices women make," he said. "We will listen to testimony tomorrow. I believe you will both confess." With that, he turned and went out the door.

Irmeltrud, who was still on her knees, fell forward onto the door sobbing. She hammered on it, and a small, mean part of me thought that this was retribution for the night I hammered on the door she locked against me.

"I don't understand," she raved. "I was only seized this evening and upon the sunrise I must stand trial? Künne was kept here many days; you've been here nearly as long. Am I not to have time to reflect upon my accusation?"

"He didn't threaten you with torture."

"Oh, God," she said. "I know why." Her palms stilled on the door. "I heard he was to move on to Flußstadt. We have heard reports of witchery there. He's trying both of us on the same day so he can be freed to pack up and leave." She dug her fingernails into the wood. "Güde, do you know what this means? There will be no three days of wait like Künne had after her water test. They will rule on us together, tomorrow. And he believes both of us to be guilty."

She gouged her way into the wood, her face a twisted mask. "We will be put to death," she said in a rasping whisper.

———

Into the small hours of the morning, I watched her rebuke herself and stare at me in wild anger. She mourned for the children and wondered aloud what it would be like for Jost to return to the village, if he returned, to find that his wife and mother had been killed in his absence. She cursed the day she had called the friar to our house to accuse me, but without taking a second breath she scolded me for living when all others my age were dead, and for continuing to eat when there was no food to be had. She muttered that she wished she had killed the cat. She recalled to herself that my mind was faulty, that I had forgotten about Alke's burned nightgown.

"You were become like a child," she said. "You had to be told things."

While she ranted and walked our tower, I sat in a daze. Hours later, she stilled. She went to sleep upon the straw, leaving no room for me.

I sent my mind out into the snow, seeking my son. I drifted up to the slits and looked through the limbs of the tree, where the moon sat on a branch like an owl. It curved like the yellow slant of an owl's eye. The air held the thick odor of the storm's passage. I pressed myself forward until I felt the steady night wind across my face. Below me, the stones of the tower slanted down, down, until they embedded in the thick snow at the bottom. I prayed to the air: *If I must burn tomorrow and never inhabit this world further, let me see my son one last time.*

I did not care who gave me wings. I was tired, exhausted beyond conception, my throat dry. The coldness of the air was welcome; it smelled of the sweetness of the snow and the evergreens. I felt more of this world than of the dank dimness beneath me, with my daughter-in-law sleeping fitfully on the straw. I was already of the forest I surveyed at a bird's height; I saw the tree branches as a home, a place to sit and nestle my beak within my feathers.

And since you have signed the book, you can take a form as well.

What do you wish, Güde? An owl? Shall we sail into the night together?

With the next gust of wind, I gave myself to it.

I unfurled my wings and felt the slight tug in my skin where the feathers attached. My sharp ears heard all the rustling across the village, the branches complaining of the cold, the crackles and sparks from the fires, a couple awake and rutting, murmuring and tossing while the straw beneath them released a wintry odor. And I heard my kin in the woods, hooting, and then I lost my sense of Güde-ness. I was only an owl.

I flew over the cottages and the wide expanse of the meadows. My quick wings moved me over the pines until the village was far away. I trained my eyes on the moon. I flew over a clearing and saw moving shapes. I circled back and let myself drift on a current as I watched the wolves pad into a formation and then sit upon their haunches. Of one accord, they lifted their heads, exposing their throats, and howled.

I was between them and the moon, so it seemed that their song was meant for me, all wild and full of animal hunger. Lust and heat and fur and fangs. No prey. Nothing to hunt.

Hunt . . . hunters' party, my mind sang.

They keened for sinews, the snap of bones, the clog of fur in the throat when swallowing. They sang for prey, for aught to eat, for prey, for prey. I had prayed once too on my knees for a thing that never came. I might better have prayed to the moon's slip and all the forest creatures and the air in crystals and the earth veined with ice. I yearned for meat like these wolves; I understood the urge to devour. I was an animal too. The unearthly cry made the humans in the far-off village shiver; I heard a child pull a blanket up, heard the rutting couple pause. I was seized by pure wonder to catch the sound before the moon did. The friar sat bolt upright, terrified. I heard his prayer and his uneasy slump back into the bed. The heavens opened and gave us soft flakes of snow, and I retreated to a tree branch, my claws gripping it. I tucked my head into my neck and prepared to let the snow gather on me. Feathers folded into each other, compact and formfitting like the stones of the tower. The wolves below were sinking under coats of snow, losing their wolfness. I too was sinking under the weight of the snow and losing my form. It was time to sleep, although I untucked my head to stare again at the wolves. *Time to sleep, but Irmeltrud's on my straw. . . .*

The air beat with silence. I did not notice when the wolves stopped howling, but the silence was so profound it was as if they never had.

Below, the wolves shook off their snow. They rose upon their hind legs, and as I watched, their fur blanched and retreated. The sharp ears curled and shrank. The round eyes ovaled and developed whiteness around the borders. The claws lengthened and fattened: fingers. Below me, the gray and black fur became spun wool, and the white throats of the wolves were again the necks of men.

It was the hunting party.

All alive! All alive! I fell like a bolt down to my son and he extended his arm so that I could rest there like a falcon on a glove. I have never looked upon a more welcome face, the thin expanse of cheeks, the mouth crooked into a smile. *Alive! Oh, Jost!* He extended his other hand to touch me, and it was pure love in his fingers. He touched me as gently as ever any touched, and his face was full of amaze.

"Mutter," he said gently, tenderly. So exquisitely tenderly.

I heard the other men stamping around but could not break the spell of looking into Jost's blue-gray eyes. I felt the stretching of the leagues of snow that lay between him and the Witch's Tower so far away. I opened my mouth to speak. I had seen him one last time. It was terribly hard to make him understand I was saying hello and farewell at the same time.

15

We know from experience that the daughters of witches are always suspected of similar practises, as imitators of their mothers' crimes.

— MALLEUS MALEFICARUM

I woke to the door opening and a hard crust of bread being thrown inside. As I darted to grab it, I watched the hand slide in a bowl of water and quickly withdraw. It was morning again. On the straw, Irmeltrud was waking, and I could see in her relaxed face that she did not yet remember where she was.

And then her face changed and she scrambled to the door to bang upon it, tumbling on her own numbed feet along the way. But it was too late.

I was lying on the ground by the fireplace, strangely calm. She bent over me and tore off half the bread, eating like a fiend as she trod away. "I saw Jost last night," I said. I didn't know if I said it to ease her or worry her further.

She stopped in midstomp. "What did you say?"

"I saw Jost and the others last night. They're still too far away to return in time."

"What wickedness are you saying?"

"I flew out in the night," I said. "I flew many leagues hence. And I saw the hunters' party. They had found no food."

She said nothing.

"They were touched by witchcraft too," I said. "Although I'll not say that to the tribunal."

She stared at me like a witless idiot.

"They appeared to me as wolves," I said. "Jost and all the men. They howled at the moon and were gaunt and hungry."

Irmeltrud began to cry soundlessly, with small tears forming again and again and slipping down her face. But her breast moved not and she sobbed not.

"They won't return in time to save us," I said.

"You *saw* this?" she asked finally. "By what power?"

"Either I am a witch and have been given the power to fly as an owl or my mind has abandoned me and I only think that I see these things."

She cried further. "I hope you are only addled, Güde. For all night I prayed, prayed that Jost would return, and Ramwold too, whose counsel we all listen to. And even if they could not sway the friar, Jost would rescue me somehow. He would find a cart and fast oxen and gather the children and we would flee."

"Without me?" I asked.

She turned away so that she could tell the lie without me seeing the guilt on her face. "Of course with you, Güde."

"They won't come," I said.

"I should have known the friar would think that one witch in a cottage would taint all those enclosed with her. I never should have taken the risk to accuse you."

She returned to the straw to sit, sniffling quietly as she cried.

I stood in the exact center of the tower, feeling as if I were the mill wheel. Calmly rotating, everything depending upon my ability to turn. I knew where Jost was and had said farewell to him. My mind was at peace, for I had done nothing wrong, while her mind was twisted and rotten, for she had done much wrong. She had been as Judas with a false kiss in the garden, condemning another to die. And sewed within my skirt hem, I had a way to ensure that my death would not pain me.

I also had an extra *Pille.*

If I chose to share it.

It was my Christian duty to share the *Pillen* with her. How would God and his sweet Son greet me at the heavenly gates if I knowingly let Irmeltrud burn at the stake in dire pain?

Yet she had been willing for me to do that.

The priest had always spoken of forgiveness and told the story of Christ receiving a slap and then looking the man full in the eyes and turning to offer the other side of his face for another slap. And long before the priest, Ramwold had told us of how the animals forgave one another. If a fox shall bear down upon the rabbit and take its neck between its teeth, the rabbit shall understand, for the rabbit itself bites down upon the grasses of the field. And as the large insect eats the smaller, it too is eaten, by a bird that flushes down from the air to complete a cycle.

What was I to do?

It seemed I *had* signed the devil's book since I had been allowed flight and taken the form of an owl. So then my soul was eternally damned and it mattered not what I did, and if I took cruel pleasure in hearing Irmeltrud's screams, that would be only fair recompense for my own death. But if God understood that I had not meant to sign and I was granted reprieve, it would indeed matter what I did with the second *Pille.* If I showed mercy to Irmeltrud, God might also spread mercy out before me.

A fierce hatred rose in my heart. It had never been my fault that the crops failed, year after year, nor my fault that I lived past the time that most my age died. God kept me on earth for his own reasons. Perhaps because Jost loved me. Irmeltrud was wrong to think I ate food directed toward Alke and Matern's mouths. We all had the same right to eat. It was true I did less work, but it was also true that we could feed the children only to see them die in the next year. They were still young and not past the age of danger. *Kinder* often died at their age, as much as the thought cost me to think it. And who was she to rank us according to importance? If God willed for us all to slowly starve, then she should not tamper with his design.

I stared at her, angrier than I had ever been. Her accusation had not been made in a moment of passion as her wits left her. It had been a slow plan, and I knew she had thought of it many days before she did it. What had it been like for her to open her mouth to the friar and speak those damning words? How had she *dared*?

I went to sit by her. The straw was first mine, as horrible as it smelled. She had no right to sleep there in my straw. Once again, as with the food she divided with the children, she had deemed herself more deserving than me.

"I have a question for you," I said. "When you say that you

never should have accused me, I wonder if you regret it only because you put yourself at risk. Is that what you mean? Or do you regret condemning your husband's *Mutter* to die?"

I fingered the nub at the bottom of my skirt. Her answer would affect my decision.

"I thought you were a witch," she said slowly. "You had an unholy alliance with the cat and—"

"You lie!" I cried. "You accused me because there is no food and you wanted one less mouth in the cottage!"

"Is that what you think?" She turned to me and showed a face that truly seemed filled with horror. Oh, she was a conniving one.

"I know it to be true," I said.

"You *are* a witch, Güde. You confessed it yourself this morning as you told me how you flew out to see Jost. Or else you are addled and your mind makes you speak like a witch."

"I watched you sit by the kitchen fire and plot the telling to the friar. You wanted to seize what small part I might eat and grant it to the children in my stead."

"No, Güde. No!" she protested.

"Then tell me this. What payment did you get for accusing me?"

She reddened. "Meat. But that was not why!"

"You mused and considered how the friar brought his own food with him. You gave me to him to please him so that he would give you—"

The door opened and the friar's notary entered. Both Irmeltrud and I took a step backward. "Gather yourselves," he said. "The friar and indeed the town await you."

It was in me to laugh at the notary's suggestion. Gather ourselves? What did we have here but our own filth? I turned in a circle to look at each of the stones I'd numbered. I remembered one of the old pagan prayers—*Thank you, rock. Thank you, bird*—and altered it in my mind: *Farewell, rock. Farewell, bird . . .* Irmeltrud was pale, nearly the color of her hair. She had no thought of what to do and used her shoe to push the straw back into a neatened line, then tried to tuck stray hairs back into her braids. I did nothing, cared for nothing. I did not need to leave things on this earth tidy. It mattered not.

As I passed through the door of the stone tower for the second and final time, I inhaled the fresh smell of the snow that settled around us. We followed the notary in a line like geese on the riverbank. I studied Irmeltrud's back as we went: strong and sturdy once, now it was simply a panel of bone barely covered by skin and the thin threads of her garment. As we passed by trees, her bodice was speckled with shadow; as we came into full sun I could see the dust and dirt ground into the weave. Below her cap, both of her braids had a tiny curl at the end, as if that tiny bit of exuberance could not be crushed out of her.

I was aware to be thankful, continuing the prayer and adding to it. I wanted to thank these things carefully, for I would never see them again. *Thank you, snow. Thank you for the water you send to the rivers and the beauty of your mantle. I honor the crispness I hear and feel underfoot. Thank you, evergreens, for the wood you have given us and the song of the wind through your needles. Thank you for your fragrance, which we sew into bundles. Thank you most for the sight of you against a gray sky, the green so*

Erika Mailman

thick and dark it makes the eyes ache, and for your shape like the towers of a church. As Irmeltrud walked, her arms swung naturally, but at the end of them her hands were in fists. I couldn't see the notary past her. *Thank you, gentians and buttercups that I know sleep under the snow. Your colors have brightened brides' girdles and girls' hair. Thank you for your other uses, which Künne and her mother knew.* On we walked until we reached the church. Ribbons of smoke poured from the chimneys. It would be warm inside.

Thank you, fire and smoke. Thank you.

I bit my lip. *It is not your fault what men use you for.*

The notary opened the door and I glimpsed the faces of the villagers as they all craned to look. Irmeltrud began to step in, but the notary intervened and turned her around. I took one last moment to turn also and look behind me.

There were the houses in the distance. The plot of earth that Künne was buried in. Deep under the snow, the hole we rooted the maypole in at springtide. A good bit behind me, at the end of the trail of scuffled snow, were the stone tower and the tall evergreen that grew up against the open window slots. They were so thin from this distance; how had I ever fit through them?

Beyond that, the hills were barren and snow-covered. And behind them lay the beginnings of the forest. The path that led into the forest. And no, as much as I peered and wished to see my son stepping out of the woods on that path, there was no movement there. No stirring. Not even a bird to wheel and circle. I felt the notary's hands on my shoulders pulling me back strongly, and I nearly fell. "For our sakes," he mumbled, "for protection."

I walked into the church backward, as Irmeltrud had done before me, as no doubt Künne had also done.

I stumbled toward the heat of the stoves and my neighbors' desperation. They did not have two of the enormous stools, so I went first. I had no strength to pull myself up, so two men helped, one of them the friar's notary.

"Güde, *Mutter* of Jost, *Großmutter* of Matern, you are before us under accusation of witchcraft," said the friar.

Once again I was amazed at the profusion of his robes. Three women's skirts could have been cut from that cloth. Although he spake to me, he addressed his words to the congregation. Most everyone I saw was female, for those that were able-bodied men were with the hunters' party, and they all stared up at me, looking shocked. Had my face worsened so much during my sojourn in the tower?

"Yes," I said.

I looked for, and found, the small, scared faces of Alke and Matern. They were seated on a bench in the back next to Frau Zweig. Matern was crying and now and then lurching with a suppressed sob. He was frightened enough to know he had to cry silently. Neither child was looking at me. They both had their eyes on Irmeltrud.

"And are you prepared to hear evidence against you and speak truthfully to your guilt?"

"Yes."

"We have asked who in this village shall serve as your advocate, but none will. It was the same with your sister in heresy, Künne Himmelmann."

I looked out at the gathering of my townspeople. They looked back at me shamelessly.

"This is a danger when one embarks on a voyage with Satan, Frau Müller," the friar continued. "If a man unduly defends a witch, the *Malleus Maleficarum* tells us, he himself becomes a patron of that heresy. And what man would place himself under such suspicion? But witches never think of this when they begin their diabolical tricks. They never think forward to this day, to the tribunal where no man will defend them."

I wondered in what manner the friar had asked the few remaining village men to act as my advocate. Had he knocked upon their doors in the evening? Had he sent his notary to inquire? Never had anyone asked Jost to defend Künne, and I am sure he would have.

"After Frau Himmelmann's trial, your lord took me aside and asked after the legality of the proceeding. Due to his status and ability to travel, he had heard that other trials elsewhere had been conducted differently." The friar took a moment to smooth the hair of his tonsure with both hands. "When one can only lead a small village, one must puff up one's importance. Your lord was duly shamed by his outrageous and ill-bred accusations. He fled with the hunters' party and this was a relief to both of us."

Inside me, a deep well of horror overfilled its limits. *Künne's trial was not like other people's trials?*

"The inquisition is a delicate and fine-tuned instrument," continued the friar. "Through a series of established procedures, we lead a witch through her questioning. The advocate would point out particular enemies of the witch, and do his best to influence the court that those witnesses should not be heard, as they would only wish her ill. We would consider the use of torture in the proper time, and examine the witch several times before pronouncing a sentence.

"The *Malleus Maleficarum* provides the language of our speeches: what the witch shall say to the tribunal, and the tribunal's answers. It is all of a method, according to the particulars of a witch's circumstances. But when an inquisitor sees before him a rude and rough congregation, where no man is willing to step forward to act as advocate, and time has become short for the proceedings, he may speed the course of justice."

"Speed the course, then!" a woman shouted. I did not recognize her voice.

He was speaking so quickly, and each sentence bore examining. Had our lord been right? Were we at the mercy of a friar who did not follow proper procedures? An advocate could ask that certain witnesses' testimony not be heard if they were enemies of the accused. What difference could this have made for Künne? And if a man of this village had agreed to counsel me, would I be whispering in his ear that Irmeltrud hated me?

"This is not a pageant enacted upon a roadside cart," the friar said, "where you may shout out your wishes to the players."

Irmeltrud was right—he was on his way to Flußstadt.

"We shall follow Rome's holy dictates for these proceedings, in the spirit of the law if not the letter, as Paul's second letter to the Corinthians instructs." The friar turned to look at me and I was lost in the calmness of his face. This man would condemn me to die, but his face was as bland as a weaver's running the shuttle through the warp.

"Let us pray." He led us in a prayer that I heeded not. I

looked at all the downturned crowns and marveled that all but me obeyed. The words lulled my ears and I wished, keenly and only, for Jost to return. Jost, who had been brave enough to ask the friar to let me speak my goodbyes to Künne. Who would have served as her advocate, and mine. Who knew what was right and just. While all prayed for me to confess my evil, I prayed instead, solitarily, for Jost to come. Despite the leagues of snow between us, despite the gauntness of his frame and the heaviness of his spirit, to *come, come, come, come for me and your wife.* I felt the heat of the wish exploding through the top of my head, like a beam of sunlight, only going back to the sun, not from it, and that beam tunneled through the roof of the church and into the gray, sodden air above, and to a sturdy cloud, and further up, up, so it could be seen for miles. My bright, golden wish like a pillar of fire. Could he see it through the shade of the forest?

The prayer finished, and the air resounded with the finality of the amen.

"Are there any here to speak evidence of this woman's sorcery?" asked the friar.

I waited for Irmeltrud to speak, but she did not. Someone else did: Herr Kueper, our village's cooper. His arms were thick and muscled from bending iron into the hoops around the barrels. I wondered, given his strength, why he had not gone with the hunters' party. He was a man whose body bore many dark spots, almost like freckles but black as beetles. His hair was peppered black and white and his very beard straggled.

"Of an evening, Frau Müller passed by my open door. She

did not look inside to greet me, but only passed by quietly. In stealth. But I noted her, and I noted that after her passage my cow's milk went sour," he said.

"The cow gives sour milk from her teats?" the friar questioned.

"No. Only the bucket upon the floor turned sour."

"Each time you fill the bucket?"

"No. Only the one time she passed."

"And does Frau Müller bear any ill will to you?"

He looked up at me for the first time. In confusion, I smiled at him. Was that not what one did, when a neighbor looked upon you? And equally surprised, he smiled back. Then each of us quickly rearranged our faces. We were not to smile at each other. He was condemning me to die.

"I know of no ill will between us. I only know that witches enjoy inflicting pain upon others."

"Indeed. Is there more to your testimony?"

"No."

"That shall suffice. Has it been recorded?" the friar asked his notary. The notary continued to write a few moments more in silence, then looked up to nod.

"Are there any others of this village that should wish to make known evidence against this woman?" the friar asked.

We waited.

I imagined Jost's feet pressing forward into the snow. Step. Step. The crunch of his weight delving into the snow and then the perfect marking of his foot left behind. Crisp step. Crisp step. Coming to me, to the beam of light radiating from my head. The friar looked right at Irmeltrud standing in the front and nodded very slightly. She folded her hands in front of her. They were blackened and foul, as if she had spent her days sorting charred wood.

Like Herr Kueper, she would not immediately look at me. The rest of the women, however, eagerly did. Their eyes were wide. I looked again at Alke and Matern. Frau Zweig was whispering something to them. I hoped she whispered calming words. But how could they be?

"I have seen proof of witchcraft in my husband's *Mutter*'s deeds," said Irmeltrud. Her voice sounded like the voice she used to scold Alke when she grew too wild.

"Give forth, Frau."

"She has been visited by an animal the Holy Church deems demonic, sir. A cat, whose manner of entry and leaving was always blocked, yet somehow it manifested within the walls of our cottage."

"A black cat?" the friar asked.

"No, sir, though one with black in it. It was striped, with gray and black."

"And did this beast speak within the house or cause harm?"

"I did not hear it speak, though it nestled with Güde within her bedclothes and may have spoken to her."

"Did she speak to it?"

"Lulling words, sir, such as a *Mutter* murmurs to her child."

The congregation shuddered, and I imagined what they envisioned: me suckling the cat at my breast, a foul, distorted picture of motherhood. The friar gave the notary time to catch up, then continued the interrogation. "And did the cat cause harm?"

Irmeltrud hesitated. "It put our house into an uproar," she

said. "Güde awoke one night in great terror, screaming and throwing the bedclothes from her, to say its eyes had been gleaming at her."

"A true account of demonic activity," said the friar. "We are instructed that the eyes of those touched by hellish influences are made to glow even in the darkest spaces."

The villagers rustled again, chilled at the idea of the eyes in the darkness watching them sleep.

"Jost threw the cat out into the night and we went back to sleeping. But I believe Güde is in consort with the cat, and . . ." Irmeltrud's voice trailed off.

"And?"

"I know not, sir. They are in consort, but I know not what they planned."

"Did you see results of malefaction?"

"Not truly. Other than, of course, the famine we all suffer."

A woman in the back yelled, "Is it she who keeps us hungry?" I watched all the faces in the hall change from intense and solemn interest to pure fury.

"She? We are starving, barely able to rise each day, because of *her*?"

"It wasn't Künne—it was *her*! Or both of them together."

A clod of dung hit my face. I used my arm, covered by the thin sleeve, rather than my hand, to brush it off. Then dozens of clods were flying through the air at me. In the past, people had thrown rotten vegetables at thieves in the pillory, but now every vegetable was eaten. All they had to throw was what issued from their very bodies. I watched them pull out rags balled up with excrement—they had forethought to bring them.

I began to weep in the rain of refuse.

"Stop! Stop this!" cried the friar. "We are in God's holy space. Cease at once!"

I continued to cry even as the onslaught stopped. I used my sleeve as best I could to clean myself. I glared at Irmeltrud. Of all suggestions she could make, this one was the worst: that I was to blame for this village's suffering. How could she? She who cleaved to my son and lived within the walls of the cottage my husband built. "How could you?" I cried out to her. "How can you say that I make fields falter? I am only an old woman. I have no such power!"

She stood there, still with her hands folded, her eyes cast down.

I shook out my sleeve at her, and the aim, though unintentional, was true. A smattering of defecation hit her, full in the face. She raised her eyes to me, and I saw a curious, horrible mixture of emotions. Guilt foremost, and then, rising equally as strong, hatred.

"I am hungry too!" I cried to the women. "Do you see that I am fattened and happy while you are lean? I am the leanest of all of you! I have eaten hardly a week's worth in the entire month past! At every chance, Irmeltrud has lessened the portion that was to be mine. I have eaten only crumbs, while you have eaten more!"

"The accused is not to speak at this time," said the friar.

"It is only God's will that makes the field unyielding! Blame God!" I said.

"You blaspheme," said the friar. He turned to make sure his man recorded what I said.

"It is the devil, *through you,* that makes our village hunger," said Irmeltrud. Her voice put me in mind of the icicles that develop from our roof. Ice cold, in the shape of a weapon.

I knew then that I would not share the *Pillen* with her. I would take both myself and drift into a fire-colored dream while her flesh melted from her bones in full agony. I was fiercely glad I had the power to help her but would withhold it. I began to laugh then, thinking of how she had spited herself.

"Do you laugh in the midst of such a severe proceeding?" asked the friar.

"I do," I said.

"Then this showeth the force of the devil within you, that you care not for your own bodily danger."

"You'll burn me whatever I say or do," I said to him, though I continued to stare at Irmeltrud in the worst, reddest hatred I have ever felt. "You came to our village to kill someone, and you were not satisfied with Künne, for she was silent upon the stake. You will burn me and my son's wife, and her screams shall satisfy you. Tomorrow you will go to Flußstadt and burn whomever you shall find there."

"I only punish those who are guilty," said the friar.

"Then let us make quickness of it, so that we may find Irmeltrud's guilt as well. Here it all is; I confess it. There was a prick upon my forehead. I am sure that is in Irmeltrud's list of accusations. The devil with his foremost fang did bite upon me and I enjoyed the bite. All that is corrupt in me rejoiced at his marking of me. See, the mark may yet endure if it has not healed." I gestured to my forehead and the notary paused a moment in his writing, to see if he saw the mark. He shook his head and wrote again.

"I was a friend of Künne Himmelmann, who confessed her evil and was burned at the stake for it. Do you think we were friends in village matters only? No, she shared with me all that the devil told her, and she brought me to the *Hexe* circle in the forest and bade me tarry there, to learn all the craft. There I learned how to sour Herr Kueper's milk, for he is a sour man."

I paused, wondering if I should go the extra step. Irmeltrud's fists were white with pressure as she clenched her hands. Our eyes met and I felt the pure, blank loathing between us. I next looked at Herr Kueper. He nodded that I admitted to souring his milk, but his wife looked fury-filled at my calling him sour. She lifted her lips to me in a sneer, and that decided me. I *would* take that extra step, just as I wished Jost was stepping on the woodland path toward me. And why wasn't Herr Kueper out there stepping himself, in the direst cold? Why did he stand here warm and cozy? I tasted bile in my mouth.

"Not only is he sour," I said. I slowed my voice to earn the soft inhale of everyone as they waited. "But Herr Kueper is a witch himself! I spoiled his milk, for in the woods I saw him rutting with another witch not his wife. I wished to punish him for his betrayal. His wife is not pretty to look at, but she is fastened to him by God and troth."

She hissed at me and he blanched.

"I know you are off to Flußstadt tomorrow, Friar. You must try Herr Kueper now, under accusation of witchcraft. I accuse him! He is of my circle!"

"She lies!" he burst out.

"Put his name down," said the friar to his notary. Frau Kueper screamed.

"What other accusations do you have against me, Irmeltrud?" I asked. "I think I have named them all, have I not?" The air shimmered between us. It was as if the fire had already been started. I looked down at her shoes, thinking of how her feet would soon be engulfed in flames.

"There is another thing I might speak of," she said to the friar.

"Then speak."

"This very morning, she told me of a flight she took in the night."

My heart stopped. Oh, surely she knew how dangerous this was to speak of!

"Irmeltrud, speak not of this. You shall incriminate him whom you love best," I pleaded.

I listened in disbelief as she continued. "Last night, as I slept the sleep of the innocent, she took the form of an owl and flew through the woods to find the hunters' party."

"No! False!" I interrupted her. Did she not understand what she was about to say?

"Which she indeed found!" she said. "All in the form of wolves!"

There was great outcry. All swarmed forward to hear this treachery, that the men of the village were transformed into wolves. I heard a thud as the baker's wife hit the ground in a dead faint, her skull knocking the hard dirt. Everyone was shouting. Soon I couldn't see Irmeltrud for the bodies between us. And above all the din was the friar's voice asking for calm so that the proceedings could recommence.

"What say you?" a woman screamed. "Do you mean all our menfolk are witches?"

"You wicked whore!" cried another. "The men are only seeking food for us!"

There was tremendous spitting, and though I couldn't see Irmeltrud's face I knew she was sopping wet from all the women's mouths.

"She tells a witch's lies!" I called out, and this cry was undertaken by two women nearest me. Although I had feared the worst, that Jost's return would be marked by the friar's seizing of him, it had turned the other way. No one would accept that all the men were guilty. They would gladly see Herr Kueper burn, and Irmeltrud and me in particular, but they would not accept Irmeltrud's tale. Therefore she told a witch's lies.

Soon it was taken up as a chant, and I was reminded of how we all used to intone the prayers of the mass together, but back then our voices were quiet and sober; now they were lusty and in great fervor. "She tells a witch's lies! She tells a witch's lies!"

I closed my eyes and smiled at the shouts. I had become a vindictive old woman indeed, but when would I have time to repent? I'd be burned in an hour hence, and all my shame would burn with me. Ha ha!

They fell upon Irmeltrud, slapping her and wrenching at her skirts. I was shocked at the sound of skin's mistreatment. All the touching in my long life was barely heard: caresses, long strokes. I took a fierce gladness in the rude sounds.

Finally, the friar succeeded at calming the group. "I am ordained to complete these proceedings, and we have yet another accused to question. Please! Sit yourselves upon the benches or stand a respectful distance away!"

Because they were all deadly curious what might now happen to Irmeltrud, they did as he asked. I saw my own pleased smile mirrored on all their hateful faces.

I looked out over them and saw poor Alke and Matern huddled on the bench, their heads hidden. It was an odd posture, almost as if they were crumpled in sleep, but they did not look relaxed. Frau Zweig laid a hand on each. I looked also for Herr Kueper and didn't see him. Nor his wife. "Friar!" I called, malicious in my power. "I believe the Kuepers took advantage of the clamor and have fled!"

Whom had I become? Who was I? I pushed these thoughts to the back of my head. Jost would never have to see me this way. I would be dead and gone and any tales told of me he would never believe.

The friar dispatched his notary and another man to find the Kuepers, and since the ceremony could not be recorded, we all simply waited. Now that the view was clear, I could again see Irmeltrud's face. Unable to stand, she had shrunk onto a bench in front. She was sobbing. Her skirts were torn. The villagers had done more than spit.

In the silence as we waited, I thought again of Jost's feet stepping in the snow. First the left and then the right. Then again. Cycle. Everything was cycle in our woods. A woman dies in childbirth, but her eldest daughter conceives. The beetle is eaten by the bird, which is eaten by the man. Who dies as his baby bawls in the cradle. And then a wondrous image took to my mind. Instead of the slow, plodding man step, I saw the swift trot of a wolf's paw. Ah, yes! For as much as a man struggles in the snow, a beast skims along the surface easily. Quick joy seized me. The wolf could do more than trot, it could run! It could make a journey in minutes that took a man an hour. I took up again my prayer. *Thank you, wolf. Thank you for your speed, for your cunning paws. Thank you for your strong muscles to stretch the legs and make them fast. Thank you for your breath, heaving into the air as frost.*

What did I care if he came as a wolf? As long as he came!

———

They were not long in returning, for the Kuepers had been foolish enough to try to pack up blankets and whatever else they might, rather than fleeing at once to the woods. In great shame they were brought back and put on the bench next to Irmeltrud, their hands tied together as if they were oxen of the same yoke. I looked at their terrified faces and felt no guilt. Hadn't they done the same to me? Frau Kueper tried to catch my eye and beg with hers. I looked her full square in the eye and might have shrugged for all I felt.

"We will recommence now," said the friar. "I am gravely concerned for this village. You have defiled this inquisition, all of you, with the excrement of your own bodies. Among you sit more to be accused, I am certain, for it seems Künne's unholy influence was duly worked among all of you.

"Now, Irmeltrud, wife of Jost, was listing the crimes for which she accuses Güde. Do you pick up, Frau, and continue what you say."

"She said she flew out in the night in the form of an owl and saw all our men transformed as wolves," said Irmeltrud. "But *she* is the one who tells witches' lies! I am only the one to repeat the lie here for you."

"I did no such thing," I said. "I lay on the flea-ridden straw last night as I have every night. My son's wife tells lies as twisted as her hair in its braids."

Commotion again! I watched the fingers pointing, and took pleasure at where they pointed. She was the first to bring the wretched idea to their minds, and therefore she was mistress of its ugliness.

"So you deny the charge that you told her of a night flight where you saw the hunters' party as beasts of the wood," said the friar.

"I do most heartily deny it," I said.

"You are a snake in a woman," said Irmeltrud. "I wonder at myself, that I kept a serpent penned in with me and my children for so long without the realizing of it."

"I am no snake," I said. "A snake brought an apple to Eve and coaxed her to eat. I had no apple to offer, no grain, no meat. I had empty hands with which to trick you."

"And my hands too were empty," she said.

"Enough," said the friar. "A woman can beguile whether she has anything of value to trade. Do you freely confess, Güde, to the other accusation, that you have brought famine onto this village by your malevolence?"

"No, sir, for you see I am like a bone myself."

"And what of the other accusations? Do you freely confess to souring the milk and consorting with the devil? Of accepting his bite upon your brow?"

I took in a deep breath. A denial would mean nothing, would trouble the friar as much as a flea upon a dog five leagues hence. I stared at his face, bland and yet intense at the same time. He came to a village, barely knew its people, and decided who would die. Such power.

I cast my mind back to the circle in the forest. I had eaten of unknown flesh and had surely opened my body to someone who seemed of another world. The devil. I had had the devil in me. I granted myself the will to eternally say goodbye to what this village had become. I wanted the village of tens of years ago.

"I do."

"Then you shall burn for your sins and they shall die with your corporeal body. You may come down now."

The notary stopped writing and came to help me from my perch. I tried to see Alke and Matern, to perhaps wink to show them I was unafraid, but they were still curled up as if they slept. For a moment I feared the notary should usher me out into the church yard and instantly be doing the deed, but he brought me to sit, while he urged Irmeltrud to stand. The bench was warm from her body. Frau Kueper fell upon me sideways, beseeching without using her voice, but in a daze I bore her weight without remarking it. Irmeltrud ascended to the giant stool.

"And now we have before us Irmeltrud, wife of Jost and *Mutter* of Matern, accused of witchcraft. Will her accuser speak?"

Irmeltrud's vision blazed onto me, but I had not accused her. My skin prickled as I waited to hear which villager's voice would pipe up in hatred. Moments passed. The smell of the excrement oppressed me anew in the silence. Then, finally, I heard someone stand, rustling out her skirts. "It is I who accuses Irmeltrud," said Frau Zweig.

My heart plummeted down to my feet and into the sanctified ground below.

Of course.

Of course her.

For she loved children and could have none of her own. And Irmeltrud's children found her playful and charming, and she would have none of the trouble of a bawling babe; she'd begin at the good time of life, with a girl who could spin and thresh and make merry, and a boy who laughed like a cricket in full summer and minded his elders.

I heard Irmeltrud moan even as I did, our throats in twin.

Frau Zweig walked to the front to stand before the friar. The children sat up and with great dread in their faces. Herr Zweig made no motion to comfort them.

"I accuse her, for she has spoken in serpent tongue and her incantations have plagued my nightmares. In the deepest night of my cottage, my husband and I hear her voice, trilling through the walls like a wind," said Frau Zweig.

"And the incantations had purpose?" asked the friar.

"Yes, sir. For when I woke in the morning, I found that a barrel of wine had been much changed."

All but the friar stiffened to hear that she had wine yet in her household.

"How was it changed?"

"In the stead of wine, we had urine, foul and stenchful. She magicked it, sir, to keep us from drinking it."

"This was resulting from the incantations you and your husband heard?"

"Yes."

I looked at Herr Zweig. He was frowning.

The friar nodded gravely. "And have you seen her odd about the mouth after any church service?"

"Odd about the mouth?" Frau Zweig looked confused.

"As if she had something inside, kept upon her tongue."

There was silence as Frau Zweig considered. "Now that you have asked me, I do recollect how last Sunday I spake to her after the Mass and she answered me with slurred tongue, as if she had been drinking."

"Not drinking, Frau. Certainly not. For we said Mass last Sunday and she surely kept the wine and host of Christ within her mouth, to not ingest the Holy Spirit. We might have seen her later, had we followed closely, spew the Eucharist into her slop bucket to besmirch it. This is a particular bliss to the witches, an affront to the very Lamb of God himself."

Frau Zweig's eyes opened wide. "Yes. Yes. She spake as if a wafer and wine still sat upon her tongue. And I do recall a dribble from her mouth after she spake in such a tight-lipped way . . . it was the sweet wine of our sweet Lord."

"And now you may understand further what has happened to your wine barrel. The incantations spoken in your home, as if by the wind, were Irmeltrud's speaking of the Mass backward, and she turned the wine into urine to show an abomination to God. Had you bread in the house, it would surely have become as the fetid issue of our bodies."

Frau Zweig's hand went to her cheek in horror. "To think of her voice in our home, making a mockery of everything we hold sacred!"

"It was more than her voice. The witches move so fast, Frau Zweig, that it is possible for them to open and close a door in such a fast time that our eyes cannot catch the movement. Possibly she passed by you and your awakened husband and glared at you before bespoiling the bucket."

"While we lay innocent in bed?" she asked, her eyes wide. I turned my head and watched everyone shift uncomfortably, thinking of the unholy speed of the witches.

"Yes."

"I shall never sleep solid again," said she. She picked up a corner of her apron and used it to press at her eyes. She sniffled too and I watched her squint as if about to cry.

I tried to imagine her and her husband in their cottage, appalled as they knelt and looked into their wine barrel, turning their heads away from the stench, and the look of wonderment that must have passed their visages as they considered that none had entered and therefore magic had. But I knew this to be a false scene. Frau Zweig had not had a barrel of urine but a heart of covetousness. She had empty arms curved, ready for childish embraces.

I looked over to Herr Zweig to see if he too wore a deceptive face, but I was startled to see that he looked shocked. His mouth hung open and his eyebrows lowered closer to his eyes in an anxious frown. Beside him, Matern was curled up like a babe and pulsing with his silent sobbing, but Alke was watching. Under her cap dangled tight, tight braids; other fingers than Irmeltrud's had plaited her locks.

I gasped at the look on her face: wild outrage. The sound was louder than I realized, for the friar took it to mean I tried to speak.

"Güde, keep your wicked lips closed," said the friar. "You have had your time to speak."

"I never did any such thing to the Zweig family," began Irmeltrud in a low, low voice. "I know not where they keep their wine, or even that they had any, when the rest of our village only drinks it at Mass. And if I were to find it, would I not drink it rather than—"

"Silence!" screamed the friar, in a voice as suddenly high as hers was low.

"Mutter!" cried Alke. I jerked my head back in time to see her plunge to the ground, lost to view behind the people standing in front of her, then heard the scurry of her pushing across Herr Zweig, and then into the pathway between bodies.

"Sit down, daughter!" cried Irmeltrud in desperation at the same time that I cried, "No!"

She flew to the friar's robes. Her tiny fingers were so pale against the vast black fabric that I was entranced momentarily by the contrast of colors.

"Go sit down, daughter!" commanded Irmeltrud.

"Sweeting, go back to Vater," said Frau Zweig, and I tore my gaze from Alke's fingers to her face. Vater? Vater was Jost, stepping in the snow with slow foot, with the flesh diminishing from his bones and his exhale fading in the cold air. But she meant Herr Zweig. She had already instructed the children to call him Vater.

Said Alke, "My *Mutter* is good and does all she ought. She swallows the host, sir! She sips the wine and it does not stay in her mouth. She swallows!" She clutched at his robes and I bit my lip, for she grabbed where a girl should not touch until her wedding day. I stood up and ran to Alke just at the same time Frau Zweig grabbed for her. "Go sit!" we both hissed.

"The young one is a witch too," said Herr Kueper.

Up on her enormous chair, Irmeltrud began sobbing loudly.

I pulled Alke away from the friar and a powerful smell of incense came from the released robes. I pushed her back through the throng to Herr Zweig and to Matern, who was openly and loudly bawling now, but his face still hidden. "Take her!" I cried wildly to Herr Zweig. "Hold on to her and keep her here!" He did nothing, his face still appalled and uncomprehending.

"I fucked that one," said Herr Kueper, calling from the front. "All the Müller women are witches and I fucked every one of them. The young one speaks the Mass backward like her *Mutter.* I'll tell who else is in the witches' circle if you hear my confession and free me. I am not a witch, only a man. I cannot be blamed for the spell they have cast upon me. They bewitched me, but I was there only for the rut and not for the devil. I am only a weak man, no more."

Frau Kueper called out, "What man here has not rutted with one not his wife? Shall they all be burned?"

I pushed Alke's body down, not onto the bench near Matern but onto the ground, so she was entirely hidden from the friar. "Stay here," I said roughly. "It is your life if you don't. Stay silent." I pressed my hand onto Matern's head to comfort him, a gesture as powerless as I felt, and turned to go back to the front. Yet as I turned I ran right into the friar, who had followed me.

He slapped me.

"How twisted is the web of evil in this town," he said. "I had hoped to pull the spider, fat with blood, from the web and thus destroy all wickedness. But Künne Himmelmann's threads were spun so vast in this town that I wonder if we shall ever uncover all the sticky places she fastened to."

Every parcel of will I had went into arranging myself to look as truthful as possible. This speech was the most important one I would ever make—and monks illuminating their manuscripts in cells far away should pause in their labors to hear the ring of truth in what I said. The river should cease troubling the small rocks clattering on the riverbed, and the wind should stop worrying the pennants across Germany. "Künne Himmelmann was a wicked woman, as low as you are exalted. And she did pull us all into her web: myself, Irmeltrud, Herr Kueper." I spake slowly, as honey pulling from the comb. "But she never pulled children into her influence. Never. Alke here is as faultless as a babe. See her tremble on the floor. She is a *child.*"

"Does a child open her legs to men in the forest?" called Herr Kueper, clearly enjoying his revenge.

"Künne's evil was in threes, sir. A mockery of the Trinity. So it is my daughter-in-law, Herr Kueper, and myself. No others." I was amazed at the inventiveness of my thinking. Why, sometimes I was as dulled as the whetstone, but now I was the knife it sharpens.

"Then why does Herr Kueper accuse her?" he asked.

"Because he has the blackest heart that can be conceived of." This came in a hiss from Irmeltrud. She had pulled herself down from the tall chair and come to join us at the back of the hall. She thrust out an arm and pulled me to her. "Güde was my instructor in evil deeds, and I then pulled Herr Kueper into our unholy trinity. Güde was meant to represent our Father, I was the Son, and Herr Kueper . . ."

We hugged each other in an insane, desperate hug. She saw

how deep the trouble was now. She could not plead for herself. Only for Alke.

"Herr Kueper . . . ," she faltered. "He was the Dove."

I nodded and nodded, like a dog watching the flight of a bee. "Yes," I said. "Yes. Only us three."

Suddenly Frau Zweig was there too, serious-faced. "I kept the child sleeping at my feet to protect her all night. She was never gone from my sight. She is innocence itself. Never has she joined the witches in the forest."

"Why do you all leave your places?" thundered the friar. "You, Irmeltrud. I never released you from the chair of inquisition. Güde, you are to sit in the front. And Frau Zweig, you must face this congregation and make your accusations. All must return."

We scattered with quickened feet.

"I did not leave my place," called Herr Kueper. "That is because I know myself to be innocent. I am no part of some unbent trinity. I am only a man whose rod was hardened by the conniving of women."

Irmeltrud clambered back up onto the chair. I moved as quickly as my bones would allow. I heard the friar's thud behind us as he followed. I sat next to Frau Kueper, whose fingernails scraped down my arm, making me shiver with her intensity. She said not a word, though. She knew even a whisper to me would draw attention to herself. She was already on the front bench, dangerous enough, because she had tried to run with her husband. But she had not been accused.

"Frau Zweig, do you wish to add more to your testimony against Irmeltrud Müller?"

"No, sir. It is completed now."

"Go then."

She went back quickly and collapsed against Herr Zweig, who offered not a comforting arm to enfold her. His expression changed in no way. He was still shocked by his wife's cruel deception. He knew there had never been wine turned to piss. Alke was still hidden beneath the bench and Matern a barely recognizable mass on it.

"Are there any others to tell of Irmeltrud's witchcraft?" asked the friar.

"I should like to speak," said Herr Kueper. His wife scraped my arm again, harder.

"Stand, then."

He stood and I looked at my arm with its thin dots of blood following the red tracks scratched in my skin.

"She is a witch of such terror that I cannot fully describe it," said Herr Kueper. "It is . . ." His voice trailed off.

"Yes?"

"She . . ." His eyes moved downward and I saw that his was no sharp mind to invent as Frau Zweig's had. "She enticed me in the woods. She told me she would give her body to me. I agreed, but I had no thought that she was a witch. I thought we were only in the woods to keep eyes away."

"You had no thought she was a witch?"

"No! Only a comely wench."

"But you have just now said that she is a witch of such terror you cannot describe it."

"Well, I am just understanding that now. After the testimony," said Herr Kueper uncomfortably. He pressed his hands against his hips and they left clear dark stains. He was sweating like Hensel or Jost when the mill was working on a hot afternoon.

"Did you see her work magic?"

"Yes. I mean no. I only saw her open her legs to me."

"Do you call yourself a witch?"

"Oh, no. Only a man helpless to the beauty of women." He laughed and tried to get the friar to smile back. But the friar did not rut. Nor did our priest. The holy men of the faith did not do so. I watched the friar's gaze swing from Herr Kueper's face up to Irmeltrud's. The thought in his head was visible. *Beauty?* Irmeltrud had once been handsome, but she was now warped by work and famine and the raising of children.

"So your only accusation against this woman is that she treated you as a husband."

"Yes."

"Sit down. Do we have any other accusers?"

I surveyed the villagers. All faces were tight and drawn. There was no infectious mad mood now. Everyone saw how easily those who spake had the accusation turned against them. Perhaps, like Alke, they wished to burrow close to the ground.

"Here is the evidence against Irmeltrud Müller. She has entered the home of the Zweigs, spoken the Mass backward, and changed their wine into piss. She has also unwholesomely embraced a man not her husband, and in fact the husband of another," said the friar.

"Moreover, she has made free confession here today, that she formed a mockery of the Trinity and does call herself a witch. I find it in my wisdom that she, like her husband's *Mutter,* is most fittingly to be put to death. May God find the good in these women's souls and remove what is evil."

I heard the loud sniffling of both children behind me. *Make no further sound and you shall be safe,* I thought.

The friar's hands rose from his sides until he had assumed the position of the crucified Christ. Thus he remained for long moments while my heart pounded fast in my chest.

The inquisition was over for both of us. Now we had only the fire.

"What shall happen to me?" asked Herr Kueper. "Am I to be released?"

I inhaled sharply at his daring. The friar lowered his arms and then made the sign of the cross. "Since you will not confess, you shall be imprisoned in the Witch's Tower to contemplate your deeds. You shall have your own trial."

Herr Kueper nodded uneasily. I knew he would be offered the instruments of torture. He would smell the rank issue, sweat and urine and feces, of three women's stay in the tower. He too would bury his expulsions in shame and count the stones of the wall.

"Come you down and prepare yourself for purification," said the friar to Irmeltrud. She climbed down with the notary's help. They gestured for me to stand beside her.

I did so.

"The first to be prepared shall be Güde, *Mutter* of Jost," said the friar. "You shall be naked before God, as ever Eve did move her hands in shame to cover herself."

I jolted. Already the time had come? I bent down and lifted the hem of my skirt. I felt the bulb of the *Pillen* and quickly used my tooth to bite against the stitches I'd sewed. I knew I did this act openly, with all watching, but if my skirt was taken from me, I'd surely not be allowed to touch it again. The cord was tough against my teeth and I felt the tug of the thread across my tongue. I bit at the thread but it did not break.

"Güde, let down your skirts!" commanded the friar. "What manner of frightful mischief do you make?"

My fingers pulled at the fabric of the garment, to aid my bite. I gnawed like a rat on hardened bread. Would that I had its sharp rodent teeth! The ones I had left were worn down from years of black bread.

Soon enough the notary's hands were upon mine. I screamed as he tore the garment from my mouth.

"No, sir! No!" I screamed. "Only grant me one moment! One moment!"

"What is it she sought?" asked the friar.

The notary knelt before me and spread the stitches with his strong hands far enough that he could see inside the seam. "Two *Pillen.*"

I snatched at them, but he was far quicker. He slapped my hand smartly and I shrieked at the sting of it. He pulled the *Pillen* from the hem and backed away to show them to the friar. I ran and fell upon him, feeling that his body was still fleshy and firm, while everyone else in this village was nothing but bone. He clenched his fist to his chest, but I bit it until he dropped the *Pillen,* and then I swooped to the floor, quick as an owl, to grab one. I had it in my hand and my mouth was wide open to receive it. I clapped my hand to my mouth like a child astonished, but he was so fast, so fast with

God's work. He prised my hand away and scooped the *Pille* off my tongue even as my throat convulsed to swallow it. Like Künne, I was so terrified I had no spit within my mouth to move the *Pille.*

We fought too for the remaining *Pille.* I threw myself across the floor for it, but his foot arrived first and he stepped upon it.

Pure, blank terror seized my heart when I saw his fine leathern boot come down upon the last hope for my salvation.

My twisted fingers dug around his foot, trying to lift it, and I bit at his ankle. He was unmovable. I looked up, up at his face looking down at me, compassionless.

"Please, sir, please," I pleaded.

"This is a witch's concoction," said the friar. "Perhaps it lets her fly."

"No," I groaned.

"Perhaps she takes the *Pille* and flies out of our hands and away from God's punishment," the friar continued. "Hand them here."

The notary gave forth the one in his hand and then bent, eye level to me, to slightly lift his foot. I grabbed when he grabbed, desperate, but could not match his speed.

The friar now held both, musingly turning them over in his hands and sniffing them.

I lay there upon the ground, panting, undone.

I thought of the fire and how hot it had been, even for one who stood away from it. Those flames had slowly risen and taken Künne's body, burned every inch of her until she was black and only a pile of bones and ashes. I would feel that. I would feel that *this day.*

I began to pray to God, in a hoarse, frantic voice. "Dear Lord, deliver me from the pain of this punishment. Dear God, make the flames bright but not hot."

The friar laughed. "Our Savior made his very Son suffer," he said. "Why would he spare a woman who has mocked his sacraments and allied herself with his enemy?"

"I never did," I sobbed. "I didn't sign the book. I worshiped God and I do to this day. Why would I turn to him in prayer if I did not steadfastly believe?"

"Stand up," he said.

I could not, by my wits. The notary roughly pulled me up.

"Whatever you wanted of these *Pillen,*" said the friar, "they shall not do their work." He walked to the stove at the side, the one that had boiled pebbles for Künne's grasp. He briefly turned his head to look at me, then threw the *Pillen* into the fire.

Into the fire!

I sagged, and the notary pulled me upright again. I saw the green light the *Pillen* made as they flared into flame. He nodded and walked back to me.

I looked all around, in a trance of despair. The world was a blur I could not focus on. And then I blinked and the tears flew onto my cheeks forcefully. I could not release myself to my tears; I had to keep my eyes clear. If there was any path out of here, I would not see it through the film of sorrow. I blinked again and looked at the folk around me. There was Irmeltrud, and the look on her face moved me not. The various neighbors, their wives, the Zweigs. A small boy hid his eyes behind his fists. I listened and heard not a sound. No one breathed.

"We will recommence where we once started," said the friar. "Undo her garments and render her ugliness to God."

The notary pulled my skirt past my hips. Then he knelt and lifted each leg in turn to free it. I was like a child that can do nothing for itself. He took off my boots and my woolen stockings. He undid the laces of my bodice, pulled the kirtle off, and looked at disgust at my dugs, now visible under the thin fabric of my chemise. He tugged that off above my head, roughly.

"Stand on your own," he said and stepped away.

All eyes traveled down my body. The gray, gaunt skin. My bones so apparent I was like an ancestor in the grave. I looked too and resumed my weeping. Why was I not yet dead?

"I wish to preserve our congregation from an unholy sight," said the friar. "Since Künne freely confessed to her witchcraft, we did not shave her to look for the devil's mark upon her. And thus we saw a fearsome spectacle as her hair burst into flames. I do not wish to repeat this."

I didn't know why it mattered at all, a whit, but I wanted to keep my hair. "I had the devil's mark upon my brow," I said. "It has healed, but the notary recorded it."

"Shave her," said the friar. "Perhaps she has more *Pillen* secreted upon her person."

The notary removed my cap, then took a huge knife and pressed it to my temple. He cut a chunk of my hair and tossed it to the ground. Gray and wavy, it looked like a ruined cobweb. He cut again and again until my head felt like a stubble field in autumn. Then he turned the knife sideways and shaved the remainder. I felt the cuts he made, for he was clumsy and the knife dull, and knew that spots of blood must be seeping from my head.

He stepped back and looked at his results.

Between my thighs was thin gray thatch. He picked up the knife again. Half the congregation turned from the sight, but the friar hungrily watched as the notary sheared even this from me. He made me lift my arms and took that hair too.

I bleakly watched the blood run down my body.

"You are perfectly ready now to receive God's fiery embrace," said the friar. "And so too shall be your son's wife."

I shivered with the cold and with the knowledge of the wood that waited outside for me. Like Eve, my hands crept over myself to cover the most shameful parts. One hand cupped the bleeding remnants of my womanhood and the other arm stole across the sunken purses that had once funneled milk into Jost's mouth.

Irmeltrud brushed away the notary's hands, took off her cap, and undid her braids herself, silently releasing the twists until her hair was majestic upon her shoulders. Few had ever seen her like this: her children, Jost. Her fingers moved to her skirt but froze as she heard a faint shout outside the hall.

As of one accord, all of our heads lifted. It was as if a prayer had ceased, releasing us from its holy spell.

"—are you?" came the call. "All in the hall? Where are you?"

I screamed so strong my throat nearly burst. And all around me the women screamed too, at the limits of their ability, an obscene din like wolves howling at the moon. It was a terrifying sound, such as souls may make in eternal damnation, as

Satan prods them with his pitchfork. I screamed until no breath existed in me, and then I still managed to move my limbs, to join the crazed press to the back of the hall, to the oaken doors that everyone was traveling through with haste born of hope.

And onto the snow I trod with my bare feet, leaving a little bloody passage as I went, running, to the group of men bewildered at seeing the entire village race out to them.

The hunters had returned.

16

Very often men who are not witches are unwillingly transported bodily over great distances of land.

—MALLEUS MALEFICARUM

We ran to them wailing our joy. If there had been birds in our forlorn skies, they would have flitted off, sore afraid of the din below them.

And suddenly the running was stopped by men and women lunging against each other, as if only a candle and not the full sun watched their fierce embrace. The men were much changed, ruddy with their marching and—so fine to see!— bodies *plumpened.* The gaunt scratches famine had drawn down their cheeks were gone.

I marveled at Herr Schmidt, bending down to kiss his little *Kinder* with his belt again snug at his belly, and Herr Jaeger whirling his *Frau* around as if they danced, laughing as one can laugh only when one has eaten. But I lingered not and continued looking for the one face I prized over any other. I was bumped by Herr Abendroth as I passed him and he faltered and set down Frau Abendroth. His eyes were wide and his mouth wider. "What on earth has happened to you, Frau Müller? Why do you stand unclothed and with your head . . . ?" His voice ran down and he reached out a tremulous hand to touch my shorn head, but his wife slapped his hand away and pulled him from me, whispering quickly into his ear.

I was grateful for the sorrow in his eyes but kept stepping gingerly in the thick, crusted snow, my feet sinking fair much with each step. I needed to find Jost.

I was reminded with a wince of the witches' orgy in the woods, for it was couple upon couple now, man and woman kissing and groaning into each other's mouths. Children tugged upon their fathers' legs, and were also moved into the fevered clinch.

Upon the edges of the square, I saw a sled piled high with rabbit bodies, gray and soft, with the ears all pointing toward the church. Another held an elk. They had made the trouble to keep his antlers, these starved men, so we might use the horns for our fertility dances. And then I saw that there was another sled of rabbits—they must have found tenfold warrens!—and another sled fashioned into a cagelike device.

I shuddered when I saw this last one and made no further effort to determine the beast trapped inside. I turned my head and saw another line of sleds piled with carcasses. Each man must have pulled his own. What bounty!

I scanned all this in a glance, still with the foremost intent to find my son. Just then, little Alke tore past me. I watched where she ran, knowing she had spotted him. I pushed past another couple to see.

And there he was.

Jost of the gray-blue eyes and the kind face. There he stood in his rags, but with his face agleam. He was swiveling his head around to seek among the crowd for us, his family, and I watched his neck straighten as Irmeltrud ran to him, having found him first. He kissed her full on the mouth, eyes squeezed shut in savage concentration. His hips made the movement of rut against hers, although her skirts and his clothes were thick between them. Alke and Matern hugged the legs of their father, eyes buried.

It took all I had to keep me stonelike in the snow. Finally I pressed forward and laid my hand upon Jost's shoulder. He pulled back from Irmeltrud and the look in his eyes as he turned them upon me was enough to make me lose my breath.

His look was revulsion. He didn't recognize me.

"Jost," I sobbed. "It is me, your *Mutter.*"

I held out my arms for his embrace, shaking bitterly with the cold. "I saw you in the woods," I said. "I perched upon your fingers."

He ignored this and only stared at me. "Are you crazed?" he asked. "Why would you make yourself appear so?" He did not hug me, but instead took off his shirt and put it upon me, winding the extra cloth so it covered me twicefold, tucking it under my arm to hold it. Then he stretched his warm hand to my cheek gently.

I clamped my hands to his waist and tried to pull him to me. "I have spent these many days in the Witch's Tower," I said, "and today have stood trial for witchcraft, as has your wife."

He whipped his head around to her. She was keening, her voice out of her control.

"What falsehoods has this town suffered under?" he cried. "We have found the only one who is to blame!"

"Jost, I crave you," I said. "Do not put your own *Mutter* from you."

He then submitted to my embrace, and feeling how filled with trembling the wind made me, he gasped. "Let us get you by the fire, Mutter," he said. He saw for the first time that my feet were bare, and scooped me up like a child.

"Let us eat!" came the call. "Let us skin these rabbits and eat them on the instant!" The women moaned with relief and the men pulled their knives out, advancing upon the sleds.

Jost walked toward the church, but I stopped him with a cry. "No, Jost! I can bear that place no further! Take me home."

He kissed me on my blood-matted forehead and obliged. His strong arms easily carried me, as if I were no more than a rabbit hanging from his belt. As I was carried, I watched the rest of the village prepare for the feast.

The men sat outside on stones covered with blankets the women brought, and opened the rabbits. They sat in a circle and threw the offal into the center, tossing the skins and beasts behind them so that the women could walk the outside of the circle and pick the rabbits up for boiling. I heard the shout that the alehouse offered its fires and all its kettles for our use, just as at feast time.

And in the distance, far from the merrymaking, I saw the friar talking with our priest, gesturing such that the fabric rolling from his arms made him look like a bird spreading its wings for the sun to dry them. I shuddered in Jost's arms and whispered, "Hurry!" into his ear. The friar was insisting, perhaps, that the ceremony interrupted by the men's return be taken up again.

Irmeltrud and the children followed us, Matern pulling at his father's garments, for they dared not let Jost out of their sight, so hungry for him they were.

Jost brought me inside the cottage and put me down upon my straw tick. "Bring me some warm water," he commanded Irmeltrud, but our kettle was cold. The fire had gone out, for Alke and Matern had been with Frau Zweig. The children sat on my straw and watched their father with wide eyes, motionless. He took a corner of my bedding and dipped it in the cold water, then used it to wipe the blood off my skin.

"Why did they shave and strip her and not you?" he asked Irmeltrud, turning his head. She stood over by the dark hearth with her back to us.

"I was next," she said. "They were going to burn us, Jost, for witching. Our neighbors lied to the friar and told him we had soured the milk and pissed in the . . . Oh, God . . ." She broke down, unable to continue. She sank onto the hearth, putting her face into her hands.

I stared into Jost's eyes as he did his delicate work, muscles visible in his strong arms. The bedding was now pink and streaked with my blood. The unspoken thing was like another person in the room. He rhythmically washed my face as I considered the tongue in my mouth. What would be the advantage to saying it, and what the advantage to keeping silent? Surely, by the way they had welcomed each other, the stronger bond was between the two of them.

I couldn't say it: that Irmeltrud had accused me.

The bowl of water was now as red as if it had caught the throat-rush from a slaughtered goat. Jost rose to toss it out and refill it. Irmeltrud then took the chance to stand up and walk the few steps over to me. She leaned down and whispered, "What were the *Pillen*?"

I shook my head, feeling how strange it was to have no hair tangling beneath me on the pillow. If I told her the *Pillen* were to diminish all pain, she would know I had not meant to share. We each had a secret to keep.

After he had cleaned me, she put upon me the chemise and kirtle that I had last worn when plugged bellyful with Jost, and lent to me a second skirt she had. There was no other bodice, so I pulled the blanket around me and donned the cloak I'd not had time to put on when the friar took me. I handed Jost's shirt back to him, and he slipped inside it.

"Cover your head, Mutter," he said, his eyes pained at the pitiful sight.

I pulled the blanket up over my head.

"There'll be no more talk of you two as witches," said Jost. "We found something other than food in the forest."

"What do you mean?" asked Irmeltrud.

"You will see," he said. "And no villager shall blink to look upon you. They were fools to put you up for trial. It never would have happened if the lord had stayed here to keep order."

Jost's confidence was so firm that I took a deep breath, suddenly released from fear. Of course I had known all along that Jost's arrival would cure everything.

"Now," he said, "are you hungry?"

We wrapped my bare feet in rags and walked back to the village square.

———

The smell was overwhelming. Meat! Everyone was smiling and laughing; our family was the only one yet somber. We went into the alehouse, where everyone was seated at the plank tables, singing and jesting. I looked for the friar but did not see him.

No one paid me any heed, which I could scarcely believe. Jost lightly swatted one of the men who had gone with the hunters' party, and he moved over upon the bench so that we could sit. Alke and Matern sat opposite, their gazes trained on Jost with the utter trust God grants only to children. Soon enough, a huge trencher was placed in front of Jost by the alewife. "We're told you killed the most rabbits, so you eat first," she said. She winked as she added, "And trapped the one who caused all our woe. That'll be a fire to warm my hands at."

Her eyes shifted to the right, to focus on Irmeltrud and me.

"I see your look, alewife," threatened Jost, "and it shall stop now. The village has fallen prey to utter foolishness in the menfolk's absence and it shall stop. My wife and *Mutter* are no more witches than yonder rabbit on the trencher."

"Such mischief was abroad, sir," she said, "I feared for their lives, I did. There was no welcomer sound than the shout of the men returning." She curtseyed and returned with huge mugs of water for Irmeltrud and me, her way of apologizing.

"Remember the finer days when this would be filled with ale?" asked Irmeltrud.

"Aye, well I remember!" laughed the alewife. "And Güde surely remembers too!"

They both peered at me, waiting for my senseless reply and laugh. But I could not give it. I saw that Irmeltrud was determined to resume her life as it had been before, but I could not forget what dim hours I had spent in the tower, and that I had stood, shaking and blood-covered, before the eyes of all this village. The alewife had looked too. Whether with compassion or not, she had looked.

"Drink, Großmutter," she murmured to me.

Jost handed over a hunk of rabbit meat, greasy and pungent. I made the sign of the meat and saw it echoed all across the hall. Everyone *had* been paying heed to us.

I popped it into my mouth and nearly swooned. Tucked under its gray fur, which now lay with the others in a soft, loose pelt pile on the snow outside, the rabbit had kept a sturdy flesh, salty and gamy. *Thank you, rabbit, for your meat.* I chewed the piece and then gulped down the alewife's water. I leaned across Irmeltrud's body toward Jost, anxious for my next bit. He doled it out to all of us in turn: me, Irmeltrud, Matern, Alke. This was a different order than before.

"Vater, you should eat too!" said Matern, for he noticed his father skipped himself.

"We ate while we hunted, to keep our strength up," he said. "I can wait to eat."

When the rabbit meat was exhausted, the alewife brought another trencher. We ate that quickly too, and Jost finally had his first bites. Irmeltrud leaned her head against Jost and closed her eyes. "Is it a dream that you are back?" she asked.

"It is no dream."

"And all can return to as it was," she said.

I surveyed her with a wooden feeling. How could she forgive Frau Zweig for trying to steal her children by sentencing her to die? And how could I forgive her? How could I stand the memory of Jost hugging her to him more fastly than ever he had done me?

What would we say to the friar to satisfy him?

I looked all around me. He was not here. Nor were the Kuepers or the Zweigs. Rabbit bones formed a little pile in the midst of each table, sucked absolutely white and gristle-free. A table away, children still sat sucking the bones like they were *Mutters'* breasts.

"We are finally full," said the lord, climbing up on a table to stand above everyone. "For a long time, we wandered the woods without success. We were in despair, thinking of our wives and children so far away, wishing for our return with hands full of food. And on we pulled ourselves through that thick snow, so thick that we sank to our necks sometimes."

My hand went to my mouth. I smelled the rabbit grease still clinging to it.

"We continued on, for we had no choice. We would rather die in the snow than return with nothing to offer. And one day, Jost Müller came to me with an odd tale to tell."

I looked at him, surprised. Irmeltrud lifted her head off his shoulder.

"Would you like to tell it?" asked the lord.

Jost stood. He raised his voice so it could carry through the alehouse, deep and comforting. "I will tell my tale," he said. "I slept one night, hovering on the thin crust of snow with my blanket, aware of the deep, soft snow beneath, so deep

that if I were to sink into it as I lay prone, I should surely suf-
focate and drown in it as one would the river. I lay there, trying not to move and break the thin rime that kept me safe. I
looked above me and saw the moon beaming down. I prayed
that God would keep its light cold, to keep the snow crisp."

"I saw that moon with you," I mumbled. "You howled
for it."

Irmeltrud pinched my thigh and hissed at me.

"And as I lay there upon my back, the snow beside me
opened up and a woman's head came up out of it, staring at
me with wild eyes and black hair. Only her bare head and
shoulders appeared from the snow, as if her feet touched the
ground far, far below. Or hovered."

"It was a witch," I heard the whisper.

"A witch, a black-haired witch came out of the snow,"
came more whispers. "What a fright, the moon gleaming on
the snow and her hair dark against it, a witch, a witch."

"I bethought myself it was only a dream," said Jost. "For
instantly she was not there and the snow was not marred."

"It was a witch," continued the whispers. "No dream at all."

"In the morning, I told Ramwold of my dream and he cast
the runes to see if we were in danger from the spirits of the
woods," said Jost.

I could easily see it, for I had seen it so many times: Ramwold pulling the calfskin bag from his belt and scattering
onto the white cloth, barely visible against the snow, the
many sticks, each with a rune carved into it. I remember,
years ago, watching Ramwold cut the letters into the sticks,
the rough slashes of his knife. He was a young man, then,

making his own set since his father had died and the runes were to be buried with him. As he carved, tears had flowed down his cheek into his beard, but he ceased not his toil.

I pictured the men of the hunting party in a circle around Ramwold, dread-filled from the telling of Jost's dream. Ramwold said the prayer and then, with his eyes cast heavenward, crouched and picked up three of the sticks without looking at them. The vision reminded me of Künne's hand casting about in the water for three pebbles.

His hands would have gathered the twigs, as spindly-seeming as his very arm itself after age and the never-harvest had worked upon him. And then once he had them, he could lower his glance and look at the markings.

"Tell what they were," said Jost now, "for I have not the skill."

Across the room, Ramwold stood. As always, the bag of runes dangled from his belt, with the odd ends of the sticks poking the sides. He smiled.

"Two of the three sticks were merkstave," he said.

I nodded, though few others did; it seemed the rune lore was becoming lost to Jost and those of his age. When a rune was merkstave it meant that it lay in opposition to its meaning: either the marking upon it was facedown or upside down. It was usually a dark sign.

"The first rune was Isa, the ice," said Ramwold. "When naturally positioned, this is a sign of frozen motion, stillness— something each soul comes across in the course of life. But in this merkstave position, it means that there has been a plot, a cunning and guileful plot, to cause the slowness."

Not a whisper purged the air. We all knew what the slowness was: the fields unwilling to do their task. So who would plot this for us?

"The second was Jera, the year of good harvest."

Still no sound.

"In the merkstave position. Meaning a bad time, harsh change. Famine."

I looked at Jost. He watched Ramwold as carefully and respectfully as a child would a father. He had never had the chance to listen so to Hensel. Maybe the old rune reader had taken up such a position in Jost's life.

"The third stick, which lay straight and centered as the trunk of a tree itself, was Perthro, the woman's sign. A secretive and mystery-filled rune, this one is like a woman with her thoughts raging beneath her cap. And so said the runes," said Ramwold.

"And so do we listen," we all responded in unison.

"Ramwold spake to us of what he understood from the runes," continued Jost. "Our bad fortune was not a punishment from God but a trick from one with feminine qualities or a female."

"The one in the cage!" screamed someone, and there was hubbub suddenly. Benches were scraping back and mugs were smacking down upon the board, accompanied by scolds and angry words.

"Wait!" cried Jost. "Allow me to finish my tale."

I watched the company settle with a sick feeling in my stomach.

"No sooner did Ramwold collect up the runes and refasten the bag to his belt than a woman stepped out of the trees to speak with us. She was shaking with the cold and as hungry-looking as any of us. She had not exactly the face I had seen in my dream, but because her hair was dark, I knew it was she. She begged us for food, and I laughed heartily. 'It is your doing that we suffer so,' I told her. 'The runes have told us, and here you are upon the instant. If you ask us for food, it is a bitter contrary wish, for you did indeed cause the lack of it.' This she denied most strongly, but her hair was like a raven's wing upon the blankness of the snow around us. It had been marked by Satan's dark fingers as he clenched her locks in passion."

I knew it had to be she, the one who had pressed my soul into an owl's body, who had brought me to the place where the devil presented his book to me.

"We made for her a cage and put it upon a sled. She ranted at us and stretched her arms through the gaps such that we feared even to come near. Ramwold made a charm and put it upon the snow at the east side of the cage to weaken her power. For one entire night we listened to her fume and shriek. The dream did not return to me, although all night I thought of her slipping through the wooden bars, sinking into the snow, and silently tunneling her way to my side. The next day, as we moved ourselves and the sled farther on our journey, we saw our first elk. It fell to our spearing and we ate of it and found then more elk, its brethren, and many rabbits and squirrels and other beasts. And we filled our sleds with the goodness, always taking care to keep the charm on the snow before her, and prepared to return home."

I could only think: had they given this poor woman of the elk or rabbit or squirrel meat?

"We have brought her back with us for justice to be meted

out," said Jost. The clamor began again but he raised his voice and again gained the village's attention. "I have heard dire news of my wife and my *Mutter* being accused of witchcraft during my absence. I am ashamed for the thought of it, and to see my *Mutter* in such a state. But I do understand that you did not know what we men in the woods knew, that there was one source for all this mischief. And now that we have delivered her up for punishment, I want no more talk of Güde or Irmeltrud."

There was a roar of approval, and then the hall did empty out, for all to run to the sled and taunt the one who huddled there. For that had been what I saw from the side of my gaze and tried to discard: a woman kept like a beast in a cage.

Outside, the crowd circled the little cage. I could not see above all the shoulders nor through the bodies, so I followed the young boys' example and climbed up onto one of the meat sleds now emptied of its rabbits. The wood grated against my shins through my thin, borrowed garments, and my arms were barely strong enough to hoist me up, but young Fritz Plattler helped pull me up. I could now see that the villagers stood an arm's distance away from the cage. The charm still lay on the snow on the eastern side, butting up against Frau Winkel's shoe. Inside the cage, Fronika sat curled in the corner with her dark hair tangling from her cap to mass around her thin, frightened face. "May I have some food?" she called out in a hoarse voice. "I smell the rabbits you boiled and I am starved, for I have not eaten for many days!"

"We have been starved far longer, for your doings with the devil!" cried someone.

"No! No!" said Fronika, but her voice was so hoarse that it carried no conviction. It was as if she refused a glass of ale in better times, rather than refused that she had brought famine down upon a village. "Why do you blame me? I have had naught to do with the devil."

"I remember her from Whitsuntide and other fests," said one of the older women. "Yes, Michaelmas too! She would come for the food, for she and her sister were sore beset to fend for themselves. And look at her now, ruining all of us. For shame! We fed you!"

Fronika bent her head and began to cry at the mention of her sister. This surely was not the same woman who'd visited me with fury in her very skin! She was weeping for her sister, rather than avenging her death. My vision went hazy. Fronika blurred in her cage as did the jeering villagers. Were this woman's words true? Fronika had come for our fests because she was starving, even while we then lived in plenty? I tried to call back a memory of her, skulking around the madly dancing couples, her drawn face, her hands holding bread and sausage against her skirts as if to hide them from view. . . .

And I had understood this? That she was then hungry?

So . . . perhaps . . . I had thought of her when I myself became hungry?

This wasn't the Fronika of the nighttime rides. She had no ardor to her. She had the soul of a dog limping from a years-old kick.

"Well you may cry, Frau! For we have found you out and you will serve your punishment!" cried someone.

She made no reaction. The Fronika of my nighttime visits would have raised her eyes, gleaming with intensity and hatred, to spew a reply. And she would have wrenched at the bars until they split. Or gnawed at them.

This was a woman who had no courage to her.

Someone pulled at my skirts. It was Irmeltrud. She wanted me to reach out a hand to pull her up onto the sled, but I had no strength. Fritz Plattler pulled her up and she gave both of us a careful smile. Then she turned to the woman in the cage below her and called out stridently, "Mistress of the woods! Do you see me and my husband's *Mutter* standing here next to me?"

She lifted her head, showing her red, tearstained face. I watched her eyes very closely. There was not a whisker of recognition. She nodded tremulously.

"In yonder yard there are two stacks of wood. One to burn me and one for Güde," said Irmeltrud. "I was about to die for your malefaction. A pure, innocent soul tortured by flames because of you. You!"

"I don't know you, Frau. I have done no mischief!"

Irmeltrud laughed, a ripe, rippling sound that seemed to go on long after she stopped. "Done no mischief? We are nothing but bones and the hope of skin here, Frau! And the village came to blame my husband's *Mutter* and then me for all the trouble: milk souring and chickens removed of their eggs. We were about to *burn* for your deeds, do you understand?"

A flicker of fear crossed her vacant, sad face. She used her long hair to dry her tears. And then she pitched herself forward until she was on her hands and knees. The villagers shouted and backed up. The cage was not tall enough for her to stand up in, so she crawled its length until she was as close to Irmeltrud and me as possible. "I'm sorry you were blamed if there was something you did not do," said the woman nearly in a whisper. "But perhaps then you can understand that I am too in that position: blamed for something I did not do. This village has been kind to me. I have eaten here in the past on feast days and no one ever asked why I brought nothing to the table I supped at. My sister and I had to manage for ourselves in the woods, eating what we found only. Always we were hungry. She was shy unto fear of death of others. I was the only one she trusted. I came here and filled my pockets for my sister. I was *grateful* to your village. Grateful! *Grateful!* Never would I raise my finger to do ill to any of you."

"I am the one possessed," I mumbled to myself. "For this woman never transported me upon her hair, never did she."

"A fine speech," said Irmeltrud. "But I have heard tell that even demons get soft voices and hide their horns."

"*Ja!* Don't be tricked!" yelled Ramwold. He and Jost were at the other end of the circle, and Fronika turned her head to look at them. If Jost had indeed killed her sister in rabbit form, would not she then quake to see him and cast her ire his way? But she slowly turned her head back to us for the remainder of Ramwold's speech. "She traveled as far as our hunters' party did! How did a mere woman come so far in the snow if not assisted by devils? The runes told us of her deceit."

"I don't care what you do to me," she said dully, "so long as you give me some food."

It was then that I saw the flash of black and white at the edge of the crowd, and fast I pulled myself down off the sled. My heart began a hasty race in my bosom, like a rat bolting across the floor. Irmeltrud remained up there; her face was calm and level.

"What be the meaning of this?" called the friar.

"Come and see for yourself," said someone, and I heard the steps in the snow as people moved to make room for him.

"Who are you?" I heard him ask. The intimate privacy of his voice made me shudder. Someone in front of me stepped to the side to pick up her child, and thus I had a full view of him while mostly hidden myself.

"I am Fronika of Steindorf," she said.

"And why are you pressed into such device like a blackbird?"

"They blame me for this village's troubles. And I am nothing but hungry!"

"Feed her!" he commanded.

"No!" said Frau Schmidt. "Why give her the precious food she denied us?"

"*Feed* her!" rumbled the friar. "Even our tower's prisoners were fed."

I, who knew the friar, understood that the kindness was not true. He was like a hunter who releases an animal from a trap, only to kneel in the snow and cleave its throat. It was my own grandson, Matern, who raced into the alehouse to fetch meat for Fronika.

"Thanks be to you," she said, stretching out a thin arm to him. She ate like a dog, moaning in the back of her throat as she gulped chunks down entire. Little pieces hit the sled floor and she grabbed these up quickly, as if one of us would sneak into her cage and take them first.

"Enjoy it, witch; it is surely better than child's flesh," taunted one of the villagers.

"At least you face your death with a full stomach," sneered another.

Someone reached out and shook her cage, hard enough that she fell over onto her side. She did not sit up, but remained eating as she reclined. If she was a witch, she would have supped in the forest as I did. But she was famished beyond all reckoning.

Finally, there was nothing more for her to eat. And Matern, who had made a second trip into the alehouse, presented her with a mug of water. "Sit up," he whispered.

Fearless child somehow. Perhaps his father's return had bolstered him.

"Tell me now why you are thus trapped," said the friar.

"I was in the woods following the men's footprints, thinking they might have food to offer me. And when I came upon them, they seized me, saying I was of a dream. But I was only hungry, seeking a meal. I was never in anyone's dream! And then they put me into the cage, saying I was the cause of all this village's hunger."

"And how was this determined?" asked the friar. "And, more importantly, by whom?"

"We called upon Ramwold's wisdom," said Lord Obermann, coming to stand next to him. "He read the runes, which told us that this woman had been our source of misery."

The friar's jaw tightened, and I winced. I stepped to the side so as to be better hidden. Only one of my eyes peered past the shoulder of the *Frau* before me.

"He *read the runes?*" the friar intoned.

The lord looked amazed at his anger. "Indeed," he replied.

"The Church has soundly denounced such pagan and foolish means. Every time you throw down the heretical collection of sticks, our Savior suffers. You must cease this profanation instantly. You, sir, must pay special heed to make your confessions to God," he said, pointing to Ramwold.

"We respect the church and its holy lessons," said the lord. "But the runes have also spoken and we have listened. What further evidence do we need that this woman bewitched our harvest and sent all the animals far from here?"

"Interrogations are best left to the church. We have the most recent information; we have the *Malleus Maleficarum* to guide us in questioning women and learning of their deceit," said the friar.

"But we are certain of our findings," persisted Lord Obermann. "No sooner did we capture her than all manner of beasts presented themselves to our spears. We ate that night for the first time! And here we have brought back a feast's worth, while she stays harmless behind the charm."

"The charm?" asked the friar.

Lord Obermann pointed to Ramwold's charm lying in the snow before the sled. The friar picked it up and cast it far beyond the crowd. It landed near Künne's burying place.

A hiss rose from our village. I sank down, hearing the sound arise from the woman I cowered behind. Her child too offered what sound it could.

"Stop that!" yelled the friar.

But the hiss continued.

"Fetch it!" commanded Lord Obermann, and it was again Matern who jumped to do the bidding, racing through the crowd to retrieve the charm. Ramwold began a chant to counter Fronika's malefaction, to counter her until the charm could put in place again.

"By God, stop that unholy sound!" yelled the friar.

Matern stooped at the friar's robes and put the charm back into the snow. Then, praise God, he quickly buried himself into the larger, taller bodies of the crowd. I didn't want the friar's eyes on him, ever.

As soon as the charm was in place, the hiss ceased.

"I see you are all caught up in these pagan fears," said the friar. "Let me interrogate the woman, as Rome calls for us to do, in a proper way. And then we may know for sure what danger she poses to the village and select the punishment that destroys her powers."

"Burn her now!" screamed someone.

"Before our food spoils!"

"She may reanimate the beasts and they will run back into the forest!"

"Burn her! We have the wood ready!" And then the cry that made me put my fist to my mouth to bite: "This fool of a Dominican doesn't understand that this woman cursed us!"

But the danger of the insult was quickly dispelled by numbers, for many more added their words. "Didn't Rome tell you how to recognize a witch?" and "The runes let us eat! We would still be starving with your stupid book!"

"You ridiculous idiots!" shouted the friar. "The runes are no better than asking the snow! You are heretical fools to pay heed to sticks with symbols on them. Christ's very jaw drops in horror for this village. Only a proper, Christ-ordained interrogation can demonstrate this woman's guilt."

"The runes told us to gather the hunters' party! If we had not been in the woods, we would not have met our foe! The runes helped us twofold," argued Lord Obermann.

"You dare to argue with a representative of His Holiness

the Pope?" asked the friar. His face was red with rage. I did not know how the lord continued to stand there fearless. As they stood there with their backs turned to the cage, Herr Baum opened it. Fronika screamed as he pulled her out, but the sound was quickly swallowed by the village's roar. The friar and Lord Obermann heeded the hue and cry not, still passionately arguing, their arms flailing and smoke gusting from their lips in the cold of the day.

They pulled Fronika so fast that her feet didn't touch the ground. I thought of the first time I'd seen her, how she'd hovered with her feet near my head, above me. But this was the kind of hovering a human woman might do as her man hustled her too quickly.

The villagers continued to roar and suddenly my hiding space was gone as the woman in front of me surged with the crowd to move toward the burning place. I was forced then to move with her, to keep myself away from the friar's sight. Quickly, running, we moved to the two stakes that had been erected in the ground with the carefully piled faggots around them.

They had been meant for me and Irmeltrud, but if I could remain invisible, I might not serve my time with the flames.

"Pray your last backward prayer," taunted Herr Baum.

"No, God, no," Fronika was screaming. "I believe in the Father and the Son and the Holy Ghost! I am no witch! No, God, please!"

The village entire was united in extreme fury. They were like wolves upon a rabbit. This was the sort of crazed anger I'd feared I would face. I couldn't believe the noise; it was a calamity of shouts. As Fronika was staggering, forced by men's longer legs across the snow, I stayed with the woman ahead of me and over her shoulder I saw the face of her tiny babe, staring at me, screaming with all abandon. I put my hands over my ears but then took them away. I needed my hands to keep my skirts above my feet so I didn't trip on them. If I fell, I'd surely be stepped upon like a stone in the mud.

Now there were five men surrounding Fronika, shaking their fingers in her face and screaming at her such that she shrank down into a crouch. They tried to push her up onto the pile of wood. The baker produced rope by undoing the cord of his britches. "Let me have her before we burn her!" he yelled. She twisted her body sideways away from him. He grabbed her waist and began to gather up her skirts.

"No!" cried one of the other men. "Don't foul yourself! A witch can murder by her contaminated fluids!"

All the same, they had to push him back. Finally he gave up. His wife, Frau Bäcker, was on her knees in the snow, gagging. He did not even notice.

They succeeded in pushing Fronika up to the stake, and they used the baker's rope to tie her to it. She screamed for her very life and I wished that I might stop all of this, all this madness, and restore order to the village, put kindness back in everyone's face, but this was an impossible thought. I could only take care for myself now, huddling behind the woman afore me and making sure I caught no eye.

For it did not escape my notice that there were two stakes up there.

And Fronika took only one.

17

We have often learned from the confessions of those who
we have caused to be burned, that they have not
been willing agents of witchcraft.

— MALLEUS MALEFICARUM

To cover all of her hair, they put a rabbit pelt over her cap and pushed the stray locks under it. I touched my own stubbled head. How was it that in the matter of hours we had switched fates?

"Any last words?" asked Herr Baum as he stood next to her with a torch. He was not the only one. In the late afternoon dimness, a dozen or more held fire, eager to touch it to her skirts.

Already coming loose, her dark hair mingled with the gray of the rabbit's, an odd sight. Strangely beautiful. Her lips were full red and lush in the white zone of her face. Had she only not been so thin and strange, living in the woods, she might have been the beauty of any village. The one who the men wished to partner with, her small hand gripped as the dancers honored the grain mill, her skirts flouncing with the kick and twirl. She might have been the one they all winked about as they threaded the ribbons of the maypole, her virginity they craved.

How different her lot would have been if she and her sister had not had to fend for themselves in the woods.

"I will say one thing," said Fronika.

Herr Baum waved the torch impatiently.

"I brought nothing ill upon your village," she said simply.

A unified shout from the crowd greeted her words. "Wicked liar!" they were all saying. "Bitch with a twisted mouth!"

"And do you pray to God?" asked Herr Baum quickly. A cinder from his torch drifted down onto his arm and he smacked at it with a swear.

"I pray to God for my salvation, in this realm or the heavenly one," she answered.

Herr Baum nodded and without an instant of hesitation put his torch to her skirts. They didn't catch instantly, as she was wet and cold from snow seeping into her cage, but in a moment a dry fiber caught and the skirts began to smoke.

The other torchbearers either climbed the pile of wood or leaned up onto their toes to touch fire to Fronika's new trap. She screamed at each blaze, even though she couldn't yet feel them. I felt the people on my right press into me, smashing me. They were making room for someone who was entering the crowd.

"Stop!" cried the friar. "You are not observing proper Roman protocol!"

Herr Baum, still standing next to the shrieking Fronika, whirled his torch toward the friar. "Fuck your Roman protocol!" he snarled. "We are Germans!"

The friar drew himself up and even from behind I could tell he wore the face he had when he showed me the pear. A face with all the compassion of an ice-blasted field. "Shall I make the report to Rome that this entire village relies on the reading of runes? Shall I say you reject Christ's teachings and embrace heretical pagan beliefs?" he asked. "Do you understand that the holy army would quickly descend upon this village?"

"You create trouble that doesn't exist!" cried Herr Abendroth, the kind man who had stopped hugging his wife to ask why I was naked and shorn. "You come here and get the young women pointing fingers at the old ones!"

I heard my name spoken throughout the crowd. Güde . . . Jost's mother . . . she was no *Hexe*. . . . I lowered my head, frightened. Nor Künne . . . nor Irmeltrud . . . none of them were *Hexen*. . . .

The woman before me turned her head and nodded. I heard only a snatch of her words, "Good Güde, who—" The baby peeped out at me, his face solemn.

"Do you dare to—" the friar began, but he got no further.

"Set those robes afire!" screamed Herr Kueper. It was the first time I'd seen him since the hunters had returned. He grinned in the flickering light of Fronika's fire like a demon himself.

They seized the friar. He was fast, running and darting between them, but it was the length of his robes that undid him. It was child's play for them to grasp the voluminous folds and bring him to an abrupt stop. Soon enough, they hoisted him up onto the second pile of logs, flailing and threatening them with the Pope's vengeance, but they laughed at this crudely. Fronika was now burning in earnest, writhing as the hairs on her arms caught fire. She twisted on her pole with the agony of every inch of her in torment, and she screamed, a wail no human voice should utter. Her eyes were open wide and her mouth a black void such that I saw the pinkness of her throat beyond. She blinked in terror, her face moving through a dozen expressions within a mortal moment, screaming and crazed with anguish as her body transformed to smoke.

Next to her, the men worked to tie up the friar, tearing a sashlike strand from his robe to make a rope. The smell clogged my throat again, the smell of human flesh rendering to oil and then to ash. I couldn't stand it.

"God will favor you, Fronika!" I screamed to her, but she was not possessed of reason anymore. She was a flame, a scrap of something fluttering in the wind, bright and flickering and somehow, although no longer human, creating the most damnable shriek one could ever hear. Irmeltrud was suddenly at my side. She had Alke and Matern's hands in each of hers. I could tell by the sharp profile of her knuckles that she was clenching the children's hands so hard it hurt them.

"I was so frightened about the second pyre," she said. "I thought myself to steal up to it with a torch and set it aflame just so it couldn't be used but now *he* shall burn there!"

She fell to her knees, and because they were connected, the children went to theirs too. "Oh, thank God Jost returned!" she keened. "My God! Güde, it would have been us!"

I was struck dumb as Lot's wife. I looked past Irmeltrud to Fronika's fire. For it was fire now, not woman. A blaze that took the rough shape of a woman, but could be anything tall and narrow. A pine tree, a maypole . . . she was only a pillar of fire.

And the men were now taunting the friar, flashing the torches past his face. The robes were bunched and folded to tie him to the stake. His eyes followed the path of the torches, intent and terrified. I thought of the cats of yore, mousing in the mill, how they'd track the movement of a fly or bee, moving not their heads but their eyes only.

Oh, the cat. The cat I'd thought was Fronika. No. Surely not. A demon had possessed me and now I saw clearly. Fronika was a woman. The rabbit Jost had killed was no sister, but a beast of the wood only. I had seen no dancing. I had no man rut with me under the moon. There was no book, nor had I signed it.

I had a mind that was crazed.

I coughed and spat onto the snow. Was I breathing in Fronika? Was her will and her spirit infusing through my breath?

Everyone moaned and coughed for the odor. There was no more screaming. Fronika was gone.

"I can't see," said Irmeltrud, coming to her feet again. "The smoke is so thick. But I want to be sure he burns. Come, children."

She pressed on through the yellowish smoke so that she could witness the friar's end. I had no such desire. No matter what, I would never be safe.

The first scream was so high in pitch I would have thought it a woman's. And he screamed as Fronika did, over and over.

I turned my back on the spectacle, seeing the smoke furling behind me as I walked. I would not sleep. No, never again.

My mind took me evil places when I slept.

I would remain awake eternally.

I saw Jost on the edge of the crowd. He was crying. "Mutter!" he said, and came to me. He embraced me and his wet cheek gave the tears over unto me. "How has all this vileness come to us?" he asked. "How, Mutter, how?"

I held him while he sobbed out his love of the field and the mill and working to grind the grain, and the men singing the end of day with a mug of beer coming to the lips, and the red-cheeked wives and the board full of food. How he wanted only the smallness of neighbors squabbling over tiny injustices, and the priest and Ramwold leading together. How the village would thank the runes and thank the birds and the deer and elk and skies, how we would be thankful ever after and bless every aspect of the world that offered itself to us. How we would live long lives and die on our straw tick, easily. Cozily. We would hold hands and dance with each other, carrying each other's weight and flying as much as our heavy feet would let us.

Flying as much as our heavy feet would let us.

Flying.

Oh, God, to fly.

I kissed my son goodly on each check and put him from me. I was too distressed in mind to bear his distress as well. I walked away from the square but I did not send my steps home. I knew home had gone up in smoke like Künne, like Fronika.

18

IN THE YEAR 1509

"What will happen if there is no food again?"

I could see that she hadn't wanted to ask it, but her mouth had issued it anyway, the way the well bucket sometimes yields a toad. She looked down at the board full of thick elk slices, the circlet of cheese, and the mug of hot, thin milk. At my right hand was a loaf I hadn't cut into yet, with a dough braid on top that I had crafted while smiling about her hair, now bright and thick again.

Alke was a wise girl. She was unseduced by the fields plumed with grain, the cows sturdy enough to beget calves. Behind her daily smiles and her light voice singing as she did her chores, she still remembered sitting with her family to eat of snow.

I wanted to laugh and say, *Alke! For shame! There shall always be food.* But I couldn't say that. She had many years of life ahead of her, and who knew when I was long in my grave what the fields would say to the town? Who knew what tremendous wind might shake through the forest and send the animals scattering far away?

[244]

I stood up and went to her side of the table, lowered my old limbs down, and gathered her into a hug. We clung to each other, both remembering.

"I dream about the fire all the time," she said, beginning to cry. "Mutter made us build that fire!"

"You were only a babe."

"I was not!" she stormed, her head pressed against my paps. "I heard that man tell Mutter, and I understood everything. But all I cared about was the food he promised."

It had been two harvest seasons since then, and this was the first Alke had talked of it. I had hoped that, emerging from childhood, she had released these memories.

She pulled away and looked straight into my eyes. "And Künne was your friend," she said in a low voice.

"We are none of us blameful for things we did from the asking of our parents," I said. I waved an arm in the air to show her how, like smoke, her fears should waft. She winced and I know we both thought of Künne's arm, sore and bubbled. "You were a *child,* Alke. You knew as much of the world as what was contained in the eye of my needle."

"No, I *knew,*" she said.

"You didn't know," I said simply. "Because if you were old enough to know that you would feel this way now, you would have run away into the snow."

We sat quietly, taking no heed of the food, honoring the thought of Künne and Fronika.

"I spake for her," said Alke finally. "I stood up in the church and begged for her life. But not yours. And not Künne's."

"You were a child," I said again. "What child doesn't value its *Mutter* most?"

"Mutter will go to hell when she dies," said Alke. "She traded fire in this life for endless fire after."

I did not answer. I didn't know what I thought of heaven above us or hell deep below, the fires supposed to be constantly stoked and tended. I was afraid to tell her what I feared: that both places were kingdoms of air. I had been to the churchyard to sit above Hensel's bones and to the spot where Künne's blackened remnants lay, and when I listened to the earth, it told me they were still down there. And for all the praying I've done in my life, I fear that prayers are bits of grain the birds drop to the winds.

But if Alke needed to hear that Irmeltrud would twist forever in the great maw of the devil, smelling the burning flesh of thousands and knowing that stench was her own as well, then I would let her keep that small, bitter gift.

"If there comes a day when the food is scarce again," I said, "you must equally divide what you have."

She nodded strongly.

"It is wrong to say that one should eat more than another," I continued. "Or that one deserves nothing. Give it out with the hope that more will come."

"I know," she whispered. "That is what we should have done."

"Yes," I whispered back.

A knock came at the door and jolted us out of our quietude. And Libeste came in without waiting for a response, as she always did, instantly making the *Hütte* small with her huge, red cheeks and eyes as large as plates. I smiled to see her; no one could come near the spirit of this girl and not smile.

"Alke and Güde!" she cried, as if we were a field away and she had to call for our attention. "Come, come! The sheep is giving birth!"

Libeste and her family had come soon after the events that Alke and I were talking of; they had moved into the Kuepers' abandoned *Hütte.* They were from the monastery city, like the friar, and had never been famished. They came into our village like wildly singing birds, arousing us out of our stupor and making a clear path for us to ease our way out of pain. In my mind, I thanked them daily for coming. They had saved all of us.

They had brought with them five fluffy sheep, all well fed, that they set up on the hillside where Irmeltrud's family's flock once roamed. When the grass came in that spring and I saw the bounce of the sheep's progress from hillside to hillside, I sank to my knees in the sweet-smelling grass and cried. Is there ever a vision as hopeful as those life-crazed, oiled, and softened beasts? With their black noses and feet and the sturdiness of their hay-bale bodies, they told me to move my mind, keep searching for sights that could bring me joy.

And now the dame of the group was giving birth.

"Ah, but you didn't eat yet," Libeste said, looking at our untouched board. "Hurry, then, hsst!"

And because I knew that food was a gift, and one that could be taken away, I plunged my hands into the loaf and pulled out a still-warm chunk for Libeste. Her broad face became broader with her delighted grin. "No one makes bread as well as you do, Güde," she said, as her strong white teeth bit into it.

They ran ahead, hair flying from under their caps like May Day streamers, and I plodded more slowly. To see sheep birthing! How different the world was.

I stepped past the place where the blood of Künne's goat had spilled, now covered by edelweiss I had asked Alke to bring back from the meadows, for we now lived in Künne's cottage, the two of us.

While Fronika, poor Fronika, was tied to her pole and burning for being a woman no one understood, and the friar was giving his life in exchange for the dozens he had doubtless taken, I had walked straight to Künne's *Hütte*. I had set to work gathering the bristles in the corner, torn from her broom. Once I had them together, fat in my fist, I tied twine around them. Then I held the bundle out at arms' length and looked at it. *Did they really think a woman could use this to fly through the air?* I remembered wondering. *Was that why it had been ripped apart? Or did the men think she had hidden jewels in the tight weave?*

To me, it was nothing more than the fields brought inside to do a woman's bidding. I set the tip down onto the ground and began to sweep. The familiar sound had comforted me. *Swish swish. Swish swish.* I swept all of Künne's tumbled belongings into the center of the room. There was little I could save. I pulled out her gowns and took them outdoors to flap the dust and dirt from them. I found her salt cellar, miraculously unbroken, lying on its side. This I gave a kiss and put onto the sill. I heaved with all my strength and righted the table.

But everything else, save a few branches of herbs I didn't recognize, was broken and useless and for the fire. I made several journeys to the hearth with my arms full, putting Künne's belongings where previously only wood went. And then I began the fire, to clean the *Hütte* and make it mine.

Künne's cottage was far enough that I could not hear the friar's mortal screams. Our two fires both burned without knowledge of the other.

The night of the burning, no one came to me. As I curled up on the ground as I had in the Witch's Tower and slept with my ear pressed to the earth, I wondered what they all thought. Were they in the woods looking for me? Surely the smoke from my chimney had alerted them.

In the morning, Jost brought my straw bed, and his little girl. "Alke wants to live with you," he said.

And I opened my arms and gathered her thinness to me. "Yes," I whispered fiercely.

We have never spoken of this, but I can only imagine Irmeltrud's face when, after all of it, she lost Alke anyway. Five times has Irmeltrud come and stood at our door, three times in snow and twice in mud, to beg us to let her in.

But I have looked on that face enough in this lifetime. I remember, if she does not, how she sealed the door against me and ignored my hands beating against it. A door is only a plank of wood, but I am grateful for its ability to preserve me from that which would punish my eyes. When we do see her, we give no sign.

Herr and Frau Zweig have still not had a child.

I have never seen the cat again, but Jost tells me he finds

half-eaten mice in the mill, and I am hopeful that the beast will someday find me again, mewing at my new window.

A marker was erected for the friar's grave, and a band of men came long ago, clad in black and white like him, to sprinkle holy water upon it. They were told the friar and his notary had died of fever, and they believed the lie. The notary has never been seen again. When the friar was seized for the pyre, some saw the man run to the woods. Herr Baum pursued him and the tales say he returned with a blood-covered knife. This is all reported through hushed words and significant silences.

Fronika has a grave that is a stretch of land like any other. If the villagers do not keep telling each other where she lies, the place will be forgotten.

In remorse, a tiny cross was put upon Künne's grave, as best as anyone could see where it was. *By the tree,* I reminded Jost. *Remember how the man threw the shovel?* I am hopeful that the cross marks the right place.

There is a holy trinity of places I will not go: the church, where last I feared for my life and Alke's, my old *Hütte,* and of course the woods.

Until the earth gave it freely, Jost brought us food. Last season the grain came, and this year all seems well again too. The seeds are deep in the dirt and sending upward their green shoots, he said. The runes were such that the entire village had pressed their lips to the magicked three that foretold the good harvest. In a line they stood reverently, Jost told me, to pass the sticks among them and kiss the goodness there.

He also brought us wood when winter yet stretched its

painful fingers through the walls of the cottage, and brought water every day or two. Even in winter he did this, when we had naught to do but open the door and gather the snow. My son is a solitary pure lily in the bramble, and I love him for it.

One time I asked if he had seen an owl in the woods and spread his arm for its talons to rest upon. "I was feverish with hunger," he said. "I saw strange things I question now. Did I truly see a woman's head emerge from the snow?"

I have opened my reedy throat and sung the song until it lost its meaning, until the evergreen trees staved into the ground so I do not fly.

Matern is more like a man after all this. When he sits in our cottage to visit, I see no sign of the child who raced around my skirts to keep a toy from his sister. Jost is teaching him the trade, now that there is something to mill.

Sometimes my mind clouds and I think that Alke is Künne. When she sighs and tells me her true name, her blue eyes troubled, I kiss her hand and think, with a stab of delight, *Maybe that was a visit from Künne, and not a falsehood of my mind.*

I dream of Fronika sometimes. She crouches in the cage upon the sled and everyone spits upon her, as they spat upon me in the church. She is calm, though. Her eyes are patient and sad. In my dream, I whisper, "This will soothe," and I spit the *Pille* right into her mouth. Our lips touch as if we kiss.

I wake up crying. How can anything soothe anyone ever again? I walk the floor of this cottage as if I were the small dead creatures in the ground beneath, the dried spiders whose legs curl into balls, the rodents whose sharp teeth sink into their own diminishing lips, the worms that roll witlessly with the earth's breath.

But then in the dim firelight, I look at Alke's face in sleep, untroubled, sometimes even with a slight smile. And then I see quite clearly what soothes. This child. This growing woman who will wear white for May Day and race Libeste across the meadows, as Künne and I did. This being whose life I value more than my own, for she is here today because of me.

I saved Alke, *I saved her!* As I stood in the inquisition that day, with Herr Kueper's black mark already upon Alke's head, it was my own mind, which had failed me so many times, and still fails me yet, that did its utmost deed of my lifetime.

My mind, mine! That grayish place was bright as a knife blade that day, and I was able to come up with the one explanation that would suit the friar. The trinity, I had said. There were only three witches. And as Alke was a fourth, she was freed. Even if the hunters had not returned, she would have lived.

I shall never be able to say how that came to me, but I am grateful for that more than any other single thing in my life. When I see Alke giggle with Libeste and her throat work as she downs her frothy milk, when she comes so sweetly to me each night to deliver a solemn kiss in worry that either of us should not wake in the morning, I am flooded with joy of the most dazzling kind. I feel like Mary in the moment of annunciation, when a dove crafted of fire nestled its beak in the crook of her neck and spake.

That girl who huddled under a bench is now strong-backed and fast on her feet. She is more beautiful than her parents ever would have supposed. She is a shimmering, wholesome sign that there is good in the world. I look upon Alke and my heart, finally, released from the wracked pieces of crockwork that held it, beating moistly, *flies*. Over the evergreens like my spirit never did, like Fronika never did, in tandem with owls and swallows and hawks . . . my heart *flies*.

19

It took yet another season for more good to come.

The alewife came to my door in tears. Her daughter Ilg was in childbed and the babe would not come. "Can you help?" she asked me.

"I don't know anything," I said.

"But surely Künne left you with some herbs, whatever she gave me when I struggled?"

Alke stepped to the door beside me. "When the village dragged Künne to the stake, they took all the knowing of herbs with her." Her voice was defiant and she flicked a cleaning cloth between her hands as we will do to shoo a bird.

"You know nothing?" the alewife asked, her voice breaking. "Ilg can barely breathe for the pain. There must have been something here in the *Hütte* when you came to live here, Güde. That was not so long ago. Please!"

"I'm sorry for poor Ilg," I said. "But surely you know that the men spilled Künne's herbs and killed her goat. It was worse than when rats sack the grain bins. Everything was ruined."

She stared at me piteously, tears rolling down her cheeks. "She told you nothing?" she asked me one last time.

"Nothing," I said. Alke sent the alewife back with some bread so she'd have something for her hands to do.

Ilg lived but the baby didn't. However, something good came of this. The alewife spread the news of the night Künne's cottage was thieved. Some women had known, as their husbands had brought home goat meat with no good explanation. The rest were angry.

And as they thought over my friend's battle with the boiling kettle and the way she had fearlessly faced the flames, they began to be ashamed. At various firesides around the village, Jost told that he was now unsure of Fronika's guilt. I began to notice that rather than glancing away to avoid the evil I might still harbor, people looked into my eyes with sympathy.

After consulting with Ramwold and casting the runes for a solution, the villagers sent for a glassman to come from Stuttgart. They knew he could not create a stained glass window for the church, given the subject matter, so they constructed a special tower just to hold the glass. It was round, like the Witch's Tower, and stood where the stakes had erupted in flames years ago. I was there the day the men brought stones, tumbling in their carts, to build the tower.

The stained glass was meant to memorialize our wrongly murdered women.

The glass story moved from the bottom to the top, so closest to my level gaze was my dear friend Künne depicted in her pebble trial, her arm glowing vicious red and her face filled with savage despair. Then, moving up the window, were the hunter's party, all the men treading in snow, and the dark-haired girl confronting them, their eyes wide with fear and mistrust. Finally, at the top, where my neck hurt to look, Fronika and Künne burn together, mouths round with woe and the flames consuming their bodies. Ringed all around are angels weeping behind their wings, standing in pools of gray tears, their feet sogged.

Although these burnings were separate, the glassman chose to render them together and I don't believe either woman would mind. The friar is absent from the window; it is as if Künne had put her hand in boiling water of her own will, and as if the friar had not been the third in the trilogy of fire. I'm pleased by the omission. We need nothing to remember that man by. His absence from the windows means that he is not honored, and is also to fortify the lie of his death by fever, to protect the village.

There is a small fireplace in the tower, to keep us warm as we look up at the glowing sprawl of colored glass. But I prefer to stand outside on winter evenings, when the fire makes the images glow from within. I feel the flakes of snow against my cheeks and look at the unreal tints that the glassman created. It is otherworldly and causes my eyes to drift closed.

Nothing can bring Künne back to me, but that window brings me comfort.

Künne and Fronika's names aren't on the glass. But each child shall be told whose agony flickers through the molten glass, and they shall tell their own children. Tierkinddorf will remember.

The glassmaker has long since returned to Stuttgart now, but one day I saw him eating a sausage outside as he rested during his labor, and made myself known to him. He told me a beautiful thing, that he believed that the glass in the window was forever moving, although too slowly for our eyes to see.

"I blew into the glass and it continues to move with my breath," he told me. "It presses against the lead soldering as if wanting to overflow."

I'm glad of this. I like to think Künne is moving her arm out of the kettle, that Fronika is turning to run away from the hunters, that the flames will easily subside and the women step down from their stakes and rejoin the world.

Author's Note

Although *The Witch's Trinity* is a work of fiction, it describes a world that was very real. No one knows how many women were executed for witchcraft over a four-hundred-year period. A major trigger was the publication in 1485–86 of the *Malleus Maleficarum,* the witch hunter's bible. Gutenberg had built his press just thirty years earlier, and this allowed dissemination of the book in unprecedented numbers. One misconception is that the Catholic Church was entirely to blame for this holocaust. Secular courts were just as eager, and sometimes more so, to capture and punish witches. Although women were largely targeted (the title *Malleus Maleficarum* gives the word *witch* a feminine gender), it is important to note that in the 1300s men were named as witches as frequently as women were. And northern countries such as Scandinavia equally targeted men and women throughout the craze. The idea that midwives or healers formed the bulk of the accused has now been disproved, but it is still understood that the elderly, the poor, and people outside of society were the main targets. These unfortunates suffered the torments of imprisonment, torture, and death by hanging, decapitation, impalement, or being burned alive.

Several years ago, I learned that one of my ancestors, Mary

Bliss Parsons, was accused of witchcraft in 1600s Massachusetts. Although she faced the accusation twice (and possibly a third time, but the court documents have disappeared), she was acquitted and lived into her eighties. In the following pages, you can learn a little bit about her story.

MY ANCESTOR GOODY PARSONS[1]

Living in California, far from the New England I grew up in, I received an e-mail a few years ago from my mother. "Someone sent me this link," she wrote. "Our family has a witch in it." I clicked on it to find a complex Web site devoted to Mary Bliss Parsons, who was forced to defend her innocence twice. My connection to her traces back eleven generations through my mother, an only child and the last of our particular line to bear the Parsons name.

I marveled at the story that unfolded. No one in my family had ever spoken of this true black sheep, because none of us knew. Mary's husband, Joseph Parsons, was spoken of proudly whenever lineage came up: he was one of the founders of Northampton, Massachusetts, where Smith College is today. But his rumor-tortured wife was never mentioned. I asked my mother to send me some genealogical materials, including photocopied pages of a 1912 family history that goes on at length about Joseph but does not mention Mary's lifelong fight against accusations of witchcraft. To my amazement, when I located the original book in San Francisco's Sutro Li-

---

1 *Goody* is short for *Goodwife,* an early and less prestigious form of *Mrs.*

brary Mary's troubles *were* documented. Someone in my family had very specifically chosen which pages to photocopy—and left out Mary's trials altogether!

Perhaps shame lingered, or perhaps the relative responsible for the photocopying felt Mary's story was moot since she was acquitted. It is a myth that the accusation of witchcraft always carried with it an immediate death sentence. The magistrates of New England ruled more sensibly than we might give them credit for and New England history is full of stories of witchcraft acquittals.[2]

Learning about my ancestor was absorbing and ultimately sobering. She and her husband lived for a number of years in Springfield, Massachusetts, neighbors to Mary Lewis Parsons and her husband Hugh.[3] Beginning in 1649, Mary Lewis Parsons experienced witchcraft troubles of her own. I will not give all the details of her well-documented case, but for our purposes, the important thing is this: in 1651 this neighbor and her husband stood trial, she for causing fits in the minister's children, he for a dozen acts of mischief.[4]

2 More than a quarter of the people accused of witchcraft in seventeenth-century New England were acquitted, according to *Entertaining Satan* by John Putnam Demos.

3 Genealogists have been unable to establish a familial relationship between Hugh and Joseph Parsons. It is possible, but quite unlikely, that they were brothers.

4 Here are the bare bones. In 1649, Mary Lewis Parsons was accused of slander, for calling another woman a witch. Found guilty, she paid twenty-four bushels of Indian corn to avoid the alternative: twenty lashes. After this, she began losing her mental faculties. Later testimony revealed that Mary believed more than one person was a witch; she told a neighbor that she suspected her husband. In 1651, husband and wife stood trial, she for causing fits in the minister's children, he for a dozen acts of mischief such

Springfield consisted of only forty-seven households in 1651; undoubtedly turmoil over the case plagued the small community. My ancestor reacted strongly to her similarly named neighbor's situation. When the minister's children were having fits, she (a grown woman with four children of her own) was also having spells. One Sunday, she had to be carried out of Sabbath meeting along with the enchanted children. During another fit a neighbor carried her home. He said, "I discerned that she did not understand herself nor where she was." Chillingly, Mary cried out a warning that witches would creep under someone's bed. In her spells, she struggled with such power it took two men to hold her. Other neighbors saw her fits, later testifying, "Shee would looke fearfully somtymes as if shee saw something, & then bow downe her head, as others did on theire fits about that time."

Why was Mary Bliss Parsons having fits? Was she epileptic? Was she part of a group delusion, three decades before the Salem hysteria? Was there ergot in her bread?[5] According to a neighbor's later testimony, my ancestor believed her fits were the result of being locked in the cellar by her husband,

---

as making an ox tongue disappear from the kettle it was cooking in. During the time of examination, their five-month-old child died. Mary confessed both to witchcraft and to murdering the child and was sent to Boston for further trial. She was acquitted of witchcraft but found guilty of murder and sentenced to die by hanging. Due to her extreme illness, her execution was postponed and it is believed she died in prison. Hugh was originally found guilty of witchcraft, but his wife's confession got him off the hot seat. In 1652, he was ultimately acquitted. He left Springfield and remarried.

5 Behavioral psychologist Linnda Caporael introduced a theory in 1976 that ergot poisoning (from a rye fungus) caused the convulsions and hallucinations of the Salem witchcraft trials.

Joseph. She claimed the cellar was full of spirits she threw her bedclothes and pillow at, but they would not leave. *Bedclothes and pillow* in the cellar? Did Joseph lock her down there so often her bed was stationed there? After fighting spirits in the basement, Mary was washing clothes at the brook and spirits appeared to her in the shape of poppets (dolls). Seeing the tiny, fiendish specters caused her to fall into her first fit.

In 1654, Mary and Joseph Parsons moved to a new town, Northampton, nineteen miles away. Joseph and others had negotiated with Native Americans to buy the land then called Nonotuck. As a fur trader, Joseph dealt often with native peoples and spoke their language, at least enough to trade with them. As a seventeen-year-old in 1636, he had witnessed the deed of cession for the land that became Springfield, just sixteen years after the Mayflower landing.[6]

A founding father in Northampton, Joseph held many civic offices and began buying up land, becoming wealthy. He and Mary had their fifth child Ebenezer, in May 1655; he was the first white child born in Northampton.

Another family also moved from Springfield to Northampton: Sarah and James Bridgman. Sarah was eight years older than Mary, she had married a man whose finances and social standing were modest, and she had lost several children.[7] In the same month that twenty-seven-year-old Mary gave birth

6 Springfield was bought for eighteen yards of wampum (shells on strings), eighteen coats, eighteen hatchets, eighteen hoes, and eighteen knives. Northampton was bought for two hundred yards of wampum, ten coats, and a few trinkets.

7 When Joseph died in 1683, his estate was valued at more than £2,000. James Bridgman's estate was a mere £114 in 1676.

to healthy Ebenezer, thirty-five-year-old Sarah gave birth to James, who died after two weeks. Sarah had previously lost a newborn about eight years earlier, and she lost another, named Patience, in February 1656.[8]

Several months after squalling Ebenezer arrived in the Parsons family and sadness visited the Bridgmans, Sarah's eleven-year-old son John wandered out to look for the family's cows. Some strange force struck the boy on the head, making his hat fly off and causing him to nearly fall to the ground. John thought it was an unseen bird; continuing on, he stumbled, fell, and put his knee out of joint. Back at home, a surgeon set the knee but John was in "grievous torture," his mother later told the courts, for about a month. One morning at dawn John shouted out, waking his parents. He told them that Goody Parsons was trying to pull off his knee and "there shee sits on the shelfe."

The frightened parents responded that there was no one on the shelf and struggled to keep the violent boy in his bed. After a time, he quieted and said Goody Parsons was running away, a black mouse following her. He repeated this many times with so much vehemence that they feared for his life. Soon Sarah was telling Goody Branch (a Springfield woman who presumably came for a friendly visit) her fears about

8 Although the *timing* of these sad events was exquisitely painful for Sarah, the two women were basically neck and neck in their fertility at the time of the first trial. Sarah had experienced three newborn losses, while Mary had undergone two. Both at the time had four healthy children at home who would indeed grow to adulthood. However, after the trial, Mary went on to be über-fertile, giving birth to fourteen children total, with nine reaching adulthood. Sarah ultimately gave birth eight times, with only four living to adulthood.

Mary Parsons' character. Several other women were there to hear this gossip; the news was too large to be contained in Sarah's small Colonial home. It spread and other neighbors recalled strange interactions with Mary Bliss Parsons; one can imagine the suspicious glances and pinched faces on the dusty lanes of that small village.

Perhaps inspired by the slander trial of the other Mary Parsons, Joseph Parsons filed a slander suit against Sarah on behalf of his wife. This was a risky thing to do, given Mary's history in Springfield. And it also put his wife's reputation on trial. Proving one is being slandered means proving one is innocent of the tales being told.

Dozens of people testified, both for and against each woman. This showed extraordinary interest and involvement: Northampton only consisted of thirty-two households at the time. Springfield also contributed a few witnesses. Mary was said to have fits; speak of witches; make spun yarn diminish in volume; cause a cow, sow, and ox to die; be able to locate her house key even when it was hidden by her husband; and go into the water and not be wet.

We can look back at these accusations and wonder at a world where if a cow died early and unexpectedly, magic had to be the reason. Unable to elevate scientific explanations for natural (and naturally frightening) phenomena above their superstitious beliefs, the early settlers heard rough whispers in the wind and believed that sentient forces were behind them.

A neighbor, William Hannum, testified against Mary during the slander trial. They had fought about the volume of yarn his wife had sold her, and the next morning one of his cows lay in the yard, sick. He got the beast to her feet and fed her unceasing meals of "samp pease wholesome drinks eggs etc." but the cow died two weeks later. The same week, Hannum said, he witnessed Joseph beating his child for losing a shoe. He testified, "To my apprehension he beat it unmercifully, & his wife comeinge to save it, because shee had beaten it before as shee said, he thrust her away." The next day, neighborhood talk was about how Joseph had "in a sort beaten his wife." Hannum jested about it and when word got back to Mary, she confronted him angrily. That same evening, his pig, who had four young piglets to nurse, went missing. While he was looking for the pig a neighbor told him he had seen a sow in the swamp. "I went thither and it was my sow & there shee stood with her nose to the ground looking steadily as if shee had seen something in the ground. Soe I drove her home & before noon that day shee died. Shee till now was a lusty swine and well fleshed," testified Hannum.

Hannum also stated he had lost his ox to Mary's evil influence. He had joined his two oxen with those of Mary's brother and another man's to break up some ground. Mary scolded him for abusing her brother's oxen, because he had put them in the middle where they were "always under the whip." Hannum disagreed with her assessment and she went away furious. Three days later, he was driving his oxen when a rattlesnake bit one on the tongue "and there he dyed." Is it any wonder that the ox died in this way, when it was clearly Mary's venomous temperament that was responsible?

"Thse things doe somethinge run in my mind that I cannot have my mind from this Woman, that if shee be not right shee may bee a cause of these things, though I desire to look at the over-rulinge hand of God in all," concluded Hannum humbly.

Mary's strong character and willingness to scold neighbors created hard feelings that led to testimony against her, but it also permitted her to stand up in court confidently and speak on her own behalf (attorneys did not generally represent litigants, especially in inland towns). Says a chronicler, "Mary Parsons was apparently a proud and nervous woman, haughty in demeanor and inclined to carry things with a high hand; she belonged to the aristocracy and evidently considered herself a dame of considerable importance."[9] Another report has her "possessed of great beauty and talents, but . . . not very amiable . . . exclusive in her choice of associates."[10]

Hannum briefly appeared in court a second time to answer a question about the cow, and a week after his testimony about the untimely farm deaths, Hannum and his wife came before the court a third time with some surprising news. They admitted that Sarah Bridgman's husband had "hiared them to downe to Springfield to give in there testimony." Why were the Bridgmans so deeply against Mary, to the extent of pressuring the Hannums to testify against her? Entrenched bitterness is my best guess. After all, Joseph chose Sarah as the sole defendant in his suit, when seemingly half the village was passing rumors. She was still raw from the death of her newborn Patience four months prior.

Moreover, she was losing the case. Previous to the Hannums'

9 James Trumbull, as quoted in *The Parsons Family* by Henry Parsons, vol. 1.
10 Mary Walton Ferris, as quoted in *Entertaining Satan*.

testimony, four people had testified on Mary's behalf and only two for Sarah—one of those being herself. Sarah seemingly scrambled to fortify her case, coercing neighbors to testify and coming up with a grimmer accusation herself. On the same day in August that Hannum gave that compelled testimony, Sarah testified for a second time. When she had first spoken in June, she had focused only on her son's injured knee and upon other neighbors agreeing that Mary was "not right." But with Sarah's second chance to speak her piece, she added a much more sobering allegation: she spoke of May 1655, when her sickly son James was a newborn. Sitting with James on her lap, she said, a "great blow" came upon the door. At the moment she heard this sound, her child "changed," as she put it (from healthy to ill).

"I thought with myself and told my girle I was afraid my child would dy," said Sarah. She sent the girl (presumably her oldest daughter, Martha, then twelve) out to answer the door, but Martha found no one. After the girl came back in, Sarah peered through a hole in the door and saw two women walk past the house with white cloths on their heads. The eerie sight spurred her to send out the girl yet again, who found no one outside. "This made mee think there is wickedness in the place," said Sarah.

As we know, James was not long for this world. It's interesting that Sarah never actually *named* Mary Bliss Parsons in relation to this incident, although she freely referred to her in the testimony that expanded on her description months previously of John's knee being pulled by an invisible force. James had died shortly before John's knee trauma, so why hadn't Sarah mentioned it the first time she testified? As if somewhat ashamed, she only briefly spoke of the dead child in this amplified declaration, and devoted twice as much explanation to the knee episode. Most tellingly, James Bridgman testified right on the heels of his wife, confirming the knee grabbing but not mentioning the doomed newborn at all.

After Sarah's second testimony, neighbors rallied in force to combat the increasingly serious allegations against Mary.[11] On August 18, 1656, thirteen testified (formerly the largest number on a given day had been six), and every single person testified in Mary's favor. Of these, seven rebutted the charges about the dead farm animals (including, as mentioned above, the Hannums themselves); one said Sarah had a grudge against Mary; two were Mary's parents; and three women came forward to rebut the new charge about James. Hanna Lanton, Sarah's next door neighbor, said that she had come to dress the child soon after his birth and that he had a "louseness" (looseness; i.e., diarrhea). She thought the child had a cold. Hanna Broughton who also came to nurse Sarah confirmed that James was sickly even before Sarah rose from childbed. Neighbor Anne Bartlett added that the baby was groaning from sickness right after its birth. Further, she had asked Sarah how the child was, and Sarah responded that he had "the louseness still which it had at the first and if it continueth I feare it will be the death of my child." Anne was with the baby the night he died. He

11 Besides the Hannums, three other witnesses would end up changing their negative testimony against Mary Bliss Parsons to positive.

had another attack of diarrhea, and Sarah had said, "Thus hath it been from the first."

It was all damning testimony against Sarah Bridgman, and on September 8, 1656, a bond for her arrest was issued. However, the constable responded that Sarah was not able to appear without hazard to her life. She was pregnant again (the historical record does not show a birth date for this child, so possibly she miscarried). In the following days, more witnesses would show for Sarah, then several for Mary, and finally a decision was rendered.

Sarah Bridgman was found guilty of slander and ordered to publicly apologize to Mary Bliss Parsons, both in Springfield and in Northampton, within the next sixty days. If she did not comply, she could pay a £10 fine instead. She was also ordered to pay Joseph Parsons' court costs: 7 pounds, 1 shilling, and 8 pence. It is unknown whether Sarah made the humiliating public acknowledgment or simply paid the fine. The case was over, but in such an insular environment, feelings doubtless continued at high pitch. When Sarah and Mary next met on the street or in meetinghouse on Sabbath day, we can only imagine their emotions and reactions. But the interactions were short-lived. Sarah died in 1668 at the age of forty-seven.

Eighteen years later, in 1674 and at the age of forty-six, my ancestor found herself in court again for the charge of witchcraft. Sarah's daughter Mary Bridgman Bartlett, who was four years old at the time of the slander trial, had died very suddenly; her bereaved husband, Samuel, and her grudge-holding father, James Bridgman, filed suit against Mary Bliss Parsons.

Unfortunately, testimony in this case no longer exists, but the original complaint states that Samuel Bartlett believed his wife died "by means of some evil instrument." James Bridgman, similarly, "strongly suspects she come to her end by some unlawfull & unatureall means." Whatever the "diverse evidences" the two men showed to the court were, they reflected badly on Mary, who was warned to prepare "to answer what shall be objected against her." The witnesses were also warned to back up what they'd already said upon oath.

After a preliminary trial in Springfield, the case was referred to Northampton. Mary once again vigorously proclaimed her innocence, while neighbors provided more testimony against her. A committee of "soberdized, chaste women" examined Mary, performing a survey of her naked body to see if any marks of witchcraft showed on her flesh. Eighteen years earlier, during the slander case, William Houlton said Sarah Bridgman was so suspicious of Mary that she wouldn't be satisfied until women searched her three times. Sarah Bridgman's wish now came true posthumously. We can only imagine Mary's humiliation at having neighbors poke and prod her. We have no record of what those women found or did not find but the report was sent along to Boston with the testimonies; Northampton, less gracious than last time, referred the case to that city, making Mary post bond to be sure she'd appear. Witnesses briefly pulled Mary's twenty-four-year-old son John into the case, calling him a witch as well, but he was dismissed.

The Boston grand jury indicted Mary in early March 1675 and imprisoned her until her trial in mid-May. We can assume

Mary was confined in a cold cell with a dirt floor, and mixed in with men and women together, which may have provided its own dangers. The prison might have reminded her of the cellar her husband had locked her into, where she believed she encountered the spirits that caused the first fits that drew attention to her as a witch.

On May 13, 1675, she faced a jury and spoke for herself. In attendance was no less a personage than the governor of Massachusetts. Again, no transcript survives, but the final record does summarize the decision. Despite Mary Bliss Parsons' initial indictment for "not having the fear of God before her eyes" and for having "entered into familiarity with the divill and committed several acts of witchcraft," the court proclaimed her not guilty. She was released. Twice now, Mary Bliss Parsons had effectively and persuasively argued her own innocence of witchcraft.

The Parsonses stayed in Boston as Joseph pursued real estate purchases. They eventually moved back to Springfield, perhaps finding it friendlier in the end than Northampton.[12]

There were several unfortunate reverberations from Mary's witchcraft battles; people wouldn't let the scandal die. Ebenezer Parsons, the child who thrived while the Bridgmans' son faded, died in a surprise Indian attack at Northfield, Massachusetts, in September 1675. Mary's Boston

12 Some historians believe the move to Springfield was precipitated by yet another accusation against Mary. In 1678, Northampton resident John Stebbins died, believed killed by witches. He was Samuel Bartlett's brother-in-law; this familial connection spurs the surmise that one of the unnamed suspects in the inquest was Mary Parsons. No action was taken after Boston reviewed the evidence.

acquittal had taken place that same year in May. Cruelly, neighbors put out the word that this was God's retribution for Mary's false exoneration. "Behold, though human judges may be bought off, God's vengeance neither turns aside nor slumbers," wrote one historian, imagining how the criticism was worded.[13]

Second, in 1702, a slave named Betty Negro was indicted for cursing and striking a child. The child, Peletiah Glover Jr., told the court that Betty claimed his grandmother (Mary Bliss Parsons) "had killed two persons over the river, and had killed Mrs. Pynchon and half-killed the Colonel, and that his mother [Hannah Parsons] was half a witch."

Fortunately, Mary was not pulled into court again; instead, poor Betty was lashed ten times by the constable (who was Mary's nephew). It may have helped that the two justices of the peace were Mary's son Joseph (and thus Peletiah's brother-in-law) and John Pynchon, who had testified favorably in Mary's slander case.

Joseph Parsons had died in 1683, while Mary continued as a widow for almost thirty years, dying in 1712 at about eighty-five. She was confused and unwell at the end, to the extent that two of her sons, Joseph and John, took over her estate in 1711.

The rumors have finally quieted. Some of Mary's own descendants—including me—were unwitting of her alleged misconduct. My heart goes out to my ancestor, whose life was marred by continuing gossip—and strangely enough, it goes out to Sarah Bridgman as well, who seemingly only sought an

13 Trumbull, quoted in Henry Parsons' book.

explanation for the hard luck she endured. Sarah and her family chose to scapegoat my ancestor . . . a shameful decision, but one supported by the culture of the time.

———

Note: Fortunately, there is much material available on both Mary Parsonses; unfortunately, sources often contradict each other. Moreover, it's difficult to interpret these events through the filmy veil of 350 years. The anecdote of the hidden key, for example, strikes me as something whose meaning is lost to culture and time. Was it commonplace for husbands to commandeer the home's locks? Was it understood at the time as a teasing gesture or an abuse? Some researchers think Joseph was locking Mary up to keep her from sleepwalking. I am grateful that chroniclers have fastidiously logged the details; I take responsibility for all errors.

SOURCES

Burt, Henry M. *The First Century of the History of Springfield; The Official Records from 1636 to 1736, with an Historical Review and Biographical Mention of the Founders.* Sections about Mary Lewis Parsons posted as "Witchcraft in Springfield: Hugh and Mary Parsons." American Local History Network, http://www.usgennet.org/usa/ma/county/hampden/hist/witchcraft.html, accessed October 2006.

Demos, John Putnam. *Entertaining Satan.* New York: Oxford University Press, 1982.

"The Mary (Bliss) Parsons Witchcraft Trial." Center for Computer-Based Technology, University of Massachusetts, http://ccbit.cs

.umass.edu/parsons/hnmockup/home.html, accessed October 2006.

Parsons, Gerald. *Our Parsons Heritage.* Baltimore: Gateway Press, 2003.

Parsons, Henry. *Parsons Family: Descendants of Cornet Joseph Parsons.* New York: Frank Allaben Genealogical Company, 1912.

Acknowledgments

I am indebted to my agent, Marly Rusoff, and her partner, Michael Radulescu, and to my editor, Allison McCabe. I have found our collaborations to be absolutely energizing and fruitful and I'm grateful to be working with such wonderful people.

Thanks to Joe Quirk for loaning me Teofilo F. Ruiz's *The Terror of History* audiotapes, which inspired this novel, and to Teo himself for reading the manuscript and graciously answering my never-ending questions. Thanks to readers Jennifer Lee and Maria Strom, to the Oakland Schuhplattler group for teaching me the Miller's Dance, and to Herb Schmidt for help with German words. Thanks to Tamim Ansary, Joe Quirk, and Gary Turchin for their years-long support and friendship, and all the other members of the San Francisco Writers Workshop. There are many wonderful books out there about the European witch craze; one I particularly liked was Jeffrey Burton Russell's *Witchcraft in the Middle Ages.* Of valuable assistance to my research on Mary Bliss Parsons was John Putnam Demos' *Entertaining Satan,* and I thank Mr. Demos personally for reading my essay. I somewhat altered the song "I Must Go Walk the Wood," a lyric dating to 1500, found in R. T. Davies' *Medieval English Lyrics.*

I also want to extend appreciation to the Web site agentquery.com, which connected me with my agent and whose staff rooted for me. Thanks also to Alan Howard, Cathy Clarke, Kenneth G. Hecht Jr., Scott James, and Melodie Bowsher.